Dragonfly

Dragonfly

JAXN HILL

WestBow
PRESS
A DIVISION OF THOMAS NELSON

ISBN: 978-1-4497-4483-0 (e)
ISBN: 978-1-4497-4484-7 (sc)
ISBN: 978-1-4497-4485-4 (hc)

Library of Congress Control Number: 2012905790

WestBow Press books may be ordered through booksellers or by contacting:

WestBow Press
A Division of Thomas Nelson
1663 Liberty Drive
Bloomington, IN 47403
www.westbowpress.com
1-(866) 928-1240

Printed in the United States of America

WestBow Press rev. date: 5/10/2012

Dedication

❖ For my niece Caiti who shimmers, too, and my step-daughters Amanda and Erin, who sparkle and shine.

❖ And for my friend Torstein-Doffen whose kind heart gave me this idea.

(I could keep going because God has given me so many fabulous people in my life, but I'll have to save some of them for another book, another day. Love you!)

Jaxn Hill
February, 2012

Table of Contents

1

"**G**et a job!"

Torstein wasn't begging, but the Big Guy thought he was. He was doing the opposite of begging—he was *offering*. He had a bag of sunflower seeds, and he was offering them to people who passed by. It was kind of weird—but Torstein was a weird guy. Like, who's going to take sunflower seeds from a stranger on the street? Especially one that looked like Torstein. He *looked* weird. For one thing, he always wore this bottle green coat, like he was leading an electric St. Patrick's Day parade. I don't think he had any other coat, but he gave the impression of being the kind of guy who had a hundred coats—probably really great designer coats—but chose to wear that one every day, like a costume.

He really could have used that advice—"Get a job!—but I never saw him too concerned about that. He seemed to prefer trying to hand out sunflower seeds to people who could have cared less. Every once in a while a kid would take a handful, but even then, you know the kid was wishing it were M & M's.

I was there the day Maggie first passed by. She had an entourage. There must have been seven assistants flanking her, left and right, with cell phones, pagers, PDA's. Everyone had something to remind Maggie where she was supposed to be and what she was supposed to be doing. One of those seven must have flinched because somehow a bag of sunflower seeds got shoved in Maggie's face—the assistants had let Torstein slip through! They'd been gliding along in phalanx, but he must have weaved in between them.

It was kind of comical. When someone handed Maggie a phone, she talked. When someone handed her a PDA, she texted. When someone handed her a clipboard and a pen, she signed. When Torstein handed her the bag of sunflower seeds, she grabbed a handful. I think it was force of habit. I think these seven assistants had been programming her actions so long, she just assumed Torstein was one and did what he prompted automatically. Then—boom! She stopped. The whole phalanx stopped. She was standing there with a handful of seeds, staring at Torstein in his green coat. And I think, for her, for the first time in a long time, all her entourage disappeared. And for a minute, there was only her and Torstein.

And she put some seeds in her mouth and spit out the shells, and laughed.

It happened like that sometimes—instantaneously.

Other times...well...Torstein was patient.

There was this crack addict named Angel in a ratty old building on the block behind the city street where Torstein met Maggie. Angel never even looked at Torstein—she didn't look at any men, really; they were just business to her. I doubt she even noticed when Torstein was offering her sunflower seeds. She didn't think men gave away anything for free. But she had a kid, maybe 5 years old, Sully. Torstein would give the kid sunflower seeds, and other stuff—sandwiches. He'd tell him, "Take this home to your mom. She needs to eat." Like crack addicts ate anything but crack. I think Sully ate all the sandwiches himself. Who could blame him? He had to be hungry.

One day Torstein took Sully into the bodega, gave him some money, and showed him how to buy bread and peanut butter and jelly and milk. Torstein told him to keep the bread and milk and jam in the fridge...After that sometimes he'd give Sully a few bucks for groceries. Everyone thought maybe Sully was *his* kid. Someone even asked him. He said, "Sure he's my kid. He's yours, too. If his father and mother abandon him, shouldn't we take him in?"

So Torstein was Sully's hero because—well, who else ever gave a damn about him? But Torstein was trying to get to Angel. Only once a person's on crack, nothing gets to them but the promise of more crack. At least, that was my opinion. I mean, Torstein was a great guy. My brother and I had fallen victim to his Irresistible Charm almost exactly the same way Maggie had. We wanted to stick by him and see what would happen next, no doubt. But for Angel, she wasn't sticking by anyone except the guy that could get her next fix to her. I figured she'd be happy if Torstein took the kid off her hands completely and she never saw either of them again. But like I say, Torstein was patient.

2

The green coat made Torstein look like a dragonfly. It was that kind of green. And he was light on his feet, almost dancing when he walked...he shimmered. It wasn't so much what he said that captured people's attention, because usually he didn't say much at all. It was more just the way he *was*. He was like a flame, a green flame, and some people were drawn to him like moths. I was, Maggie was, my brother was. Little Sully never had a chance. He was devoted to Torstein almost from the first handful of seeds.

But the Big Guy? His immediate response had been that snarled, "Get a job!"

It sounded rude, but Torstein wasn't put off at all. He said, "I'm surprised anyone with a job like yours would tell me to get a job!"

Then it hit me: we knew this Big Guy. It was Bruiser, one of the Big Guys who collected protection money for Nikolai, the Russian mobster who terrorized the legitimate business owners and ran the illegitimate businesses around here. Yah, Bruiser had shaken my old man down every week for a few bucks. For protection. My dad used to own the fish market. He'd given it to me and my brother, and we'd sold it. But I still remembered Bruiser.

The Big Guy, Bruiser, I thought he'd just pound Torstein into the pavement there on the spot. After all, Torstein was quick and light on his feet, but big he was not. He wasn't any taller than me, and slighter. Bruiser could have laid him out with one sucker punch, easy. But he just said, "Everybody's gotta make a living," as if he had to justify himself to the nut-job on the street offering everyone sunflower seeds! I was floored.

Torstein said, "I don't make a living. And yet, here I am, living. Care to join me?"

And the Big Guy, he reached out and took a handful of sunflower seeds. And he laughed. Torstein laughed, too, and did a little two-step around the guy. That about killed me—crazy man in the green coat dancing around ol' Bruiser the collections man.

But that was Torstein's Irresistible Charm. Some people couldn't say no to him. Not that my brother and I had tried very hard. We'd first run into him the day we signed the papers to sell the fish market. It had been bought by a big gourmet food chain that wanted the great storefront space for merchandise, and wanted access to our dad's vendors of fresh fish. The ocean was just 20 miles away, and our dad knew all the old fishing families from when he used to fish. His market had always had the best fresh seafood.

So my brother and I had been ready to celebrate. We thought we'd done remarkably well on the sale. That day, Torstein didn't have any sunflower seeds. He'd just been standing on the street when we came out of the broker's office; almost like he was waiting for us, though we'd never seen him before.

We thought, like the Big Guy, that he was panhandling.

He said, "Looks like a party, boys!"

My brother said, "Heck yah it's a party!" and he pulled $10 out of his wallet and handed it to Torstein. We were feeling generous.

But Torstein just smiled and gave it back, saying, "I'm not that cheaply bought. Where are we headed?'

My brother, still thinking Torstein was a beggar, started laughing and said, "You've got guts, I'll give you that." My brother, he was a tough guy—what he valued in himself and prized in others was daring and fearlessness. He was one of those guys who had a good brain if he'd use it, but often preferred to settle things with his fists if that's what it took. He was impressed that somebody he thought was a beggar was turning down money and inviting himself to party with us. He figured Torstein must be as fearless as he was.

So we took him out to party with us. We'd been following him since then…or not really following him anywhere, because he hardly every went anywhere except for a few city blocks around where we'd met him.

Every now and then, someone else seemed to see in Torstein what we saw in him, and they'd start coming around, too, a couple of days a week, or every day for a week straight, and soon they'd just be part of the crowd. We didn't *do* anything but watch him dancing with his sunflower seeds or listen to him tell a story ...

... but somehow it seemed important. Apparently, to Bruiser it seemed important, too. He stopped doing his collections. I guess Nikolai got someone else to take over for him, but he wasn't happy about it. He sent some other thugs to talk to Torstein, but Bruiser got in the way and told them unless they'd come there for sunflower seeds, they ought to go right back the way they came.

Later that day, Torstein told us he wanted to visit the ocean. It would be our first journey with him.

3

W e took the bus to the shore. There was this crazy man who'd appeared that spring. He dressed in camo and had a deep, booming voice. I guess he was homeless, and the beach police must have been afraid to try to run him off because he was a pretty large and sturdy looking individual. His deal was, he went into the sea every day, in the shallows where people swim, and if you got too close he would grab you and dunk you under.

At first people were *freaked out* by it. But as the days grew hotter, and more people crowded the shore, and nobody drowned, it got to be kind of a game. Kids would try to see how close they could get without being dunked. The guy was fast, though, and he could catch most people—grab them, pull them under, let them up. It was pretty funny to watch, actually, girls in bikinis shrieking and sputtering, teenaged boys jumping and splashing to try to evade his long arms. We stood watching from the shore, laughing and carrying on a bit, cheering for the best looking girls—he *always* managed to grab them I noticed. But he caught almost everyone.

Then suddenly Torstein said, "He's my cousin, you know." We were all stunned! Was this another Torsteinism, like Sully belonging to all of us, or was he making a statement of fact that he and the Dunker were blood relations? Torstein looked nothing like the Dunker. Torstein had short, straight almost black hair and a hooked nose. He was one of those short guys like a gymnast who is slightly muscle-bound, so that saved him from looking too delicate. But the Dunker, he had about a yard of gnarly dreadlocks streaming out the top of his head, a kind of bulging forehead and dark eyes set deep under it. He was well over 6 feet tall, taller even than our Bruiser.

Sully had come with us to the shore, and he'd been having a fit to try his luck with the Dunker, only he couldn't swim. I didn't bring any trunks, so I wasn't going in the water. I was just there for a corndog and a gander at the bikinis. The Dunker was in water up to his waist, but that would have been almost over Sully's head, so he couldn't go alone. Before we could ask Torstein if he were serious about the madman being his cousin, he had whipped off his coat and shirt, and was stripping down to his shorts, saying to Sully, "Let's do it! Let's try if he'll dunk us!"

He held out his hand to Sully, and they went splashing out into the water. Sully had just been wearing a ratty old pair of shorts and a t-shirt. That's what he was wearing when the Dunker lunged at him, grabbed him by the shoulder and yanked him away from Torstein, plunged him under the surf—then lifted him back up and launched him like a missile through the air, back toward shallower water. Sully was screaming and laughing all the way. He splashed down in about 2 feet of water and came scrambling back toward us on the shoreline.

Meantime the Dunker had grabbed Torstein, but didn't dunk him. He gave him a big old bear hug. Clearly they knew each other. Sully was standing with us, watching, and said, "Why doesn't he dunk him?"

Other people splashing around, waiting for the game to continue, were wondering the same thing. Even Torstein, it seemed, was wondering. The Dunker had let him go and was backing away from him, shaking his head, no. Torstein was gesturing to himself and the water—he'd come to be dunked, clearly, probably the only person who came with the purpose of being dunked, and the Dunker was refusing. Except—it was a ruse!

Just as Torstein was about to give up, already turning away, the Dunker's right hand shot out and grabbed him, twisting him around so he tumbled toward the Dunker who caught him, dunked him, and brought him sputtering back up. At that same moment, a crazy seagull dive-bombed them and landed on Torstein's shoulder—and bit him on the ear! That was the kind of weird stuff that happened to Torstein. He was still recovering from the surprise dunk attack, and he just laughed at the bird and shooed it away. Then he came wading back to the shore, with the Dunker beside him. They were both laughing.

Torstein said—and I am not kidding—"This is my cousin, Duncan."

Duncan the Dunker?! We all shook hands, but it's hard to keep a straight face at a moment like that. Which is why it's great to have a kid in the crowd. Sully piped up, "You dunked me and you *threw* me!" The Dunker's response was to grab him again and toss him in the air. He was that big of a guy, to toss a five-year-old in the air. Sully started squealing, and the awkward moment was over before it really got started.

So, yah, apparently Torstein and the Dunker really were cousins.

Somebody asked the Dunker what he was doing, shoving swimmers underwater. He said in this booming voice of his that it was his destiny. Seemed like a lame destiny to me. And when the weather cooled off, it was going to be an impossible one. But why argue with a crazy man?

4

aggie had never been married. She said she'd been married
to her job. She'd never had children, and she didn't know
any more about them than the rest of us did. But she did know about
fashion. When she'd spit out the shells of those sunflower seeds Torstein
gave her the first day, she also spit out her place in the corporate world,
her power suits and six-figure income—but she nevertheless remained
a fashionista. When she saw Sully, half dry and covered with powdery
beach sand, his old shorts and t-shirt hanging on him half sodden with
sea water, she took him in hand. She made him shower at the public
stall, dried him off and marched him into one of the chic boutiques on
the boardwalk, like Beach Babies or Jovenes Solimar, and bought him
swim trunks, khakis, a button down shirt, a sporty windbreaker, a pair
of deck shoes and some kind of toddler sunglasses. She combed out his
hair, and when she stepped out of the shop she glared at us, daring us
to laugh.

We all thought of Maggie as a tough girl. She'd been a commodities
broker in her other life, and apparently a really good one who never lost
a deal and never paid more than she'd bid. She knew how to dress for
success, but we'd never considered she might know how to dress a little
boy. We were amazed. You could tell Sully was amazed just to have
a shopping bag from a retail store with real clothes in it just for him.
Maggie barked at the rest of us, "Just because you go around looking
like bums doesn't mean Sully has to!"

She had curly auburn hair and white skin that she never exposed to daylight if she could help it. She had beautiful brown eyes, a small, snubbed nose and a roly-poly figure. She grabbed Sully's hand and flounced past us down the boardwalk like a queen on the red carpet with her little jester flying along beside her, looking back over his shoulder to wave his shopping bag at us. Torstein gazed at her bemused and said, "What a woman!" We followed her down the way, and before we were back to the bus stop that night, we were all dressed in khakis and button down shirts with deck shoes. And, for Torstein, his same old electric green coat. Maggie had given up the corporate world, but she hadn't given up her money-market account and her Gold Card.

She'd bought Sully that sporty windbreaker, but none of the rest of us had a coat except Torstein. The rest of us were starting to shiver because the sun was setting and the breeze was coming strong off the water. It was still 40 minutes before our bus—and Torstein decided we might as well walk, walk the 20-odd miles back to the city.

"It'll take us 5 or 6 hours even if we go at a good pace," said this one cool blond guy named Ferdy. "And what about the kid?"

We didn't have to walk all night, Torstein said. "We'll stop for dinner somewhere, and get a hotel or something."

Ferdy hated that idea. He was our money man. When my brother and I first started spending time with Torstein, that's how he introduced Ferdy: "This is Ferdy, the money man. You got any money, you give it to Ferdy. You need any money, you ask Ferdy." Ferdy had been at school with Torstein. They grew up together. Apparently he had always managed Torstein's money for him. He was an accountant, or had been. When he got permanently caught up in Torstein's Irresistible Charm, he'd given that up. Now he was our treasurer.

"We don't have enough money for a hotel," he said. "You gave a lot of our money to the Humane Society." Torstein would do stuff like that. He gave away a lot of money. And he didn't have a job!

"Oh well," he said. "If Sully gets too tired, someone will give us a place to sleep."

So we started walking.

5

Torstein was carrying Sully on his shoulders. The kid was small. I'm guessing he was a crack baby, and he never got enough to eat, so he was slender and I'm guessing short for his age, too—though I don't exactly know how old he was or how tall he ought to have been.

I was walking with my brother and Bruiser a little behind Maggie and Ferdy. Bruiser had tried to apologize to me and my brother about the protection money; he recognized Peter, my brother, from the fish market. We told him not to mention it, that our dad made more money than God from the fish market and we hadn't done too badly on the sale, so everything evened out. Bruiser was kind of a nice guy when he wasn't threatening you.

We could hear Ferdy asking Maggie, "Why'd you buy us these clothes?" He was always curious about any expenditure.

"Because I bought new clothes for Sully and didn't want you guys to be jealous."

"Why'd you buy them for Sully?"

"Because he looked like a kid nobody cares about," she said.

"He *is* a kid nobody cares about," Ferdy said.

"That's not true!" Maggie said. "Torstein cares. And Angel."

Ferdy just laughed at that. It made me want to laugh, too. If Angel had cared, she'd have been the one to get new clothes for Sully. Somehow.

The neighborhood along the shore was pretty tony, upscale shops and beach boutiques, then narrow streets of pricey condos and homes sandwiched onto long lots designed to make the most livable space close to the water. A few blocks later we were into a commercial area with seafood joints, nightclubs and more shopping. Ferdy grudgingly shelled out for fish tacos from a roadside stand—fresh fish we'd seen them carry in the back door: a big halibut the cook butchered and cleaned in about three minutes. My brother and I had grown up in the fish market and appreciated the skill and the preparation—just lemon and garlic butter, then right onto the grill. What could be better?

Fortified, we continued our march. The sun had set, and we had left the beach town behind. It wasn't two miles later we were in a concrete-walled slum with a few old houses, that had once been genteel, stuck between tall new tenement projects. Lots of broken streetlights and slow-moving cars on the street with that deep bass note booming behind tinted windows. We all sort of drew together, flanking Maggie like her old entourage, but the divine madman who led us seemed to sense no danger at all. From some pocket in his coat he had produced a bag of sunflower seeds and began offering them to the people who passed. There were no takers. We'd decided to stick to surface streets on our trek home because it would be easier and safer than walking alongside the highway, but right then I wondered if we hadn't made a mistake.

Ahead of us, Torstein had just offered to carry a bag of groceries for a little old lady who'd been hurrying, as best she could, up the block. He was telling her, "I'll carry these for you. Here, have some sunflower seeds."

She smiled at him and said, "Are you all going to the church?" I don't know if she thought we were all dressed alike because we were some kind of band or what.

"We may," Torstein said. "But we'll get you home first." And we did. She lived in one of those tiny old houses that people actually used to raise 3 or 4 kids in 50 years ago. It had a little postage stamp of a lawn and a little front porch that could barely hold Bruiser, Torstein and Sully. The rest of us stood in the street as they walked her to the door and handed her groceries in.

"Thank you, dears," she said, and gave them each a swift kiss on the cheek. "I hope I see you again."

"You will," Torstein said. "Some day soon, you'll be seeing a lot of me." That was the weird kind of thing he used to say to random people.

The little old lady set her bag of groceries down inside the house, then came back out on the porch and gave Torstein a long hug. "I'll be waiting for that," she said. "I'll be waiting."

I knew Torstein wouldn't lie, but really, when would he ever see her again?

6

A couple miles more, and we came to her church, a little oasis of green lawn with a shining white church building. It was lit with street lamps and floodlights for a carnival. Some games, some kiddy rides, some cotton candy and saltwater taffy, and a little petting zoo. In the center was a big "Fellowship Tent" with tables and benches and punch and cookies, and a bake sale.

Maggie asked for a volunteer to go see the carnival with her and Sully, and Bruiser went. He said he wanted to ride the bumper cars! Who'd figure him for a big kid? He was at least 50 years old because he'd been collecting from my dad 20 years back ...

Torstein sat down at one of the tables in the "Fellowship Tent," and my brother and I went to get drinks and cookies for us all. The pastor came running up to us, calling, "Welcome!" He introduced himself, Pastor Ruiz, and told us to make ourselves at home. Torstein already had: he was offering sunflower seeds to several people who had joined him at the table.

He was telling them what a fine carnival this was, and what a nice looking church, and although he still had on his bright green jacket, somehow he didn't look as eccentric as he normally did.

Sitting under the "Fellowship Tent" where the punch and cookies were free, offering sunflower seeds to everyone seemed quite normal. And his sunny smile was reflected in bright faces all around him. It was almost as if it took this specific atmosphere to make Torstein look at home. Back in our neighborhood, he was just the freak in the green coat trying to get strangers to eat sunflower seeds, the madman with the sort of manic passion to share with everyone who passed by. Under the "Fellowship Tent," there *were* no strangers, and sharing was the norm. The sort of complete, happy *acceptance* of everyone that bubbled out of Torstein at all times seemed to bubble out of all the people under this tent.

We stayed until the carnival ended at 9 p.m., then we helped Pastor Ruiz and his team tear down and load up anything that had to be sent away from the grounds that night. He offered to drive us back to the city in the church van, but when Torstein told him we were enjoying our walk, he offered to let us sleep in the basement of the church.

The next morning, the "Fellowship Tent" was still there, but now the people from the church were serving breakfast. It was Saturday morning, and apparently they dished up a free breakfast for the homeless (and anyone else) every Saturday. They invited us to eat, which we were happy to do, and Torstein made them take $100 to help with the costs. Ferdy protested harder than Pastor Ruiz did, but in the end Maggie, my brother and I split the cost from our own pockets. We didn't mind. It was a good breakfast and there were at least 20 of us eating—maybe 25, so that was cheap for breakfast. And they packed a snack for Sully to take with him too.

Sully didn't want to leave. I think he thought the basement was a fine place to live, and the carnival happened every night. Pastor Ruiz explained that the carnival had just been a special event on Friday night, but that Sully was welcome to come back to have breakfast any Saturday...Sully sulked a bit, but since he had that box lunch to take with him, he consented to go along with us. He wasn't happy about it, but he went. He'd really enjoyed the cotton candy and the bumper cars.

7

We started down the street again, and a funny looking little guy came following us. He was so small, he looked like a kid, but when you saw his face, he was a grown man. He had bright red hair, not like Maggie's auburn curls—he was a real carrot top. I recognized him from the night before. He'd been talking to Torstein under the tent, and I noticed he'd taken a few handfuls of sunflower seeds.

He didn't know it, but he was caught. Torstein's Irresistible Charm had taken over. It was intoxicating what happened when you were drawn to Torstein. You felt accepted, welcomed, loved, wanted. Everything else you used to think life was about, it didn't seem to matter anymore. It had happened to this funny looking little guy.

"Hey, can I come with you?" he said.

"Sure," I said. "But we're walking to the city."

"Great, I live in the city," he said. "Listen, who is this guy, Torstein?"

Torstein was sort of two-stepping along at the head of the group, and I guess it looked like some kind of parade because we were all dressed more or less alike.

"He's just our friend," my brother said.

"Yeah, yeah," the funny looking little guy said. "But why do you guys follow him? And why are you all dressed alike?"

I started laughing. "We don't follow him—he just wanted to go to the shore, so we all went. And the clothes…we just got them yesterday on a lark."

We *did* sort of follow him, but he hadn't really gone anywhere before, not out of the neighborhood where we'd met him. This 20-mile walk from the coast, we were really seeing the world.

The funny looking little guy said, "Don't you have anything better to do?"

Well, it was a good question, wasn't it? But no, I didn't have anything better to do. My brother and I didn't have the fish market to run anymore. Peter, my brother, was quite a bit older than me. He was married, but not so you could notice, and both his kids were in school. I was a single guy. But really, what could be a better thing to do than watch and see what Torstein would to next?

Still, the question kind of annoyed me, and I snapped back at the funny looking little guy, "Don't you?!"

"Sure, sure," he said. "I got my job to do, but last night, talking wit' your friend, I dunno. I got to wondering if my job was that great, anyway."

"What do you do?" my brother asked him.

"I work for Nikolai, back in the city, you know? I get information for him. Listen, just telling you this, I could get in a lot of trouble, OK? But you gotta tell your boy to watch his back. Nikolai don't like anything too unusual on his turf—don't like people like Bruiser quittin' him for no reason."

"He send you to spy on Torstein?" my brother asked.

"Sure, yeah, but…like I say now I'm not so sure I want to. Maybe I can just stay with you guys and Bruiser."

He seemed sincere, but if Nikolai were already sore at us, what would he think if we took Bruiser from him and the funny looking little guy, too? He seemed to sense what I was thinking because he said, "Don't worry, I'm nobody to Nikolai. If I don't report, he'll just send someone else. He won't mind losing me like he would about Bruiser."

He walked along with us in silence for a few moments, then:

"I wouldn't have been able to tell him much anyway. My whole report would have been that your boy wanders around giving sunflower seeds to people and rubbing elbows with other maniacs like the Dunker. That's not much of a threat to someone like Nikolai."

8

The little guy had a point. We were no threat to Nikolai. But I didn't like that he was even aware of us. The little guy had a name—Franz. Of all things. Small as he was, with a name like Franz, he must have gotten his backside kicked every day in school. Probably how he got over was spying on people, getting information they didn't want broadcast and using that for protection. Sneaky. But smart.

He caught up to Torstein and told him everything he'd told us. Torstein gave him some more sunflower seeds and told him he *should* report to Nikolai—that we had no secrets and if Nikolai was interested, he could come and join us himself. That was how Torstein looked at the world.

We covered a lot of ground that morning. The street we were on, Seventh Avenue, now led us right through the suburbs of the city, block after block of single family homes with green lawns and automatic garage doors. At each corner, Sully stared down the street at the houses, like he thought that was summer camp or Disneyland down those streets. There might be kids in a yard running through a sprinkler, or a lady walking a dog. Sully would stand and watch until whoever was at the back of our group would grab his hand and pull him along.

"Let's stay here," he finally said. I guess he'd never seen a suburb before. I don't know how he thought we could stay there. He'd taken it hard that we couldn't stay at the church—maybe he thought these people might let us sleep in their basement like Pastor Ruiz had. Maggie picked Sully up and started carrying him. He was small, but he was too big for her. I took him from her, and noticed she was crying.

"What's wrong?" I asked.

"I could have had a house like these," she said. "And 2.5 kids, and a dog."

"You still can if you want, Maggie," I said. "I don't guess you're 40 yet, and people keep having kids right up to 43 or 45 these days."

Maggie gave me a funny look, but before she could speak, Sully, who'd been listening, said, "Yeah! I'll live with you!" That made Maggie cry harder.

We were crossing a major intersection. On one side of the road there was a strip mall and grocery store, and on the other side a big park. Torstein was heading to the park, but he'd sent some guys to the grocery store, so I guessed we were stopping for lunch. I didn't know what was wrong with Maggie, or how to help her, but she grabbed my arm and said, "Thanks, Andy. I know you mean well." Then she hurried forward to walk with Torstein into the park. Sully wriggled away to run ahead of them.

My brother, who'd been walking a bit ahead of us, dropped back beside me. He said, "I think we need more dames in this outfit. You're terrible at comforting a woman."

Thanks, Pete.

9

W̶e made a picnic in the park. It was Saturday and a lot of suburban families were doing the same. We sat on a little green slope that rolled down toward a duck pond, and after lunch, Torstein started telling a story.

"Once upon a time there was a typical suburban family with a mommy, a daddy and two children. They had a dog and a cat and a mortgage the could manage, an SUV that was paid for and a BMW financed at a low 3.5%. They were very happy."

Some kids had been rolling down the grassy slope toward the duck pond, but then they began to move in close and hear the story.

"Every day the daddy went off to work at 7 a.m. and the mommy got the kids up and ready for school. Then she cleaned up the house, organized the dinner she would cook later that night, and went for her tennis lesson. At four o'clock she picked up the kids, helped them with their homework and started dinner cooking. At six p.m. the daddy would call to say he would be late and not to hold dinner, and then at nine she put the kids to bed and waited for the daddy so she could re-heat his dinner and sit with him while he ate it."

By now some of the parents of the suburbanite kids had joined the crowd listening to the story.

"It was a good life and it probably would have gone on for many years, interrupted only by fabulous vacations to Disneyworld and occasional bouts of melancholy until one day the Mommy was diagnosed with a terminal illness. She had just one year to live. Everyone was very sad! They cried and cried. The mommy tried to be strong and keep everything as normal as possible for the kids. Then she realized: in just one year, she would be separated from them! Would they remember her? What would they think about her? Would they care that she always had dinner ready at 6 p.m.? What would they tell their own children about her?

"The mommy realized, keeping everything as normal as possible was the last thing she wanted for her last year on earth. And the daddy agreed. If there was just one year left for them to be together, he didn't want to waste one minute of it on their normal routine. They sold the house, sold the Beamer, moved in with grandma and grandpa, squandered their savings so dad could quit his job and spend one amazing year with his wife, just playing with their children and loving each other."

Sully was not liking this story, you could tell. The little brow was wrinkled across his tiny forehead. He liked the idea of playing with the kids every day and loving each other, but the reason for it all—the dying mommy—that sounded harsh.

"Did the mommy die?" he asked.

Torstein grimaced a little.

"In a way, yes, she did. She got weaker and sicker, and one day she died. But in another way, she lived much longer than other mommies, because her memory shined so brightly in the minds of her children and husband and parents. After the funeral, the family was poor. The daddy had to try to get some new, better job, and they had to move into an apartment in the city rather than their nice suburban home. He drove the paid-for SUV instead of his plush BMW. But he and the kids had something they'd never had before…they really knew for the first time just who the mommy had been, and what a wonderful woman she was. They missed her more than ever, but they knew she'd loved them more than anything. And at the end of her life, the mommy had something she'd never had before, too. She was able to say that for this one year, she'd really lived, and she'd really loved. Which in the end is the same thing."

Sully still wasn't convinced that this was a good story.

"Did the Daddy get the kids a new mommy?" he asked.

Dragonfly

"I suppose so," Torstein said. "But this time, he found a lady who already knew how much more important it is to love, and to be loved, than to have a nice home in the suburbs and a tennis lesson every Thursday. It doesn't take a terminal illness to teach that lesson…we can all learn it, today." He paused and smiled at Sully, then said, "Now, who wants some sunflower seeds?"

Most of the suburban parents who'd stopped to hear the story now took their kids by the hands and led them away. They hadn't liked the story much, and they didn't want their kids taking sunflower seeds from strangers.

10

We still had miles to go to get back to our neighborhood. We threw away the remnants of our picnic and packed up what was left over so it was easy to carry. As we started to walk away, a young woman came up to Torstein and said, "In your story, the woman had a family to lavish her love on in her last year. What if she'd had no one?"

Torstein said, "No one has no one. If she'd been single, she could have lavished her love on kids like Sully, or people in the old folks home, or AIDS babies in Africa."

"So you think the only way to die, knowing you've really lived, is *volunteerism?*" She was walking along with us now, and she sounded kind of mad.

Torstein offered her some sunflower seeds. "No," he said. "I think that the only way to judge if you've really lived, before you die, is to ask if you've really loved. Not if anyone else loved you, not if you loved *anyone* else, even, but if you loved…everyone."

"Everyone?! How can you love everyone?"

"You start with loving the people closest to you, and work out from there."

We were reaching the edge of the city block that the park ran along. We'd be crossing the next major street in just a few steps.

"If you're dying to live, why don't you come along with us and figure it out?" Torstein asked.

Dragonfly

She stopped now at the edge of the street. The signal light would tell us to walk in just a few seconds. Would she come?

"Where are you going?" she asked.

"To the city. You'd be welcome."

"You're walking?"

"Yes, it's just a few more miles. We might be there by nightfall."

She had taken a handful of sunflower seeds from the sack, but she hadn't put any in her mouth. Now she stood there holding them, looking at Torstein in his green jacket with his sparkling eyes. Clearly she could be happy with us. The light was signaling for us to go, and we'd all started out into the street. Only Torstein lingered with her, and then he started to waltz out into the crosswalk, doing that mincing dance that always made me laugh. I don't know if it was the best choice at that moment, because it *did* make him look a bit like a lunatic, and this woman had been on the fence anyway.

She stayed on the sidewalk and watched him go. Then the light said "Don't Walk," and she obeyed. The last we saw of her, she was standing on the corner with her fist clenched around a few sunflower seeds she hadn't eaten.

11

Torstein caught up to us and said, "That was the devil you know."

"Huh?" I'd never before heard him say anything about any devil before.

"She hasn't got any life back there, but it's all she knows. We offer her a new life, a real life, and she doesn't take it. She's afraid to take it. There's a saying: better the devil you know than a new god."

We were going easy because of the kid, stopping frequently, but now we were at the outskirts of the city, the industrial edges with warehouses and factories. Fewer hospitable places to stop, occasional chain-link fences and big parking lots. It was late afternoon and the sun was beating down on us and the concrete around us. Torstein had taken off his green jacket and was carrying it. Maggie was walking beside him and she said:

"That girl was right, you know. Without a spouse and children, what's the point?"

"It doesn't take a spouse and children to make a legacy if that's what you want," Torstein said. "Already yesterday you were more of a mom to Sully than Angel's been. And, Maggie, you never wanted kids before. When I first saw you, I saw a career woman all the way. No time for kids."

"I got pregnant once," she said. "I was just a teenager."

I was a few steps behind them, and I hadn't wanted to hear that.

But Torstein seemed to take it in stride, and Maggie hadn't taken any particular care that no one else should be listening.

"I'm sorry," Torstein said. "That must have been scary."

"It was."

She drew a little closer to him, but I could still hear her voice ...

"I had a little girl."

"I bet she was beautiful," Torstein said.

"Of course she was!" Maggie's voice was a little husky; like she was crying, or laughing. Maybe both. "I gave her away you know? Put her up for adoption. Since then...I always wondered...where she was, how she was. Who she was."

"Then you decided, instead of making babies, you'd make money. And you did that, Maggie, you did that really well. You did the best you could for your child, and you've done very well for yourself."

"But what's the point?" she said. "If I die in a year, like the lady in your story, or in 50 years, who will remember? Who will care?"

"That depends on what you do with your year, or your 50 years. You don't have to get married and have children to make a difference. Other people besides your own children can remember you and cry at your funeral. Look at me. I'm a single guy. You think no one will cry for me?"

"You're different," she said.

"No denying that!" he said, laughing. "But I'll tell you something. I'm not going to have a funeral. What would be the point?" He spotted a convenience store in a strip mall ahead and whistled to get everyone's attention. "Pit stop!" he called. "Big Gulps!"

We swarmed into the place, 20 or 25 of us all together, and the clerk looked sour. He gave up the key to the bathroom with a great show of reluctance. And when we all began to line up to pay for our small purchases separately, he seemed incensed. We knew from experience it worked better this way than trying to get everything on the counter and pay for it all together and then dole it back out. But I don't think that would have made the clerk happy, anyway. Nothing about us was going to please him.

Sully was picking out sweets, and Maggie was putting them back and trying to interest him in a cold, hard apple from the refrigerator section.

My brother and I got bottles of water, and Torstein got Gatorade. He was the last one to pay, and he offered the clerk some sunflower seeds.

The clerk motioned to a rack of sunflower seeds for sale and said, "I think I have enough sunflower seeds, buddy."

"I see that you do," Torstein said, handing over the money for the Gatorade. "Perhaps I can offer you something else."

"What are you , a smart ass?" the clerk barked.

"No," Torstein said. "I don't mean to be. You seem unhappy here. Why don't you come with us?"

"Why don't you get the hell out?"

Torstein laughed. He was sort of impossible to offend. That was part of his Charm.

12

Sully was getting tired and fussy. Torstein consented to catch the bus the rest of the way downtown. In fact, he sent everybody home when we got into the city. Franz said he would go report to Nikolai and find us the next day. My brother Peter and I went with Torstein to get Sully back to Angel's place.

There were police cars outside the building. Peter said, "If the police are busting Angel, they'll take Sully away."

Torstein thought it over and said, "She'll be out in a day or two if they do arrest her. Can you guys look after Sully 'til then?"

"I can, or Maggie will, I bet," I said. I didn't know what Pete's wife would think if he brought Sully home. She wasn't home that much herself, but you never know. "You guys stay here with Sully a minute. I'll go check."

I had never actually been to Angel's apartment, but Sully told me what number it was, and I went into the building. What a dump! It smelled bad in the dark hallways, but there was nobody in them—the people who usually peed in the stairwell must have disappeared at the arrival of the police, who were in Angel's little two-room apartment. The door was open, so I stuck my head in, and Angel started shrieking at me:

"Have you seen Sully?! Sully's gone!"

I guess she'd come down sometime that afternoon, remembered that she had a kid, realized she hadn't seen him in a while, and called the police—something none of us would ever have expected her to do.

I said, "Yeah, he's downstairs with Torstein. We took him to the beach."

Angel started cussing a blue streak at me, and the police grabbed me by the arms. One of the officers said, "You know where the little boy is?"

They hustled me down into the street, and Angel came along behind us, screaming that we were kidnappers, and, I think, murderers, but she didn't mean that, I'm pretty sure. She was really worked up. Torstein and Pete brought Sully over, and Angel grabbed him and held onto him while she kept screaming at us about kidnapping, and the police arrested us.

Sully got really scared when he saw them cuffing us—he started screaming then for them to let us go, and he squirmed free from Angel and started kicking at the policemen and hanging onto Torstein. It was a bad scene. When Angel saw what Sully was doing, she started screaming at him to get back and shut up, and that made him more frantic than ever.

Finally Torstein knelt down—with his hands cuffed behind him—and Sully wrapped his arms around Torstein's neck, just sobbing. Torstein kept saying to him "It's OK, Sully, it's OK. Everything will be all right in the morning. Just go on with your mom. I'll be back tomorrow ..."

They put us into an interrogation room together. A detective named Waverling was pretty sure we were kidnappers, and worse. "What'd you guys want with that kid?" he demanded. "Are you perverts?"

We'd put in a call to Vic Mondino, one of Torstein's friends who was a lawyer. He'd been with us on the trip to the beach—in fact, he'd barely gotten home when we called. He'd told us to say nothing until he arrived, but Torstein answered the detective anyway:

"We just took him to the shore. He wanted to see the Dunker."

"Another pervert?" the detective sneered.

"My cousin. You've heard about him. He dunks people in the ocean?"

"Torstein," I said. "Vic said not to say anything until he gets here."

"It's OK," Torstein said. "Detective Waverling understands." He turned to the detective and offered him some sunflower seeds.

Dragonfly

Waverling didn't accept any seeds. His next words surprised me. "I hear in addition to being a pervert, you're mixed up with Nikolai, too. Got some of his muscle working for you."

Torstein shook his head. "I got nobody working for me," he said. "And I never met Nikolai."

"I hear things," the detective said. "Big guy named Bruiser running with you now. Nikolai's wondering what you're offering that he's not."

"Oh, well, that's easy," Torstein said. "It's a lot more fun being with me than strong-arming people. You should try it."

The detective got mad then. "Who am I strong-arming?! I didn't strong-arm any one of you. I never touched you at all."

Vic arrived then. He'd called Maggie and sent her to Angel's apartment, where the officers were still taking her statement. Vic said he was pretty sure once Maggie explained things, Angel wouldn't be pressing charges. He allowed us to answer a few questions, but 20 minutes later, we were released. Angel hadn't filed charges, and Sully hadn't been molested, so they had no reason to hold us.

As we were leaving, Torstein invited Detective Waverling to come visit us sometime. I was hoping he wouldn't. I didn't know if he was on the take, or what, but I didn't like how we kept running into Nikolai.

13

Franz came back the next day, with his girlfriend. Beautiful woman, taller than itty-bitty Franz. And, no offense intended to funny looking little guys, but you had to wonder how *she* ended up with *him,* and the only possible explanation was: poor parenting and low self-esteem. Franz told us she was a dancer, but there was no place in the city for a dancer to make a living except the exotic dancers in the clubs Nikolai owned. And the woman looked like a stripper ...

She had this great blond hair like a lion's mane flowing back, and too much make-up on a naturally pretty face. She was wearing a black tank top that showed off the goods and these great tight jeans. She was like a walking shot to the hormones. And little Franz, he kind of strutted beside her, wanted all of us to know she was his.

Torstein elbowed me in the ribs and said, "Put your tongue back in your mouth!" Which I did.

Franz said, "I don't want Tawny shaking it for losers at the club no more. She's gonna move in with me."

"How do you feel about that, Tawny?" Torstein asked.

"OK," she said.

"You like dancing?"

"I don't mind," she said. "It's the only thing I'm good at."

"Not the only thing," Franz said, and he said it loaded, there was no mistaking what he meant, and she gave him a look that was pure broken-heart. These big baby blues about to fill up with tears. She couldn't believe he'd said something coarse about her, three minutes into introducing her to his friends. I guessed he'd told her that she was going to stop stripping and be a lady, and now he'd cut her down in front of us.

It was embarrassing for everyone, and more so because, rough as some of the guys in our group were, Torstein had made us see the value in each other…no one even made nasty jokes around Torstein. Somehow it seemed like that stuff just wouldn't fly with him, like it would be *extra* obscene to say something like that in his earshot.

I guess Franz felt the weight of everyone's horrified stares, because he said, "Nah, baby, I mean you can do a lot of things."

She gave him a crooked half-smile then, afraid that she had misunderstood what he meant, after all.

Torstein offered her some sunflower seeds, which she happily accepted.

"You're welcome here any time, Tawny. In fact, I was just hoping someone like you would come along. There's a lot of small kids in the park across the way every afternoon, and I was hoping to find a lady who might be interested in doing story time with them. Did you ever hear of a book called *Where the Wild Things Are?*"

OK, the stripper/story lady? I wasn't sure this was one of Torstein's better ideas, but Tawny seemed amenable. She took the book and went off by herself to read through it a few times, and later that afternoon, we presented out first story time. She got a pretty good response—maybe five little kids sat through the entire story, but a lot of drunks and bums had crowded around to hear the story, too.

The little kids gave the Tawny hugs before they ran off to do whatever they'd been doing before we crossed the street and invaded their park. The drunks and bums would have given it a go, too, but the rest of us standing around waiting for her discouraged them.

Tawny looked up, all smiles.

"That was great, baby," Franz said. "I told you, you can do a lot of stuff."

14

Story Hour in the park. That was a new addition to our repertoire. At first the drunks and bums turned up to ogle Tawny, but Maggie sized this up pretty quick and told Tawny the truth, I guess...I don't know exactly *what* Maggie told her, really, but she started appearing for story time dressed in Bermuda shorts and button-front shirts. She still looked darn good, but she didn't look quite as much like a stripper. And I think the bums and drunks liked to hear the stories.

We'd all wander to the park about 3 p.m. and sit and listen to the stories. Tawny would practice the day before; she took her job very seriously. Sometimes the kids would ask her to read it again, and she would. Other days they would wander away, and we'd sit there with the homeless guys and talk about what was wrong with the world and how much better they could run it.

Torstein didn't talk a lot in these bull sessions, but if someone actually opened up and shared something personal, he was...sympathetic. He was the best listener in the bunch, and he didn't have this built-in guy thing where he would suggest what could be done to fix the problem. Some loser might be drunk enough to tell us how his dad or his uncle or his step-dad had abused him as a kid...and Torstein *wouldn't* say, "That loser! We oughta track him down and beat his face in!" No, he'd say to the guy, "That must have really ruined your childhood. How did you cope?" or he'd say, "Child abuse is a tragic cycle. Do you have kids?" and get them talking about why their crummy life ended up this way drunk, alone, homeless.

Dragonfly

And of course, he offered them sunflower seeds.

After Story Hour, Tawny would sit with us and listen to the yahoos defend their sorry lifestyle (drunks almost always blame someone else), but every once in a while, she would say something that cut right to the heart of it. And she wouldn't even seem to know it.

Once this smelly freak was telling us that he'd had this great job at a car factory in California (which, do they even make cars in California?!) until the elitist liberal losers in management had made it impossible for an honest man to make a buck. Oh, yeah, he'd been this very big deal with headlights or tail-lights or something, but when he tried to show them how backward it was the way they were doing it, and how much money he could save them doing it his way—they made his life a living hell. And eff him if he was going to work for sons of guns who didn't recognize a man of genius when they saw him! He was so far advanced of the guys who were supposed to be his *superiors* that it wasn't even conceivable they were shafting him for lack of initiative. It was straight-up jealousy. So he quit.

It was lies from start to finish except maybe he did, at some time in his sorry life, have a job for 30 minutes and tried to tell the boss how to do things, then got mad and quit. Maybe.

Tawny was buying it, though. I think she thought they probably did make cars in California, and maybe this genius really had figured out a way to make them more cheaply, but she said:

"You know what, though? Even smart as you are, it didn't do you any good to quit. I mean, because then you didn't have a job at all. And now look where you are."

So, yah. Tawny was no genius. But she wasn't any dummy either. She was the Story Lady.

15

I told you about the Dunker's voice. Awesome, deep voice, naturally projecting, like an actor. These days, he'd started speaking out—in addition to dunking people.

We heard that he was preaching sermons down on the shore, with that gorgeous voice. Mainly he was talking about the serious trouble some of our citizens were going to run into if they didn't mend their ways. Particularly, he was knocking the people who:

❖ Sold drugs.
❖ Sold sex.
❖ Sold weapons.
❖ Abused women.
❖ Stole or vandalized.
❖ Set a poor example for children.
❖ Used air conditioning.

The usual stuff you'd think a mad prophet would preach about, except for the air conditioning, I'm not sure where that came in. Most of us had air conditioning in our places, even if we didn't use it that often. I guess from living outdoors he'd become convinced that filtered air was bad for you.

The funny thing was, the Dunker was getting a following, just like Torstein, but only his following was mostly made up of younger kids, surfers, skaters, like that. And they were taking him seriously, I swear! A bunch of them had cut their hair in crew cuts (which made no sense since his dreads were about three feet long), and they wore t-shirts with a line drawing of the Dunker on them, with a catch phrase printed on them:

"The End is Near."

Franz had heard that the skaters and surfers were starting to annoy Nikolai because they'd left the shore and would go through different neighborhoods where people were committing these offenses and preach at them—or turn them into the cops if they wouldn't repent. They were sort of like those Red Beret vigilante groups, except that they were also anti-air conditioning, for the most part.

When Franz told us this, we were rolling on the ground laughing, but Torstein said, "Duncan isn't a fool. His methods may be strange to us, but he's right on target with what he's trying to do. The only thing is, what he wants to do can't be done by preaching, by setting rules. It can only be done by turning individual hearts."

"Turn or burn, that's what the surfer punks are preaching now," Franz said. "And if they keep getting in the face of Nikolai's soldiers, they're gonna be the ones burning."

"You want to go back to the shore and warn your cousin?" I asked Torstein.

"No," Torstein said. "But maybe we can go back and visit him, and see these surfer punks for ourselves."

This time only a few of us went, and we drove our own cars instead of taking the bus. We had gone late in the day; we knew the Dunker would be out in the waves until people started leaving the beach. We found the Dunker, and a couple of his surfer-skater followers in a parking lot, embroiled in a fist-fight with some of Nikolai's thugs, just as Franz had predicted. Bruiser and Franz had come with me and Pete, Jack and Jazz, and Torstein.

Bruiser and Pete ran out ahead of us to help the Dunker and the surfer punks. Pete was a scrapper. Back in the day, before he got married, he used to get into all kinds of brouhaha's, and I think he'd kind of missed that since he'd settled down and become a family man. He waded in, fists flying, but Bruiser just started grabbing people by the neck and flinging them out of the fray.

I was thinking it would have been a rout if not for Pete and Bruiser, but then the Dunker sort of *exploded*. That's really the only word I can think of for it: he had been grappling down in a crouch with one of the thugs, when he suddenly sprang upright, flinging the thug (who was no lightweight!) forward so he crashed into another thug—the Dunker's crazy hair went flying as he shook his head and *roared*. I swear it, he roared! Then he reached out, grabbed the shoulders of the thug he'd just thrown off him and the one he'd caromed into, and he smacked their heads together, just like a cartoon.

And they obligingly toppled to the ground, dazed, just like a cartoon. I expected to see little animated bluebirds flying around their heads.

After that, the other thugs ran. We heard sirens in the distance, so we decided to beat feet, too. We ran up the boardwalk, and the iron-fisted Dunker was laughing. He'd put his arm around Torstein's shoulders and was dragging him along as we turned the corner into a little blind alley behind a couple of bistros.

Still holding onto Torstein, the Dunker said to his own followers, "This is the man you should be following. He's the one with the real hope for the future. Compared to him, I'm just a messenger boy."

Torstein shook his head. "You're more than that, Duncan, much more."

"Why were those guys trying to beat you up?" Bruiser asked.

"Because they fear the truth," the Dunker said portentously in that awesome voice of his.

"You got something more concrete than that?" Bruiser asked.

One of the skater punks said, "Nikolai's yacht was out, and his little niece came by on her jet ski. Duncan tried to pull her off and dunk her."

"She got away," the Dunker said ruefully.

"You know, you shouldn't antagonize Nikolai," Bruiser said. "I understand you have your job to do, and you can take care of yourself when it comes to a fistfight with a couple of thugs, but...they're just ground-floor with Nikolai. He's got much stronger and much meaner guys to throw at you."

Dragonfly

The Dunker laughed. "Let him come," he said. "Things are changing now. The kingdom is coming. Nikolai can't hold that back."

"Amen brother," one of the surfer punks said.

Huh. The kingdom is coming.

16

One day Tawny turned up for Story Hour with another stripper. She was young, I don't even know if she was 18. She was trying to look tough, smoking a cigarette and wearing these crazy high heels, but she looked like a kid playing dress-up. We got a renewal of interest in Story Hour from the bums and drunks in the park when she turned up. But Franz seemed pretty nervous.

While Tawny was reading the story, he told me, "Nikolai ain't gonna like this. Tawny wants Mari to move in with us, to stop stripping. Nikolai, he's a businessman, and he knows he's gonna lose strippers from time to time, so he didn't pay too much attention when Tawny quit —but now, this kid? She's new. She's only been on the stage a few nights. He hasn't pimped her out yet, and he's planning on getting top dollar for her. This ain't good."

I didn't want to know this. To tell you the truth, I'd never been in a strip club at all. Pete and me, we grew up in a pretty strict Catholic household, and our old man never showed any interest in stuff like that...I guess it was Franz's business to know this stuff, but it wasn't mine. All I could think to say to him was, "I guess it's the girl's choice, isn't it?"

"Sure, sure," he said. "It's her choice. But what does she know? She comes here from Podunk Idaho thinks she's gonna be some big deal in the city, but instead she's starving until she goes to work in the club. She doesn't like doing it, but she's got no place to go and nothing to eat if she don't. Tawny screws up the mix if she takes her in. And it's *my* place. I'm the one who's gonna take the heat if anyone finds out. And someone'll find out. Nikolai's not *that* interested in Torstein and what's going on down here right now. He's curious, but he's got other more important stuff. But if it gets back to him that Tawny and Marigold both are hanging out here telling stories to the homeless…and that they're living in my pad…it's gonna be trouble for me."

"Did you tell Tawny this?"

"She don't care. She says if they can't live with me, they'll get a place of their own."

"Why don't you let them do that, then?"

"One, how they gonna afford it? And two, look at Tawny, man. I don't wanna lose that."

"You got a problem then."

"Don't I know it."

The new girl, Marigold, she was staring at Tawny as she read the story. Today it was *The Giving Tree.* That's a good story, even for adults. But Marigold was, you could say, enchanted. She had stubbed out her cigarette, and she was sitting cross-legged with her hands in her lap, leaning toward Tawny with a smile on her face, her mouth hanging a little open, like a kid absorbed in a story. At the end of it she clapped her hands and said, "I remember that story! I read that book a long time ago!"

There were only three other little kids that day; the rest of the Story Hour audience was grown men, and I don't know if any of them even heard the story. They were all staring at Marigold. She had on shorts and a halter top with her crazy high heels, and she looked like that youngest babe in the Victoria's Secret catalog, but only dressed more like the Frederick's catalog.

One of the homeless guys got up and walked up behind her and started running his hands through her hair. Franz was off like a shot—he was a little guy, but he had this energy like a bantam rooster. He shoved the guy away, pretty hard, but the guy didn't fall down. He backed up a few steps, holding out his hands, palms up, and saying, "Easy now—I didn't mean nothing…"

"Right you didn't," Franz said. "You leave these ladies alone. All you guys, you don't touch them!"

The regulars at Story Hour knew Franz, and they didn't make any response at all. The guys who had come just to get a look at Marigold backed off, mumbling. Torstein said to Marigold, "He didn't scare you, did he?"

She shook her head, and lit a new cigarette. She wanted to be tough again. She said to Franz, "I could have handled it."

"Yeah, yeah," he said. "I know. Look, Mari, you wanna come here and tell stories with Tawny, you're gonna have to dress like she does."

"Whatever," said Marigold, waving her cigarette at him.

"It's all right Franz," Torstein said. "No one will hurt the ladies."

17

I'm not quite sure how it happened. Tawny and Marigold ended up moving out of Franz's place and moving in with Maggie. She had a nice three-bedroom condo in the city, and she put them in one of the bedrooms. It made Franz pretty crazy. Tawny told him she still wanted to see him, but she didn't want to live with him.

"She's grateful as heck and all I gave her a way to get out of stripping, but she would rather live with a complete stranger!" he fumed.

Torstein laughed at him. "Maggie's not a complete stranger. Maggie's been helping her all along, ever since you brought her here. Who do you think helped her get the clothes she's wearing now? And besides, if you want Tawny to live with you, you could propose marriage, you know?"

Franz rolled his eyes.

"Although, I doubt Tawny would marry you. I think she's enjoying catching up on some feminine company right now."

It was story time, and Tawny and Marigold were sitting together in the company of 4 little kids and about 10 homeless guys. They were mostly old guys; they weren't going to give the ladies any trouble. They just seemed to like to sit and listen to them. Marigold helped Tawny tell the stories sometimes, doing different voices. They practiced at home.

They had told Maggie they didn't want to take charity from her, so they'd gotten jobs as waitresses in a diner. They weren't making the same money they had as dancers, but they were meeting nicer people, and it seemed to be making them feel more worthwhile. They worked the swing shift from 4-11 so they could always be here for Story Hour.

And they'd befriended Angel. Franz was wary about that. He still felt protective of both women, and he was afraid Angel would get them hooked on crack. Sully had started bringing Angel to Story Hour, and when she wasn't jumped-up, she seemed to enjoy it. She would stay after and talk with Tawny and Marigold. And sometimes Maggie. Angel seemed shy around Maggie. She knew Tawny and Mari had been strippers, but I guess in her mind she thought Maggie was a "lady," and somehow too good for her.

Just now Sully and Angel were crossing the park for Story Hour. Angel looked OK, not too messed up. Franz growled. "I really don't like that crack-head sitting with the girls," he said, for maybe the 10th time since she started attending Story Hour.

"It's cool," Torstein said. "If love is stronger than hate, it follows that light is stronger than darkness, and good is stronger than evil."

Franz looked at Torstein in confusion. "You wanna explain that, Master Yoda?" he asked.

"Tawny and Marigold are on a good path—in large part thanks to you, Franz. You gave them a way to escape the darkness. Now they're inviting Angel to follow."

"Yeah, or else she'll get them hooked and they'll be worse off than they were stripping."

"That's why I say we have to believe that love is stronger than hate," Torstein said.

I wasn't sure. Was love stronger? Was good stronger than evil? I was glad that Tawny and Mari were discovering they could have normal lives with their self-esteem restored...but I didn't forget what Franz had told me when Marigold first showed up. Was Nikolai wondering where she'd gone? Did he know already?

18

Angel and Sully lived in a rundown tenement building not that many blocks from downtown. One afternoon, Torstein asked Sully to take us to his building. The kid ran ahead of us to the building which happened to have about 10 square feet of dead lawn and dirt, a 5-foot patch, 2-feet deep, on either side of its main entrance doors. Torstein proposed to plant sunflowers there. Not the ones that he offered people to eat. He'd actually got some raw seeds to plant.

He sent me to the Home Depot for a watering can for Sully, and a little fencing to put around each dirt patch. Meanwhile Torstein and Sully pulled up the dead grass and turned over the hard dirt, to make a place for the seeds. We watered the dirt a good bit to soften it up, then Torstein measured off three little plots on each side of the doors to the building, and let Sully plant a seed in each plot.

"Awesome, Sully," Torstein said, as he helped the boy cover each seed and water it in. "These are going to come up in a couple of weeks, and then by the end of summer, I think we'll have some sunflowers."

I didn't know that much about growing flowers but I was pretty sure they should have been planted in the spring so they would already have been blooming about now.

"Then we can eat them?" Sully asked.

Of course that would be what interested him—he never got enough to eat.

"Yes, we can eat the seeds, but not for a long time after the flowers come out," Torstein said. "The flower will come out, and the seeds will grow in the middle of the flower. When the flower dies, then we can get the seeds out."

"You have to roast them, too," Pete said, "before you can eat them."

"That's right," Torstein said. "You wouldn't want to eat one of these raw sunflower seeds. Not much flavor. Once we harvest them, though, we can soak them in salt water, roast them, and they'll be delicious."

"How soon?" Sully asked.

"Oh, in the fall," Torstein said. "A few months from now. But the main thing I think we're looking forward to here is the flowers themselves. They're going to be big, and bright yellow, and very beautiful. Even if we don't get any seeds out of them at all, they'll give us something else, something beautiful to look at. Don't you think this entryway needs something beautiful to look at?"

It certainly did. There was graffiti on the front of the building, one of the double doors into the place hung crookedly on its hinges. There was no kind of lawn other than these two little dry patches of dirt, just the sidewalk and then the street. I guess if you lived there and had a car, you had to park around behind the ugly high-rise.

Sully agreed that something beautiful to look at would be nice, but he was still wondering about eating the seeds. Free sunflower seeds to eat was a big bonus to him. He always took some whenever Torstein offered. In fact some days he would come up and ask for some, even before Torstein could offer.

"We can cook them when the flower dies?" he asked.

"Yes," Torstein said. "Or we can leave them on the flower, and they'll drop to the ground and bloom again next spring."

"The seeds?" Sully said. "They just fall on the ground?"

"When the flower dies, the seeds fall, yes. But then they sprout in the spring, in the new season. You'll see."

A couple of weeks later, the seeds did germinate. I wasn't sure of Sully's abilities to keep watering them, or his neighbors' abilities not to stamp them down when drunkenly staggering into the entrance of the building late at night. But the little fences around them seemed to help, to keep people from tramping them. By mid-summer, they really did have six pretty sturdy, bright yellow flowers blooming.

Dragonfly

The building still looked like crap from the outside, but the flowers looked gorgeous, they actually were like big sunbursts standing in front of that ugly tenement. It occurred to me, they were sort of like our Story Ladies, Tawny and Marigold, shining in that park full of drunks and smelly homeless people. And Torstein, too, shimmering in his green coat against a drab downtown background.

19

An old booze hound named Sig used to stumble out of a bar called Sharky's some evenings and pass by Torstein and the rest of us on his way home. He was always too bleary-eyed to do more than blink and shuffle along on his way when Torstein offered him sunflower seeds. He had a little Jack Russell terrier dog that went boozing with him. The dog would sit outside the bar and wait for him. If Sig didn't come out by closing time, the dog would go in and get him, guide him home.

It was a great dog—Sully used to play with it outside the bar. He tried to take it home, but the dog knew he had to wait for Sig. He'd play fetch with Sully and do tricks, but he wouldn't leave with him, or anyone. Every once in a while, we'd see Sig and the dog, Tartan, on their way into the bar. Sig always looked a little shaky on his way in, but he was always blotto on his way home. Torstein asked Franz to find out about Sig. He was curious why anyone with such a good dog would be killing himself with the booze.

Franz was really good at that stuff. In a few days time, be brought us the most unlikely news: Sig was a policeman. Sig Scarr, a detective. He hadn't found this out inside the bar—no one at Sharky's knew who Sig was. Just some drunk as far as they were concerned. Franz had actually followed him. He took the dog to work with him! The dog would sit in his car while Sig was in the police station; Sig left the window open so Tartan could get in and out if he needed to. And the dog went on calls with him when he did his investigating. The dog had even been known to find evidence. Further, Sig had a family. He had a wife, a grown-up daughter, and a teenaged daughter about to graduate from high school. Not that he saw much of them. He seemed to spend most of his time at work, and at Sharky's.

Now Torstein was really puzzled. Why would a man with a family and a really good dog be drinking himself to death? And why wasn't he doing it nearer to the station than Sharky's? There was a well-known hang-out for cops just about three blocks from the station where he could have been drinking with other law enforcement types and probably not having to buy but every third or fourth drink himself.

The next time Sig passed in a semi-sober state, Torstein said to him, "Evening, Detective Scarr."

Sig stopped and stared at the man in the green coat who knew his name and that he was with the department. Clearly he'd gone to great lengths, drunk and sober, to keep anyone around here from knowing his whole name and his occupation. "How do you know my name?" he asked. Sully was there beside Torstein, and Tartan jumped high, up into the boy's arms, and wriggled over his shoulder and ran down his back. It was a trick they did. This made Sig suspicious, too. "How do you know my dog?" he asked Sully.

Torstein laughed and offered Sig some sunflower seeds. "Sully plays with your dog outside Sharky's some nights," he said. "Why don't you come sit with us instead of going in there, and Sully and Tartan can play in the park?"

This was the same little downtown park where we'd go for story time. Sometimes we'd sit on the benches when there was a crowd and we couldn't all stay on the street without blocking the sidewalk. It was a little way down the block and across the street from Sharky's. Sig looked up the way to his watering hole, then looked back at Torstein.

"The booze will still be there," Torstein said.

Sig shrugged and fell in step with Torstein. Tartan trotted along beside him, little black and white dog on short legs, but with springs in them. He was the classic Jack Russell and could almost fly. When we sat down in the park, at a nod from Sig, the dog went bouncing away with Sully.

There weren't too many of us with Torstein that night. Me and my brother, and another pair of brothers named Jack and Jazz. Bruiser was there, and Franz. Sig Scarr looked us all over with his cop's eyes, nodded to Bruiser as if maybe they were old acquaintances, accepted some sunflower seeds from Torstein and said, "Why you always hanging out on the street?"

"I like to meet new people," Torstein said. "Whenever we're on our way to the park in the evening, we see your dog outside Sharky's, or see you going in. You never would say hello or take any sunflower seeds...I was curious why you were so intent on getting into the bar ..."

"You had my job, you'd be intent on that, too," he said.

"You could go to Wired with the other policemen," Torstein pointed out.

"No, I can't," Sig said. "I'm not like the other policemen."

"Because you're an alcoholic?"

Sig's head flew up, and his eyes were bright. I thought he was going to protest. But when he looked into Torstein's eyes, I don't think he saw any judgment or condemnation there. Part of Torstein's Charm was that he could say something like that, and people realized it wasn't a judgment...it was just the truth.

"Nah, not that," Sig said. "I'm internal affairs. I track down criminal cops. The good officers don't like me because they don't see that I'm not after them, I'm after bad cops. They don't think there *are* any bad cops. It was a promotion, moving to internal affairs, I got to be a detective. But I shouldn't have taken it. If I were walking a beat, I'd still have friends."

"You can still have friends," Torstein said. "We'll be your friends."

"You can come here instead of going into Sharky's," Jack said. "That stuff is bad for your health, and it's a depressant, too." Jack was the youngest of us except for Sully. I doubt he was 20 years old yet, and he was one of those healthy kids who did mountain biking and roller-blading and ate only healthy food.

He was a nice looking kid, and he had a great heart. But he had no idea what it meant to be a guy on the downside of 50 with a job that gave you heart-burn and a problem with the booze.

Sig Scarr looked at him and smiled. "Thanks, kid," he said. "Maybe I will."

20

Sig Scarr didn't fall in with Torstein instantly the way some of us had. I suppose because he already had a very strong addiction vying for his allegiance. He still stumbled home from Sharky's many a night, highly intoxicated. But some nights, he would come and find us after work, before he went drinking, and some nights, he would go home sober.

Little by little, if there weren't too many people around, he would share bits of his work, which was such a great source of heartache to him. A few of our city's finest had been wooed by Nikolai to help him in little ways—to warn him when a drug ring was getting close to busted, to turn a blind eye to the streets where his stable of prostitutes plied their trade, to ignore illegal betting and black-market trading...a few, sadly, had been enticed or pressured into doing more than just *ignoring* crimes and had begun to commit them.

These were the ones Sig was tasked to discover and weed out. If he found one, and got the goods on him, then his mission was to maneuver that one into rolling on another. It was gritty work, and Sig was good at it. But it required secrecy and long-term planning. He might watch a particular officer discreetly for a year before ever making any kind of move on him.

"You get to know the guy in a year," he told us one night. "He's not a criminal. He started out a good cop with a good heart. He's got a wife and two little boys, they maybe have a big German shepherd dog. He doesn't see any harm in *not* busting some pitiful crack whores.

They're just trying to make a living. And he gets a nice bonus from Nikolai, enough money to take his wife and kids to Disneyworld once a year ..."

Torstein nodded in sympathy. "How do you feel about having to ruin a man like that?"

"Terrible!" Sig said. "If it was just that, if it ended there, I wouldn't interfere. The kid's otherwise a good cop. But once Nikolai gets his hooks into them, it *doesn't* stop. He might ask the kid to bust a pimp from a rival gang trying to muscle in on that street. Now we got a basically good cop doing a favor for a mobster. Yeah, it's part of his job what he's doing, but he's doing it *because* Nikolai asked him to. It's little things, little things, and then you're in so far with the little stuff, when he asks for something big you have to do it or else you're screwed."

"Or maybe *you* turn up, asking questions," Torstein suggested.

"Yeah. That might be it, too."

We could tell, the way Sig leaned forward hunching his shoulders, rubbing his forehead, it wasn't hypothetical. There was some kid-cop he'd been watching for a year, and now either he'd discovered something horrible, or he was going to start pressuring the kid with what he knew.

"Maybe I should just quit," he said. "I could go into private security like a lot of officers do. Get out of this mess. Maybe I could just retire and spend more time down here, with you."

Sully and Tartan were rolling in the grass just a few feet away. The dog was so smart, it would run through the playground like an obstacle course with Sully, jumping over the swings from the swing-set like hurdles, climbing the ladder up the slide and running down the slide, and when Sully went hand-over-hand hanging from the monkey bars, Tartan would bite onto a rope around Sully's shoe and be carried across hanging by his teeth. It was hilarious to watch.

Sig looked up at them now, and said, "I could forget all this and just sit in the park with you."

Torstein reached out and put his hand on Sig's shoulder.

"You could," he said. "You'd be welcome."

Sig looked away from Tartan and Sully into Torstein's eyes. "Thank you," he said.

"Your wife, too, you know. Whatever we can do to help you ..."

"I've thought about it a million times. The job is getting to me, has been for years now...but I'm a good cop. And I don't like to see an officer betraying the people we're supposed to protect. I don't wanna hurt this guy...but can I let him go on down the path to hell? I don't know what to do."

Torstein's hand was still on his shoulder.

"It's not up to you to bring justice to the world. You can get out of the game."

"If it's not up to me...who's it up to?"

"What's up to you is to do justice in your own life. You can't make someone else do it. You could retire, you could spend the rest of your days discovering what it means to do justice, to love mercy...You could join us here, in a heartbeat."

Their eyes were still locked on each other, but now Sig turned away, changed the subject.

"I got wire taps a few places." He grimaced as if the idea were distasteful to him. "Nikolai doesn't understand what you're doing here. He sent a message one of the guys should check you out. You oughta be careful who you take in."

"Thanks," Torstein said. "I can afford not to be careful, because people like you are being careful for me."

"Guy's name is Waverling. I think you know him."

The detective who had taken us in when Angel thought Sully had been kidnapped.

Torstein's eyes brightened. "He seemed like a good man. I am sure if he comes to check us out, he won't be telling any tales to Nikolai."

Sig nodded. "Okay, forewarned is forearmed. I have to move on this other thing, pretty soon now. I've been putting it off, thinking maybe I'd just retire...I know I won't. I'll see it through. But I may not be around for a while. Things will get busy once I put this in motion."

"I understand," Torstein said. "We'll be here, any time."

21

"Sig's idea of justice—most people's idea of justice—is badly flawed," Torstein said.

"They think it has something to do with balancing the scales, inflicting as much suffering on a criminal as he inflicted on his victim. But you can't 'balance' one person's suffering with another's. A prisoner in jail may suffer, but he certainly doesn't suffer in the same way or the same amount as the person he wronged.

"Of course, the criminal's suffering does absolutely nothing to restore to the victim what was taken from him by the crime. And finally: the criminal himself behaves in this criminal way because of something that was done to him in his past, or something not done for him in his childhood, and so punishing him does not address 'justice' for him—only redressing the wrong done to him in the past would equal justice for him...and isn't *he* as deserving of it as his victim?"

Yah, Torstein would say stuff like this, and everyone would go... "Huh, now, what?"

He would laugh.

"OK, think about it this way. Once upon a time there was a gazillionaire named Donald. One day a former employee named Ross came to him and asked for a jumbo loan of $50 million to launch a new business. Donald lent him the money with a payment plan based on the business slowly growing over the next 10 years. But it didn't. It spectacularly failed!

"Now Ross owed $50 million to Donald, and had no way to pay

it. He threw himself on Donald's mercy, saying: 'I lost everything and I'm about to lose my house, and my kids are going to starve. I really can't pay you and not feed my family.' Donald felt sorry for him. 'OK,' he said, 'Forget the loan. You're off the hook.'

"Then Ross headed home, happy, and he saw a friend, Bill, who owed him $50. He stopped and demanded the money, because he really needed it badly, clearly, but Bill was even more poor than him! 'If I had the $50, I'd pay you,' Bill said. 'But all I have is a dollar, and I'm going to buy milk for the baby with that.' Ross got incensed when Bill wouldn't pay! He hauled him into small claims court, took his last dollar and garnished any future wages he might get until the whole $50 and interest were paid. That's justice for Ross: Bill *did* owe the $50. But Ross had already been forgiven a $50 *million* debt. Was that fair? Was it just?"

"What's garnish?" Sully asked.

"A right to someone's money in the future." Torstein was pretty straightforward about answering kids' questions with something they could understand, but with adults, it was all stories and illustrations. In a way it was like learning a new language, seeing things from a radically different perspective than you'd ever seen them before.

"So you're saying mercy is *better* than justice, is that it?" Ferdy asked. "I think we all believe that."

"I'm saying mercy and justice are very nearly the same thing at their root," Torstein said. "I'm saying if you could understand the forces that have shaped each person into who they are, from the criminals to the saints, you'd be able to understand justice, and not before. I'm saying if you could restore to *each one* what has been taken from them, expunge the devastation of what's been done to them, pour into them what needful things were denied them, *then* you could really do justice. That's what would really balance the scales."

"In a society though, you have to have laws, and there has to be a penalty for breaking the law," Pete said. Not that he was a huge law and order guy, but he *did* appreciate order in general.

"Does there?" Torstein said. "When you have a little baby, you institute rules for his own protection. The older and more mature he becomes, the better he understands the reasons behind the rules, so the less he needs the punishment for breaking them. Shouldn't societies grow in the same way?"

"They *should,* but they don't," Bruiser said. "I mean, look at me, 35 years on the wrong side of the law and never punished for it, so I just kept doing it ..."

Torstein laughed. "You're my best example then! No one punished you for breaking the law, and all on your own, you *stopped* doing it! Maybe I gave back to you something that was taken from you so far in your past you don't remember it, something that turned you to the dark side. Maybe I gave you *justice.*"

It was something to think about, wasn't it? What if we pursued *mercy* as if it were *justice*? It was a crazy idea…but in a way you could see how it could work.

22

There were at least two sets of brothers in Torstein's motley crew. There was me and Peter, and then there was Jack and Jazz. We had known their family slightly back in the day; their dad owned some fishing boats and had been one of our dad's vendors at the fish market. Actually, Jack was too young; I didn't remember him, but Jazz was close to my age. We'd helped him unload fish some cold mornings from his dad's truck into the back of the fish market. It happened that not long after we'd taken up with Torstein, we ran into Jack and Jazz—delivering fish. They still worked for their dad. We'd told them about this crazy guy in the green coat and invited them to come and meet him sometime.

They had shown up that afternoon, and then they never went back to the docks. I guess they squared it with their dad somehow, but they hadn't delivered another fish for his business after they met Torstein. What they *would* do, if we needed some money, was take their dad's old boat out in the early morning and catch a few fish. Pete and I had gone with them a few times. We were all good hands at fishing, and we could bring in a big tuna or mahi-mahi that we could sell for a few bucks a pound easy.

One morning when we'd just moored with a pretty good haul of halibut and grouper, their mom came down to the dock. She was a fish wife for sure, a little fat lady with curly gray hair pulled back in a bandana. She gave Jack and Jazz affectionate pecks on the cheek and then kissed me and Pete, too. We'd never met her back in the fish market days, but apparently her good will for her boys flowed onto whoever they were with.

We threw the fish into a big cooler in the back of their dad's truck, and their mom told us she would go with us into the city and drive the truck back. They said OK; I imagined she had shopping or something she wanted to do in the city, but no, after we'd sold our fish and were going to get coffee and then down to find Torstein, she said she'd come with us. She wanted to meet Torstein.

"My boys meet this miracle man, and suddenly they're too busy to work for their daddy no more," she said. "I want to see this man."

Torstein was delighted to meet her, and offered her some sunflower seeds right away, which she declined. Diverticulitis, she said. The seeds didn't sit well with her. But despite refusing the seeds, she seemed to look on Torstein with kindly eyes. She said to him, "My sons are fishermen. I don't know how they can be any help to you, young man. From what they say, you're trying to start some kind of revolution."

Torstein laughed.

"Is that what they told you, ma'am?"

"Not in so many words," she said. "But they say you have new ideas, new ways of thinking, better ways."

"I think maybe my ideas are old ideas. Better than new ones."

"When my boys were young, I didn't want them to go fishing. I wanted them to go to school. With an education I thought they could get out of the boats and get into an office, make some money, have a better life. So their own children wouldn't have callused hands and tales of friends washed away in the storms."

"There's nothing wrong with calluses. And someone has to do the fishing if we want to eat seafood," Torstein said.

"Someone does, but not my boys, maybe," she said. "Maybe if you're really doing something worthwhile, you can use them to help you. They're strong boys, and even if they wouldn't go to school, they're smart. They can be your right-hand men. They say you're starting a movement here. If you're at the head of the movement, maybe they can be your second-in-command. They can be a big help to you."

"Ma!" Jack said. "There's no second-in-command!"

But Torstein laughed again. He reached out and wrapped his

arms around the shoulders of Jack and Jazz, hanging between them, grinning.

"If they want to follow where I'll go, if they can march into hell for a heavenly cause, I can't think of anyone I'd rather have beside me," he said. "But I don't always get my own way. And I'd have to *be* in command in order to have a second-in-command."

Jack and Jazz laughed, but their mom nodded, all seriousness.

"I understand," she said. "Well, they're good boys. I hope they don't let you down."

"What about you, ma'am?" Torstein said. "Why don't you come and join us?"

"Revolutions are for the young," she said. She kissed the boys and gave me and Pete a hug before she left. She waved to Torstein and said, "Come and see me sometime. You should meet my husband."

"I will!" Torstein called. "I'd like to get out on the boat."

"You'll be welcome."

23

Ferdy didn't like the expense for a cooler full of beer. But we were going fishing, and beer was a necessity. Since Jack and Jazz's mother had told Torstein to come out and meet her husband, he'd been planning a day out on the water. The summer was drawing to a swift conclusion, and he wanted to go before the winds changed. We'd already had some early nor'esters, so we agreed to go the following weekend.

I don't know exactly when it had happened, but sometime in the summer, after we'd seen the Dunker, more and more people had been coming around, sitting with us in the park in the afternoons, wanting to talk to Torstein or hear what he had to say, or just be near him. Anymore, once Story Hour began, there might be a hundred people sitting, waiting for him to pass by, to offer them some sunflower seeds, to chat. They'd wait politely for the end of story time, but then they wanted Torstein.

He wanted them, too. He would move from group to group among those gathered, give away the seeds, meet new people, pick up their kids and kiss them…listen to sad stories, give away money or advice… Looking back, it's unusual that we didn't all find it very unusual. Finally it got so that from about three in the afternoon on, sometimes until midnight, people were sitting talking with Torstein, following him if he left the park, waiting for him outside if he ducked into some place for dinner.

They weren't all homeless or beggars, either (although of course, a good many were). It got so Ferdy was going broke every day or two because of the money Torstein would give away as he talked to the poor people who came to him for help, or the meals Torstein would buy for hungry families...the word had gotten out that he was a soft touch. As the autumn chill began to be felt in the earliest morning hours, we could feel change coming to our strange existence with him.

But the summer wasn't over yet. A couple more weeks remained. And we were going fishing. I think Torstein loved helping these people who came to him for advice or money or just a kind word, but I think it was wearing him out. I think he needed to get away, to relax.

Jazz and Jack's father met us at the docks and supervised the provisioning of the boat for this day trip—a cooler of beer, a basket of sandwiches, a cooler of sodas. He told Torstein his sons were good captains and that he wished us good fishing. He said not to stay out too late as squalls were predicted later in the day.

If we'd been serious about fishing, we'd have been out on the water before daylight. We didn't expect to catch much, and what we did catch we would release, since we might not find any market for it this late in the day.

Jazz was the captain and took us out onto the open sea. He would try to find some big fish for sport, he said, and we got Torstein strapped into one of the fighting chairs to try his hand. Tawny and Marigold had come along, but they were up on the bow working on their tans. Maggie didn't tan, so she said she would try fishing, and took the seat next to Torstein. Sully said he wanted to fish, too, but he was really too small, so Maggie put him on her lap, and we strapped them in together.

Jack stood between the fighting chairs instructing the fishermen on what to do once we were trolling. It wasn't 10 minutes before Maggie had a big hit on her line—she started screaming, and then the reel started screaming as the line played our fast. Whatever she'd hooked was big and strong! Jack started helping her and Sully hold onto the rod and play the fish—both of them shrieking with laughter, Sully shouting incoherently about the size and power of *his* fish—and then—bang! Something hit Torstein's line, and his reel began to sing.

My brother Pete jumped up beside him to help him play it, but Torstein was handling it. Pete just called out instructions as he watched the tension on the line and looked for the fish to break the water. Maggie and Sully kept screaming, and Jack was laughing—he'd caught a million fish more or less in his day, but you could tell he was loving this, the enthusiasm of the newbies, the laughter from Torstein and shrieks from Maggie and Sully.

Then, and you wouldn't believe this if you hadn't been there to see it, both lines straightened out parallel with one another, and at the exact same moment, side by side, two enormous billfish broke the water together and tail-walked—*wick, wick, wick, wick, wick*—10 yards toward the boat, as if they were going to jump in of their own accord. They were blue marlins, bigger than Sully, and their eruption from the sea had thrown up two twin plumes of rainbow spray as the sunlight caught the droplets of sea water that went flying around them.

"Holy cow!" Jack screamed.

"Steady, steady," Pete called.

"Sharks!" Sully squealed.

"Lord have mercy!" Maggie hollered.

Then, *splash!* The two magnificent fish dove back under the sea in tandem and dragged the lines with them.

Jazz had run out of the wheel-house to see what was happening, and now he bellowed, "I don't believe it!"

But we'd all seen it. That was the kind of weird stuff that happened when Torstein was around.

They played those fish for half an hour. Then Sully and Maggie maneuvered out of the fighting chair, and we strapped little Franz in. With my help, and Jack's, he landed their fish in another half hour. He was as excited as Sully, just beaming all over his funny looking little face. The fish was taller than he was. He and Sully and Maggie all had their picture made with it.

Torstein finally landed his fish about the same time, and let Sully have his picture made with that one, too. Then we cut the fish loose, and Torstein watched them tear away, calling out to them, "Thanks guys! That was awesome!" I fully expected them to circle back and stand up again like dolphins...but at least we were spared that.

Bruiser and Ferdy had taken their places in the fighting chairs, and Jazz consulted his fish finder to go and find them some good fishing.

Dragonfly

Torstein stood under the fresh-water shower on the stern for a few seconds, then staggered up to the bow where Tawny and Mari were sun-bathing. He sat with them until he dried off, then went below-decks and said he would take a nap. Up top Bruiser had already hooked a good-sized tuna, and Pete was helping him land it.

We had a good day's fishing.

24

The squall came up on us fast. I assume Torstein was still sound asleep in the tiny cabin below. Tawny and Marigold came running from the bow of the boat to get under cover as soon as the first big rain drops began to fall. Jazz said he better turn us back to shore, and the last two fishermen in the fighting chairs reluctantly let us reel in the lines. Everyone had caught something, which was crazy in itself—we'd batted around, and Franz had even had a chance to catch a fish of his own, in addition to landing Maggie's fish. My brother Pete and I didn't take a turn, and neither did Jack or Jazz, but everyone else had amazing luck.

Maybe the sea gods were going to make us pay for that luck, though. The first big drops of rain had fallen out of a mostly blue sky. But within five minutes, the sky had completely crowded over with roiling black clouds, laden with hard stinging rain that came down and hit the roof and the deck like the rat-a-tat sound of a machine gun. The choppy seas we'd been riding with relative ease began to build into big 8 and 10-foot waves.

Jazz was a good captain and kept the boat from turning, but we still had to pitch and roll with the rising seas. Ferdy got sick first, and then Bruiser. You can't vomit on the boat or the smell makes everyone else sick, so they would stagger to the rail and heave, holding on for dear life. Tawny got sick, and Franz held onto her as they crossed the slick deck, and anchored her with his arms while she leaned over.

Everyone was soaked, even those of us who hadn't had to visit the rail, because of the way the wind drove the rain straight at us. We'd sent Sully with the girls downstairs to get out of the weather, but Tawny couldn't stay because she had to throw up, and Sully wouldn't stay because he was five and had never had any good parental guidance.

With all the rock and rolling, all the heaving and upchucking, Torstein never budged from the little berth where he'd gone for a nap. He must have been exhausted, or the heaviest sleeper ever.

We hadn't been strictly as safe as we should have been when this pleasure cruise began, but now we passed out the life jackets, and made sure Sully was secure in his. A gigantic wave broke over the bow, and the resulting wash across the deck actually lifted Sully up and carried him forward a few feet before Bruiser grabbed him up out of the water. Several of us were crowded into the wheelhouse, and now Jack pushed up next to Jazz and looked at the instruments.

"We're not far from home," Jazz said heartily. "Things may get rough, but we'll be fine." Jack nodded. Jazz said, "I do think we oughta stuff the kid below, though. Make Bruiser go with him and hang onto him. Just in case, you know. Send anybody who will fit and who isn't sick. I don't like the waves breaking on the deck like that with people up top."

Sully started to kick up a fuss, but Jack said, "Look, on a boat, the captain is in charge, and Jazz is the captain. You do what he says or you get off." Bruiser picked Sully up, popped the hatch and descended to the cabin below. A few others followed, to clear the deck a bit. The rest of us stayed packed in the wheelhouse to try to get out of the rain. Jazz was calling for weather reports ahead of us. We knew this squall could not be very big, or there would have been reports about it earlier in the day. We expected any moment to sail out of it ...

... but instead it seemed to get worse until one crazy wave pushed the boat sideways, near 90 degrees. Jazz had been steering us skillfully into the rollers to keep us steady as could be, but this wave came out of nowhere and slapped us hard. We all went crashing into each other in the wheelhouse and anything loose on the starboard side came smacking down on top of us.

I knew there would be chaos below, judging by the relative chaos up here, as the boat lurched and—I hoped—righted itself, I fought my way to the stairs and to the cabins below. Bruiser was picking himself up off the deck. Maggie and Marigold were still in a heap up against one wall. Ferdy and some of the other guys were sitting in the floor looking a little stunned, and Sully was crying like the kid that he was...I started helping the ladies up and making sure everyone else in the crowd was okay.

At that moment, Torstein's disheveled head popped out of he forward berth where he'd been sleeping, and he grinned at us and said, "You playing Twister, or what?"

"Just a little squall," I said.

"We're sinking!" Sully screamed, running, as best he could with the boat rolling, toward Torstein.

Torstein laughed and swung his legs out of the berth. "I don't think so, Sully," he said. He picked the kid up and started walking toward the steps to go up.

"Maybe you oughta stay down here, Torstein," I said. "It's pretty rocky." But even as I said it, I noticed the boat was starting to roll a little less. Torstein just grinned at me and walked back upstairs. By the time he popped the hatch and stepped out on deck with Sully in his arms, we had sailed out of the squall...or it had blown past us.

The sea was noticeably calmer even than the light chop we'd had in the morning, and the setting sun was gleaming peacefully across the water at us. Sully's jaw dropped in amazement, and I could hear Torstein chuckling ...

"Sinking, huh, buddy? Doesn't look to me like we're sinking."

A few minutes later we were tied up at the dock, safe and sound, and Jack and Jazz's parents were serving us drinks on their patio.

25

The summer had been golden—the trip to the shore, the fishing trip, even those gorgeous sunflowers that showed no signs of drying up and dying in front of Sully's building. We were living almost under and enchantment, everything was so right.

Which was crazy, because everything wasn't right. Angel was still a crack addict. Most of the guys Torstein befriended were still drunks or homeless people with no future. A few drug addicts, too. And the Dunker, if anything, had come under worse fire for the way he was carrying on down by the water. His followers, also called Dunkers, had been causing a stir wherever they went, preaching that same "turn or burn" message he'd started preaching a few weeks back.

One Friday afternoon while we were congregating in the park for Story Hour, the bus on the other side of the street paused to let off a giant with dreadlocks and several crew-cut surfer punks. Duncan and the Dunkers had come to join us! Torstein ran over to greet his cousin and came back to the plaza in the center of the park, arm in arm with the Dunker. He introduced him around, and Duncan introduced the young men he'd brought with him. Then he told them to be on their way. I guess he'd brought them downtown to preach.

They all took off up various streets. Our downtown had government buildings, businesses, law firms, and even three or four hotels—one of them had a convention center attached, so from time to time the area was overrun with conventioneers. There happened to be a big gun show that had opened earlier in the day. Lots of vendors, exhibitors and attendees were crowding the streets. Mostly the vendors were legitimate folks who sold guns per the laws already in place with background checks and whatever else...but they attracted the other kind of gun vendors who had a sort of no-waiting policy when it came to any arms, legal or illegal. I wondered if the Dunker had brought his posse here to preach to *them,* and what kind of reception they would get.

Duncan had a cut over one eye healing, and Torstein asked him about it.

"That hired muscle Nikolai sends after us," the Dunker grunted. "We've had two more run-ins with them since that day you came. When will he learn that I'm not to be stopped by a threat of physical violence?" The Dunker himself looked practically indestructible, but his followers looked like beach-blond boys by comparison, and I was pretty sure the threat of physical violence meant more to them than to Duncan.

He sat with us through Story Hour, and he was certainly appreciative of the Story Ladies' interpretation of *Seven Chinese Brothers.*

"Swallowed the ocean?!" Dunker laughed. "I would love to have that power."

Story Hour had become a major event for folks downtown that summer. A lot of kids came from the projects not so far from downtown, sometimes with their mothers or babysitters, sometimes on their own. A lot of the homeless folks who stayed in the park or wandered the downtown streets would come, too. Torstein charmed everyone. Each day after Story Hour, he would move from group to group of those who remained after the story, speaking with each person, offering sunflower seeds, shimmering like a dragonfly in his green coat.

As he moved away from our group after Story Hour to go greet our other guests—as he called them—the Dunker stood up and said, "You're doing something good here, Torstein. But you're not being bold enough. You want to make an omelet, you have to crack some eggs."

"Did you just make that up?" Torstein said, laughing.

"You're not making enough noise. You're not cracking enough eggs," Duncan said.

Torstein smiled at his cousin, the big man with the great voice, the wild man with the gnarly dreadlocks, the strong man with the cut over his eye. And Torstein's smile was full of affection, his eyes shining with love. "From the beginning of time until now, the world's been groaning for the kingdom to come. The violent take it by force. The wise beguile it with love. You have your methods, and I have mine, Duncan."

"The ends are the same," the Dunker said. "And my way is speedier and more satisfying. Come with me, Torstein. Not a mile from here there are death dealers plying their trade with no interference from the authorities or the people. We can cramp their style."

He grinned, and I thought, *he's looking forward to getting in a fight with a drug dealer or a gun runner.*

He turned to Pete and Bruiser and said, "What about you two? You don't look to be afraid of a fight. Come with me."

Pete stood up to go. Torstein cleared his throat and gave his cousin a loaded glance. The Dunker seemed to reconsider, and said to Pete, "No, no. You've found the true way here, with Torstein. I won't take you away from it."

Pete turned to Torstein who said, "You can choose for yourself, Pete. But Duncan's way isn't my way."

"I'll go see," Pete said. He and Bruiser stood and followed the Dunker as he strode away out of the park, toward the hotels and the convention center.

"Pete!" I called. "Be careful!"

He looked back at me and grinned. "I'll be back!" he called.

26

Pete said the Dunkers—the crew-cut surfer and skater punks—were stationed around all the entrances to the convention center, calling out to passersby that guns and violence were destroying this generation, and that they were taking their lives in their hands to go into this air-conditioned hall.

But that wasn't what the Dunker himself had in mind. He led Pete and Bruiser behind the center into the parking garage where in the basement there was apparently a second, smaller convention going on—automatic weapons and guns that required no license or waiting period. How did the Dunker even know about it?

"It was all out of the back of cars," Pete said. "Cars and trucks loaded down with guns and ammo. The Dunker goes strolling in like he's walking into the Wal-Mart, and he starts shouting back to me and Bruiser about the inventory—*Enough fire power here to conquer the world, boys!*, he shouts. *I wonder if the local police would like to know about this? Or if they already do?!*, he asks us. By now Bruiser and I regret following him, but think about it—if we hadn't, he would have been walking in there alone."

Pete marveled at this. He was a man who appreciated courage, and I could tell he admired the Dunker for what I perceived as his foolhardiness. That was Pete. Truth be told, his temperament suited the Dunker better than it suited Torstein's style...but once you'd fallen prey to Torstein's Irresistible Charm, not even the Dunker could change your mind.

Dragonfly

Pete said he thought it might be the devil of a fight if the Dunker kept shouting at the arms dealers.

"You generation of vipers!" he shouted. "You killers of children and blighters of the future! Don't you know that the means by which you deal death to the innocent could be the means by which you'll die yourselves?!"

You have to consider the Dunker's remarkable voice, enclosed in the basement level of a dark parking garage. He had that amazing, booming voice to begin with, then it echoed back from all the concrete walls, ringing loud through the darkness and the half-light.

"You're making your own bed, but you may not find it so comfortable when you have to lie in it! Even now you can change your ways and stop this evil thing you're doing. If you will abandon your sordid business in murder, and follow the light to truth, you can still escape the wrath to come!"

Pete said trunks started slamming, buyers started stampeding to the elevators, and the dealers themselves started sizing up whether they thought they could take down the giant who was ruining their business...of course, they could have used their own weapons, but once the shooting started, the police would be forced to respond (whether they wanted to or not!) and the flea market would be shut down.

"You can flee the sound of my voice," the Dunker continued to bellow. "But the message will follow you and ring in your ears: you are doing evil, and evil will pursue you! You are courting violence, and violence will pursue you! You are dealing in death, and death will pursue you!"

Someone yelled back from the sidelines:

"Shut up, you freak! Get the hell out of here before we kill you!"

27

Pete said the Dunker just laughed.

"You may kill me, but the words I speak will not die! They will live in your heart and mind! They will trouble your nights and make all your days cold. Don't let this fate catch you—turn from your evil ways, now! Destroy your weapons and work for peace!"

Pete and Bruiser stood in awe that no one had attacked them yet. These were arms dealers, tough guys, thugs. Many of them were Nikolai's men. Some were individual contractors just trying to sell off guns they'd stolen or needed to make disappear. Most were individuals who were used to fighting and not used to fear. Pete said he looked up at Bruiser at one point, and Bruiser was grinning at the Dunker, as if, Pete said, Bruiser thought the gods protected crazy people, as the Amerindians used to believe.

"Andy, you should have seen it. These guys were really spooked just by the crazy sound of his voice, and that wild power that he walks in," Pete told me.

Then the Dunker started following the departing buyers to the elevators, haranguing them:

"Don't think that you've escaped the fate of these cursed ones!" he shouted at them. "Just because you don't deal in weapons doesn't make your use of weapons any less damnable! Your violent ways will lead you to a violent end! But it doesn't have to be—you may depart from this wickedness and learn to do what's right before God and man!"

Finally, the opposition turned up. Two huge gargoyles that Bruiser thought were on Nikolai's payroll came out of the darkness and told the Dunker to get out. They had guns in their hands and did not look reticent about using them. Here's what the more articulate of the two said:

"Look, jackass. I been on the phone with the boss and he's damn tired of you. You and your faggy-ass followers are causing him lots of troubles he don't need. So here's the deal. Back off. Back way off, and don't let us hear no more from you or from your crew-cut boy toys. You shut up and clear out, and we don't kill you. You keep on bellowing, and the Hilton security guards be wiping your brains off this parking lot."

Pete said the Dunker shouted back, right in their faces:

"You don't have to die—you can still save yourselves. Throw down your weapons. Desert this boss who forces you to be criminals. Follow the light of truth and you may yet live!"

These two thugs, however, were immune to threats from an apparently unarmed man. They didn't flinch, but they did draw down. At that point, Pete said, the Dunker lunged at them, grabbing the wrist of each gun-toting hand in one of his own and twisting them so hard, they both dropped their weapons!

"It was beautiful, Andy. I don't know any other word for it. He was like freaking Super Man down there. They were tough boys, and they dropped to their knees. But they jumped right back up and came after him. The Dunker punched them both right in the nose, I swear to you, each with one hand, like he's ambidextrous. They dropped, and he just turned his back on them like they weren't there and pushed the button for the next elevator up."

As he stood waiting for the elevator, he turned back to the thugs on the ground, and the rest of the arms dealers, and called out:

"Today salvation is coming! Your chance to be part of a new kingdom is here! Don't waste these moments—don't throw your lives away! Wickedness is bowing to righteousness. Evil is beginning to bow to good! Don't be caught on the wrong side of that action!"

At that moment, the elevator arrived, the door opened, Duncan, Bruiser and Pete climbed aboard and punched the button for the ground floor.

"You should have come, Andy. It was amazing."

28

Angel had a problem. In addition to her crack problem.
   She'd been coming around a lot, sitting for a few hours after Story Hour with Tawny and Marigold. She'd even gotten comfortable around Maggie, and a few times she had looked Torstein in the eye. Once she took some sunflower seeds from him. I think when she was on the street, or in the park, with us, she felt...better. I know the crack addiction weighed on her all the time. I'm pretty sure even when she wasn't high, she felt like she wanted to be high. And I know when she wasn't with us, she was doing what she had to do to get money for crack. And then, of course, after that she was getting high.

It seems like, when she was with us though, she wasn't a crack whore anymore. She was just Angel, Sully's mom. And from the few times I saw her laughing with the other ladies, or smiling when she listened to Torstein talking, or holding her son in her lap, I think she liked that. I think she liked being just Angel, just Sully's mom. And that was her problem. She would have liked to be just Angel, all the time. But the crack thing was too strong. And if she admitted that she wanted to try to beat it—then the fabric of her life would be torn apart. She'd have to leave us, get professional help, find someone to look after Sully or else lose him to Child Protective Services. That was her problem.

When Tawny and Marigold told her about the fishing trip, you could see the longing in Angel's eyes. It was just a fishing trip on somebody's old boat where we sailed into a storm that almost capsized us...but she listened to their description of it with the wonder of a little

74

kid who can't imagine such an adventure is possible just for the taking. I don't know where Angel came from or whether she ever had a vacation or even a trip to the ocean in her life…but at this moment, it looked like she'd never been out of the city and could hardly dare to dream that there *was* any place out of the city. She wanted it so bad.

Maggie was sitting with me and my brother. She had her cell phone again and was doing some business—not brokering like she used to do; she was trying to buy the condo next door to hers. She flipped the phone shut, got up and walked over to Angel. She said, "Angel, if you ever want to go in rehab, I have a place for Sully with me. He could stay there as long as you needed. And, you know, if you get off the junk, and you need a place to stay, you could stay there for a while too."

Tawny looked over at Angel, and grabbed her hand and said, "Oh, do it, Angel!"

Marigold clapped her hands like a little kid and said, "You have to, Angel!"

Angel looked down and shook her head. "I couldn't," she said.

"OK," Maggie said. "I just wanted you to know, if you ever think you can, that I'll look after Sully. He's old enough to start school in a couple weeks, you know, and you're going to have to make sure he has the things he needs and that he goes to class and all."

I hadn't thought about it, but Sully was old enough to go to school now. And it was getting to be time for school to start. But there was no way Angel was going to be able to keep a kid in school. She didn't keep Sully now; he spent half his time with us. Maggie had somehow put all this together, and she was confronting Angel with it like a pro.

"If you wanted to go into rehab now, we could get Sully moved in with me, and then he would be ready for school. I'd make sure he went, and make sure he studied."

When Angel wasn't cracked-out, or before she became a crack addict, I think she had normal intelligence and maybe even some kind of coping skills. But since the drugs had taken over her life, to her, being a mother meant calling the police if Sully didn't come home in a few day's time. The idea of being responsible for dressing and supplying him for school and getting him there every day…clearly she was unprepared for anything like that.

"I can manage," she said weakly.

"OK, good," Maggie said. "I just wanted you to know, the offer is there if you need it."

Maggie came back to Pete and me and sat down, smiling a little.

Torstein was working the crowd. There were several more kids than there had been at the beginning of the summer who came regularly for Story Hour now, plus many more homeless and even a few people who worked downtown but had started taking an afternoon break to come to the park. The story time was over, but they were all still lounging around the park, some of the homeless looking for Ferdy because they knew he was the money man. Torstein was wandering among them, talking and laughing with the children and the adults, sharing his sunflower seeds. His green coat was shimmering in the late summer sunlight, and the way he moved from group to group made him look more than ever like a hovering dragonfly.

When he came back toward us, Angel left the other ladies and went to meet him. They sat down together a little way off, and Torstein reached out to hold Angel's hand. We couldn't hear what they were saying, of course, but some time later they got up and came over to Maggie. Angel said:

"I'm going to try rehab. I would really like it if you'd take care of Sully until I get back."

Ferdy had appeared out of nowhere. He glared at Angel, but she was staring at Maggie, who got up and hugged her. "That's great, Angel!" she said, and led her away explaining what they would do.

Ferdy said to Torstein, "Who's going to pay for rehab?! We don't have that kind of money."

"There's a charity one. I met the director one time. I'm sure they'll take her. It's just a couple hours away by bus ..." he was watching the two ladies discussing the future, and he said, "When Maggie gets back I'll borrow her phone and call them."

Ferdy handed Torstein his phone. "Call now. Make sure it's completely free."

Torstein grinned at him. "OK, stingy!" he said. "Can we at least go the bus fare?"

Dragonfly

Ferdy didn't think it was funny. "Maybe," he said. "Depends how much you give World Wildlife Fund in the meantime."

That cracked me up. I told Ferdy I'd go the bus fare.

"Thanks," he said, as if this dough would have been coming out of his own pocket—the only money we had was money people gave us, or money we'd make fishing or doing some other odd job. Ferdy had even done taxes back in the spring and kicked in most of what he made. Now he didn't want to spring for bus fare.

29

Sully was happy to move in with Maggie, but he worried about the sunflowers. He didn't have a pet, and he didn't collect baseball cards or build models. I guess the only worthwhile thing he'd ever done was plant those seeds and tend to the flowers. Plus he really, really wanted to eat some of the seeds he'd grown himself.

To make him happy, when Maggie would bring him by the park, sometimes we'd walk with him to the building and let him look after the flowers and check on their progress. When they began to die, he was upset.

"What's wrong with them?" he asked Torstein. "They're all shriveled up."

"Remember what I told you about the flowers? They have to die before the seeds can drop and get ready for next spring."

"The flowers have to die," Sully repeated.

"Yes, when the flowers die, then we can harvest the seeds. And the ones we don't take, they'll fall here, and next spring they'll bloom again."

Sully understood, but he still wanted to harvest most of them. Torstein explained to Maggie what to do with them, to soak them in saltwater overnight, to roast them in the oven. She and Tawny and Marigold helped Sully with the project, and then they brought us all some of the seeds. It was funny—Torstein started this whole organization by handing out free sunflower seeds to strangers on the street…now Sully was handing them out to his friends.

Dragonfly

It tickled Torstein.

"It's perfect, Andy," he said to me. "All of you are becoming more like me."

"Maybe we should all get green coats," I said, joking. "You know the Dunker's followers all have those t-shirts."

"You don't need a coat for people to know you've been with me," Torstein said. "People will know by the way you love each other." He turned to the others who were sitting around, sharing the home-grown sunflower seeds.

"Listen, all of you," he said. "These seeds are awesome, Sully, you've done a great job. And they're more than just sunflower seeds. They're a symbol. We all saw Sully's, flowers how beautiful they were, and how they brightened up the entrance to the building. We saw the care that he took to grow them, and we benefited from their sunny appearance every day this summer. But they're gone now. If they hadn't left these seeds, there'd be nothing left of them.

"And what are the seeds? Dry, dead things that you can roast and eat, and then they'll be gone, too. Hard shells that will get tossed in the trash once the sweet nut is broken out of them. But a few of the seeds, a few of them fell into the ground when the flowers died. They're dead and buried so far as the world is concerned. Dried out seeds in a hardened shell without even salt and flavor to make them attractive to us. Next spring, though, next spring, they *will be* attractive. They'll be more beautiful sunflowers!"

He grinned at us beatifically, just as if we'd all gotten the point. But I don't think anyone had. Ferdy said, "Well at least we didn't have to pay for these." It was as good a conclusion for the sermonette as I could think of.

"No!" Torstein said. "No, idiot." He reached out and gently rapped the top of Ferdy's head with his knuckles. "*You people* are the sunflower seeds! I'm the sunflower seed! Some of us will fall so that more people can enjoy the beauty of the message we're sharing with the world. I'm one of those seeds that falls into the ground, dried and hardened in a hollow shell with nothing to make anyone attracted to me. Some of you, some day, you'll be the same. But then, when the time is right, there *will be* resurrection. And then our willingness to fall, to lie down and be buried, then it will mean a whole new harvest of beauty, the likes of which you can't imagine."

"What are you talking about?" Maggie said.

"I'm talking about the future," Torstein replied. "Some day in the future, not all that far away, I'll be the first one to fall. But I don't want any of you to be afraid. I will come back. Like the seed, in the spring, I'll spring into new life."

He looked around at us as if this all should make perfect sense, then he grinned. "Just remember this. If things should ever look very bleak, if it should ever appear that all we've tried to do is in tatters and ruins, remember this. It may look as if all we're doing here is giving away sunflower seeds and telling stories to the kids in the park. But we're in a dangerous business here, most dangerous for me. If it ever all goes horribly wrong, just remember what I've told you. The seeds in the ground look dead to everyone but the farmer. They'll bloom in the spring."

30

To no one's surprise, the Dunker got arrested.

Some of his followers, the crew-cut surfer and skater punks, came to our park and told Torstein his cousin was in jail down by the shore. They said it was trumped up charges, vagrancy, illegal assembly, that sort of thing—and they couldn't keep him in jail very long over that. But he'd sent them to ask Torstein: what was his plan? When was he going to make his move? Did he even plan to do anything decisive, or should the Dunkers be looking for someone else to get the message out?

Torstein invited the boys to stay a while with us in the park and report back to the Dunker what they saw and heard…but you could tell Torstein was sad that his own cousin would even ask if he was doing anything decisive, anything important. Torstein seemed to think there was nothing more important than giving sunflower seeds to strangers and asking them to share their lives and stories with us. And somehow, the rest of us, when we were with him, felt the same way.

But you could see why the Dunker found it ineffective. He was the one who would walk fearlessly into the lion's den and demand that they all file their teeth down! Torstein wanted to promote love. The Dunker wanted to defeat hatred. The two aims sounded complimentary, but they were actually quite far apart in approach.

When the Dunker got out of jail, he took to preaching in front of the police station when he wasn't wading in the ocean. We heard about his sermons: he badgered the officers who had arrested him and accused them of doing the bidding of organized crime. He was an equal-opportunity haranguer though, and would also preach at the people who had been arrested as they were being taken into the police station.

Franz had checked it out and said that Duncan and his Dunkers were getting a bad rep now, not only with Nikolai, but with the police. Their continued public berating of anyone they deemed criminal (and possibly a user of air conditioning) was annoying to gangstas and to public safety officers as well. On the other hand, other people seemed to be enjoying it and a crowd would gather wherever the Dunker was, to listen to his preaching and watch what he might do.

"If you got any influence on him, Torstein, you should tell him to tone it down," Franz said. "He's gonna get himself and his little band of followers killed."

Torstein's response was vague:

"There's no one like Duncan. He's got the right idea. He's doing all it's in his power to do, to stop the violence, immorality and greed that he sees plaguing this generation. Who else was doing anything to stop it? No one else had the guts to stand up, to stand out, to start shouting along the shoreline: 'Get right! Do right!' He's captured attention. He's changed some lives. And yet everyone of you sitting here, if you stick by me to the end, you'll make an even bigger impact than he has, his whole life's work won't compare to what yours will be."

"He doesn't seem to think so," Ferdy said. "Sent his friends to ask you when you were going to make your move. When *are* you going to make your move, Torstein? What are we doing here? What are we accomplishing?"

Torstein grinned at Ferdy and handed him his sack of sunflower seeds.

"We're sharing some sunflower seeds and reading some stories to kids in the park."

"How's that beat what the Dunker's doing?" Ferdy asked. "At least he's out there getting people riled up, trying to change things."

"I know, and for what he's doing, he's the best. He's alerting people that something big is coming. Something big *is* coming. It just isn't here yet. He's opening people's hearts and minds—so that when the time is right, you'll be able to share the truth with them."

Ferdy took a few sunflower seeds and passed the bag back to Torstein.

"We'll be able to?" he said. "*You'll* be able to. *You're* the one people respond to."

"I won't always be here, and I can't be everywhere," Torstein said. "Duncan won't always be here, either, for that matter."

"He won't be here much longer at all if he doesn't start pulling his punches," Franz said. "Nikolai was pretty annoyed at that stunt he pulled during the gun show."

"It was a thing of beauty," Pete said. Bruiser laughed.

"Gonna get him killed," Franz reiterated.

But I don't think any of us believed it. Who could kill such a wild man? How could you kill someone who was ambidextrous at disarming opponents? It seemed impossible to us then that one day there would be a world without the Dunker—and especially without Torstein. The words he'd said…"I won't always be here"…they rolled right off of us. He made it seem like this life we were living was the only one we'd ever had; the only one we'd ever want to have.

31

What kind of life was it?

I guess for the homeless guys Torstein had befriended, it was sort of the same life they'd always had. They still panhandled for money for booze and went to the soup kitchen for their meals. For people like me and Pete and Maggie, who didn't really have to struggle for a living, it was like going to school, in a way. We spent our days sort of learning from Torstein, then we went to our own homes at night. For the former strippers Tawny and Marigold, it was like halfway house. They were doing real jobs, but living with a successful woman who was teaching them how to be ladies—and they were also getting these sort of life lessons from Torstein.

After Story Hour, he'd sometimes sit down with his buddies in the park and tell his own stories ...

"Once upon a time there was a woman who collected the rare and priceless South Seas pearls. Her whole life was devoted to finding the best and largest and most perfect black pearls, and then she spent all she had just to posses them. She loved them. They meant the world to her. Over the course of her lifetime, she had collected 10 exquisite pearls, and she displayed them each on a separate platinum chain in her house, and only very occasionally wore one out.

"She lived in Rancho Santa Margarita, California. Can you say that Sully?"

Then he and Sully would stop and try to chant Rancho Santa Margarita, California, five times fast. It was sometimes a sort of chore to listen to one of his stories. But when they finally got over the hilarity of a city with that many syllables, he'd continue ...

"It's a city on the San Andreas Fault and prone to earthquakes. Once there was an earthquake, and in the general shaking and shimmying of the house, one of this woman's priceless black pearls became detached from its chain and rolled away! As soon as the shaking ended, she ran into the room and saw only nine precious pearls on their pedestals on their chains. On the last pedestal, just a broken chain was hanging. Terrified that she had lost one of her prized possessions, the woman began to scour the wreckage of the room, desperately looking for her pearl.

"You might think she'd be happy to have nine pearls. After all, each one was perfect and gorgeous. Each one was worth the price of a nice automobile. Together, just the nine of them accounted for a fortune. But that day, the only one which consumed her passion was the one which was lost. As much as she loved the other nine pearls—and she did—it was the lost one which needed her attention at that moment, and she gladly gave it. She crawled on her hands and knees through the debris left by the earthquake. She moved the furniture by her own brute strength, and even plunged her hands into the ashes of the fireplace grate just to be sure it wasn't there. When she finally *did* find the errant pearl, down a hole in a rug under the sofa, she was ecstatic! She carefully cleaned it off, called up the jeweler to come over and repair its chain, and lovingly placed it back on display beside the others. What was lost had been found. The world was made new."

"The world was made new?" Ferdy said. He was attuned to the fortune in the price of the pearls, and he would certainly have been crawling through the debris of an earthquake if even one were lost... but, "How was the world made new?"

Torstein grinned at him. "Any time what was lost is found, the world is made new, Ferdy. When I found you, back in the day, that was a joyful moment, wasn't it? That contributed to the sum total of all the joy in the universe. And that, my friend, makes the world new." He turned back to Sully and said, "Why do you think she looked so hard to find the one pearl?"

Ferdy answered: "Because she paid a king's ransom for it."

"Because she loved it!" Torstein laughed, triumphant. "She had chosen it for herself, and she loved it for itself, and so nothing was going to take it from her if she could help it. It's all about love, boys."

This was a frequent theme with Torstein. He was all about love.

"Once upon a time there was a man with a metal detector, a treasure hunter. Every weekend he'd scour the countryside, looking for valuable relics, coins and jewelry. Sometimes he found a dollar's worth of change, and sometimes he found a ring or a bracelet. But one day he was prospecting on some public land that was about to be put up for sale for commercial development...and the metal detector started ringing off the charts for gold! From what he could tell, there must have been a pile of gold buried in that vacant lot. It was too much for him to dig up and take with him...but the price of the lot was so high, he couldn't afford to buy it for himself. He went home, sold his house and everything he owned, raided his retirement account and borrowed from a bank enough money to buy that lot. Because the treasure he found was worth, to him, all he had."

"Was it worth more than his house and his retirement and enough to pay back the loan?" Ferdy asked. He would.

"It was worth the world to him. Look here. When you find a treasure, something worth the world to you, don't hesitate to pay all you have to get it. That's what you do to redeem something you love. It's worth everything. You all, you're my treasure in a field. You're worth everything to me, because I love you. I'll give all I have for you...and you maybe don't realize it now, but what you've found in me is worth all you have. And you'll give all you have for it."

At the time, I don't think we understood what he was saying. It was only later that most of his stories made sense.

32

We'd seen Sig Scarr, and Tartan his dog, leaving Sharky's a few times, late at night; Sig stumbling and seeming not to see us. Torstein watched him go with sad eyes. I think he'd hoped Sig would retire, maybe give up the booze. But instead, it appeared, he had gone ahead with his operation to crack the bad cop he had in his sights, try to get him to roll on any others.

He'd told us Detective Waverling might come snooping around, but we hadn't seen him.

Summer faded into fall. Angel was gone to rehab. Sully was happy living with Maggie, Tawny and Mari. Lucky guy. And Maggie had bought the condo next door to hers. It was empty then, but I had an idea what she had in mind…it seemed that she liked taking in strays. Tawny and Marigold had been good company for her, and she liked playing Mommy with Sully, too. Whether Sully liked it, I'm not sure.

In one way, for him it was great to have a home to go to at the end of the day where there was sure to be a real dinner that he didn't have to make out of jam and bread himself. But in another way…Maggie wasn't to be gotten around as easily as Angel! She made him take a bath every day, put his shoes and clothes in the closet, do any homework he had before he could come out and play with us on the street. He didn't have much homework in first grade, granted. But he was learning to read. Tawny and Mari practiced their Story Hour routines on him, and that helped him a lot to figure out which sounds went with what letters.

Ferdy was happy about this time because my dad and step-mom

had made a big donation. My mom had died a few years back. And the reason my dad gave the fish market to me and Pete was, he fell in love with this rich widow, and after they got married, he didn't need the income from the fish market. His new wife was really a nice lady; she had a lot of class. After we sold the fish market and started spending our time with Torstein, my dad and she had come out and met Torstein, and took him to dinner with me and Pete.

My step-mom, she liked Torstein, I could tell that. She took some sunflower seeds from him, and she smiled at him a lot. After that, whenever she and my dad came around, she gave Torstein money. The first few times, he turned right around and gave the money to someone else—to some bum for food, to some single mom to pay her electric bill, whatever it was. Step-mom got wise then, and she'd give the money to Ferdy, and tell him to be sure that Torstein got something nice, like new shoes, or hopefully, a new coat.

Usually, though, the money just went into the treasury, and eventually Torstein gave it to the Humane Society, or to Food for the Poor. That was one of his favorites. They always said they could feed kids in Haiti for a nickel or something insane like that, and it tickled Torstein to think how many kids he was feeding with $50 or $100. Torstein would never admit he was generous—he said he was *greedy*, greedy for that great buzz he got by making someone else happy. That was his addiction, he said, to give joy to someone else. If you had to have an addiction, that was a pretty good one. In a way, I think he infected all of us with that addiction, because the more time you spent with him, the more you found yourself giving away…

We'd just given away a lot of coats to poor kids on the block where Sully and Angel lived. It was surprising how many kids ran around without coats in the winter, and not that far from downtown—families living in the projects; I guess there were a lot of single moms and maybe some of them were addicts like Angel. I don't know. I know their kids were delighted to get new coats. Bruiser had gotten a deal on them, if you can believe it, from one of the businesses he used to strong arm!

He'd been quietly going around to the businesses where he used to do collections, and apologizing. For months now, he'd been doing it. He would tell them it had been a cruel way to earn a living, and he was sorry. This one old Jewish guy, for whatever reason, had been so touched by Bruiser's apology, he'd sort of befriended the Big Guy. Bruiser would go to his warehouse a couple times a week and have coffee with him. The guy was a clothing supplier, and he'd cooked up this deal with Bruiser to get these children's coats at next to nothing in cost.

It wasn't *nothing*, it was *next to nothing*, and Ferdy didn't even like the "next to nothing" part, but he had gone along with it. We'd gone together into the projects and gave the coats away to any kid who wanted one. It really *was* a buzz, to see how happy it made the kids. My dad had come to help give the coats away, and when his wife came to pick him up, she was impressed, and gave Ferdy back every dime we'd spent on the coats.

So Ferdy was happy. Torstein was happy because he'd had a major generosity fix. Maggie was happy because she'd scored a coat for Sully, and Sully was happy because his life was good these days. It was about 7:30, and getting dark, and we saw Sig walking toward us, hunched over, stumbling a little. With Sig, you never knew, he could be drunk already...but Torstein went running to him, holding out his hands to him, and the rest of us followed.

He was holding Tartan, the dog, cradled up against his side. That's why he was hunched over. Tartan was wriggling like a wild thing to get out of his hands and go to Sully, but Sig wouldn't let go of him. And Sig was crying. That's why he'd stumbled. As we got closer, I could see that Tartan's front leg was in a bright blue cast, all the way up to his shoulder.

Torstein took Tartan out of Sig's arms and handed him to Sully, then put his hands on Sig's shoulders. "What happened?" he asked.

Sig looked up at him with wild eyes, and pulled a crumpled paper from his pocket. On it there was a message scrawled, "He has three more. Back off."

33

We'd gone to the park. Sully had all he could do to make Tartan sit quietly with him while we heard the story. Sig had insisted, though; he said the vet said Tartan had to be kept off his feet as much as possible for the next six weeks for the bone to mend. To keep a Jack Russell off his feet seemed impossible.

"You know he stays in my car while I'm at work," Sig said. "I came out tonight, and he was howling, crying." Sig stopped, tears in his eyes again. He rubbed his eyes, clutched his forehead. "His leg was broken, the bone was snapped in two. And this note was pinned to his collar. I don't know who did it—another cop could have done this!" He was sick with worry, and fear. "Bad enough they do this to my dog. But I think: what might they do to my kids? Or my wife?"

Torstein was sitting beside him, and placed a hand on his shoulder.

"We'll look after Tartan for you until he's better if you like," Torstein said. "No one would know where he was."

"We can keep him," Maggie said. "Sully, would you take care of him?"

"Yes," Sully said eagerly. "I'll feed him and walk him and make sure he has water and make sure he doesn't get on his feet." I don't know how he figured to walk him without letting him get on his feet.

"Thanks," Sig said. "I can leave him home. My daughter gets home from school about three, and she could look in on him."

He put his elbows on his knees and hunched forward, speaking to the ground rather than to any of us. "I busted the one cop I'd been

90

working on. He put me on to two others. One of them, he's in deep. I think he's in too deep. This message has to be from him. I don't know what to do. I've never backed down, my whole career ..."

"Give it up," Torstein said. "Let somebody else take the heat. You've done your part already. Look here, Sig, justice is good. We all like justice. But you've done justice all your life, and now seems like a good time to get out of the justice business and get into the mercy business, the grace business, the business of love and compassion."

Sig looked up at Torstein with his red-rimmed eyes, eyes that were old and exhausted. He said, "That's good for you, Torstein. But gentle souls like you can afford to be loving and compassionate because soldiers like me are keeping the wolves at bay."

"I don't deny it," Torstein said. "But you've done your part. You can come out and pasture with us now. Let someone else guard the borders. I don't want to see you and Tartan get hurt, Sig. Let this go."

"If I step back, it just puts someone else in harm's way. Someone else would have to take up the investigation. Someone else would have to choose whether to face the danger or just give in."

"And do you know what I would tell him? Give up! Justice is a good idea, Sig, but it doesn't work and it's imperfect. You bring down Nikolai, another Nikolai will rise up in his place."

Sig shook his head. "Didn't you ever hear that saying, all it takes for evil to triumph is for good men to do nothing?"

"I've heard it," Torstein said.

"Then I'm surprised you tell me to quit, to do nothing."

"Oh, no, I'm not saying do nothing," Torstein said. "I'm telling you to do something much more effective than what you're doing now."

Sig cocked his head, asking, "What? Do what?"

"I'm advocating you quit studying justice and start studying love."

"And that's more effective than what I'm doing now?" Sig said, looking at his dog with his blue cast, sitting in Sully's lap.

"More effective, and more dangerous. Maybe even deadly. But it's the only thing worth doing and the only thing that can bring a lasting change."

"I gotta have a drink," Sig said. "I don't wanna leave Tartan outside the bar. You'll look after him for a bit?"

Torstein assured him that we would.

34

"See where justice gets you," Torstein said. "Ulcers, alcoholism. Your dog's leg broken."

"You're not blaming justice for what happened to Tartan?" I asked.

"I'm not blaming anyone," he said. "I just wish that Sig, and the person who did this to Tartan, too, and all of us, could understand each other, and understand what justice really is…and what love can do."

"What can it do?" Franz asked. "It can't mend Tartan's leg, and it can't get Sig off the sauce."

Torstein smiled. "It *is* mending Tartan's leg. Sig's love rushed him and the animal to the vet. Sully's love got Tartan to calm down and sit still. It's not instantaneous, maybe, but it's powerful. And it could get Sig off the sauce, too, if he trusted in it. Or it could at least show him that there's a way to get off the sauce."

He reached out to where Tartan was sitting with Sully and scratched the dog's head. The little stump of a tail wagged like crazy, but he didn't jump up and try to run around as he normally would have. Maybe he was still feeling the anesthesia, or maybe he understood how important it was to take things easy for a while. He was a smart dog.

"But Torstein," Bruiser said, "I can't see what you're proposing… what would it look like?"

"It looks like *you*, Bruiser. It looks like a man reawakened to what's really important in life."

Bruiser shook his head. "I know what happened to me," he said slowly. "But I don't think that the people I strong-armed for 30 years would think it was right that I walked away from the life scot-free."

"Because you have a good heart, and you're looking at it from the point of view of the *victim*. You're putting yourself in their shoes and wondering how you would feel. But let's try that trick from another viewpoint. Suppose Franz there had heard some juicy information about you—skimming from the collection money maybe—and he reported it to Nikolai and you got your nose broken, and Franz got a promotion. Then years later, you both land here, with me, and you know that Franz is the guy responsible for your nose getting broken. What do you do?"

Bruiser thought for a moment, looked at Franz and smiled. To Torstein he said, "Me, now? Today? Or me back the first day I met you?"

"Either you. The first day you met me or today, what's the difference? Let's say the moment you took some sunflower seeds and started conversing with me. Suppose the next person you saw with me was Franz."

"Well, I ..." He paused and thought another moment. "It's different," he said. "As soon as I met you, everything changed."

"Exactly!" Torstein said.

"What Franz had done, if he'd really done that, would have seemed so insignificant, compared to what was happening at the moment I met you...I think we would have laughed about it."

"Exactly!" Torstein said again.

"But Torstein, you don't think there's a way people who have been viciously victimized can somehow laugh about it with their enemies, do you?" Pete asked.

"I *know* there is. It's a hard road, and nobody wants to take it. But look at Corrie ten Boom. Who read *The Hiding Place*? Years after being tortured and nearly killed in a Nazi concentration camp, she was able to embrace one of the guards with genuine love. And why? Because of what Bruiser said. What was happening inside her at that moment so far overshadowed the horrors if the past, she was able to let it go, to fully and freely forgive."

"Even if you were good enough to forgive someone for torturing you—or for ratting you out to the boss," Franz said with a funny grin and a glance at Bruiser, "you wouldn't be good enough to forgive someone hurting your mother or wife or your child. It wouldn't be natural."

"What's natural?" Torstein said. "And who says you have to be 'good enough' to forgive? You have to be *loving enough*. But I think you certainly *can* learn to forgive—and love—someone who has hurt your family. Look at Steve Saint. Who read *End of the Spear*? His father was horribly murdered by some Indians in Ecuador…years later, Steve had not only forgiven the murderers, but one of them had adopted him as a grandson there in the jungle. It is possible to forgive, and everyone comes out *better* off. Steve had a new family, and his 'grandfather' was able to make up for the horrible thing he'd done. If they'd followed the natural course of human justice, Steve would have had bitterness instead of a grandpa, and the grandpa would have been dead. How would that kind of justice be of any use?"

35

He looked around at us, and I guess we all had our heads tilted to one side like Tartan trying to figure out a new trick as we tried to grasp what he was saying.

"Look, you get hurt, and you haul the one who hurt you into court, and they decree that he should be hurt, too. Does that *un-hurt* you? No. It just adds some more hurt to the world. The only way to get *un-hurt* is to forgive, to let it go, to release the one who hurt you from your debt."

I could see what he was saying, but I still couldn't see the practical application of it. Maybe it worked for Steve Saint or Corrie ten Boom… "But who could tell them they *had to* forgive?" I asked. "If forgiving your enemies is the new standard, who can enforce it?"

Torstein laughed. "No one can enforce it. It comes from inside." He laid his hand on my chest and said, "It comes from in here. Look, Bruiser was honest. He said his reaction to Franz's betrayal would have been different before he met me. But now, now he knows something that makes all the slings and arrows of outrageous fortune moot. Now he knows the power of love. It's not the important thing, it's the *only thing*. And with that power, forgiveness may not always be easy, but it's always possible. He raised his hand to the side of my face, held onto me and looked into my eyes. "You have that power in *you* now, Andy, and you'll share it. That's how this power conquers, from person to person, from heart to heart."

When you looked into his eyes, there was no way to disagree. But there were so many millions in the world who never had.

"You can't base a justice system on 'Love your enemies'," Franz said. "All that would do would be to give creeps like Nikolai the license they need to keep fleecing people and worse. You make *that* the standard, and your enemies walk all over you."

"Yes indeed," Torstein said. "That's why I say it's a hard road, and at least as dangerous as the one Sig is walking. But it's the only one with a snowball's chance of success."

"You mean the whole idea is to *let* your enemies walk all over you?" Pete asked. "I mean, I, personally, I can forgive someone a hundred times, five hundred, but that's my choice. And even then, if the person keeps coming back for more, I think there has to be a limit, right?"

"Nope," Torstein said. "No limits. If someone steals your wallet, you ought to give him your television, too. That's the kind of forgiveness I'm talking about, the kind of charity that makes rivers in the desert. Not that you can congratulate yourself for being so forgiving, but that you can really see the deep brokenness inside the person who's hurting you, and you try to give him what he needs to be whole. See the difference?"

Pete shook his head. He still thought Torstein was a dreamer.

Maggie said, "How can it happen though, Torstein? People aren't wired that way."

"Re-wiring," he said. "That's what has been happening here, among us, all along, isn't it?"

36

"You think you can escape the wrath to come!"

The Dunker was bellowing his usual line—this time at Nikolai himself. Franz was there—he saw the whole thing. He had taken Tawny to the shore. She'd not been with us the first time we went; she'd been wanting to go for a long time. The summer was over, really, and pretty soon it would be too cool to go and sit on the sand, so one day Franz asked her to go with him, and she went.

He said they sat on the sand, watching the Dunker still out there grabbing whoever would brave the chilly water. He even came out and said hello to Franz and Tawny, told them to tell Torstein hello. There weren't that many people on the beach because it was fall and the weather was not warm ...

"When I saw Nikolai arrive with his girlfriend and her daughter, I knew he only brought them because he thought there wouldn't be anybody there to look at them. Typical brooding Slav thing."

The "girlfriend" was actually Nikolai's sister-in-law. Franz said she'd been his mistress for years, and she was training her teenaged daughter to take her place, which was a pretty weird deal if you ask me. Franz said in the mob, you never knew. It might be the niece was no relation to Nikolai at all the way the "sister-in-law" got around.

But I guess the Dunker thought it was weird, too, because he recognized Nikolai and started preaching at him! He told him it wasn't right for him to be with his brother's wife—or to make a living selling drugs and guns, either. "Yeah, yeah, you shoulda heard him," Franz said. "It was real wrath of God stuff—*You're paving the road to your own destruction!* And all like that."

Nikolai wasn't taking any crap, though, he got up and got in the Dunker's face, telling him if he and his Dunker boys didn't back down and shut up, the *Dunker* was the one on the road to destruction. Franz said it made no difference at all to the Dunker, he kept right on shouting that Nikolai, his girlfriend, and quite possibly the teenaged niece, too, were all swimming in a cesspool and would die from the crap they were ingesting.

"It was pretty good stuff," Franz said with admiration. "But I could see it was getting Nikolai pretty mad. And the girl, the niece, she was peeved because she wanted to get in the water—and ol' Nik didn't want the Dunker grabbing her, you know. I didn't want Nikolai to see me there, and for sure I didn't want him to see Tawny, so I made her catch the bus home."

When Franz got back from the bus stop, the Dunker was in mid-sermon about the evils of Nikolai's business, and he was saying that neither he, nor his Dunker followers, were ever going to back down until they had exposed to the whole world what kind of sick and twisted dealings Nikolai had with evildoers all over the city. Nikolai even took a swing at him, and the Dunker grabbed his hand and twisted his wrist until the mobster fell to his knees! His bodyguards came running, but Nikolai waved them back, got up, dusted himself off, and walked away.

Franz is a jittery kind of guy, and even now he was cutting his eyes from me to Pete and Jack, the first folks he met when he came back from the shore, his hands shaking a little.

"That wasn't cool, man," he said. "I knew if Nikolai walked away, there was something bad coming. After a while the Dunker got back in the surf, and Nikolai and his—party, I guess you could say, the two ladies and his bodyguards, you know—set up a cabana and some beach chairs, but I could see the Dunker was still watching them close, he was really putting the evil eye on them. I wanted to go tell him to lay off, and I should have, you know, I should have, but I was scared. I didn't want to get into it with Nikolai."

According to Franz, everything was quiet for a while. He was hanging out by the boardwalk, near enough to watch what was happening under Nikolai's tent and with the Dunker out in the water. The niece, the teenager, she was whining to Nikolai and her mother about wanting to swim, and Nikolai was still telling her to shut the hell up—finally he told her to go ahead if she wanted, but to stay away from the Dunker. Of course, she made a beeline for where the Dunker was waiting for any unwary swimmers to happen by, and Nikolai went running after her.

"She went splashing into the surf, like she *wanted* the Dunker to grab her. Remember before, in the summer, when she'd been buzzing him on her jet ski and all? What was it with this kid and the Dunker?"

Franz looked up at us, like he expected us to have some kind of answer, but what did we know?

"What happened?" Pete asked.

"He grabbed her! He grabbed her and dunked her under, and she started shrieking and giggling like a fool, and Nikolai, he hollered something in Russian, pulled a gun out of his shorts pocket, and opened fire."

We were all staring at Franz now, our mouths hanging open.

"He shot the Dunker?" Pete asked.

"Oh yeah," Franz said. "He shot him as many times as he had bullets, I don't know, four, six times."

"But is he all right?" Jack asked, looking over his shoulder for Torstein. We were on the edge of the park where Franz had found us, and Torstein was still hovering around with his friends, dragonflying between the different groups who'd come to Story Hour and stayed late.

"No man," Franz said. "He's dead."

"Dead?!" Pete said. "He can't be dead." Which, it was a dumb thing to say, but it's how we all felt. The Dunker couldn't be dead because he was so big and loud and brave and *alive.*

"Dead," Franz said again, glancing up to us, looking around us for Torstein. "It's gonna be on the news, in the papers. We gotta tell him."

"Are you sure?" I asked. "Sure he's dead?"

"Yeah. The police came, and an ambulance, but it was too late. And the devil of it is, they're saying Nikolai thought the Dunker was trying to drown his niece. They're not charging him with any crime."

That's how it played in the newspaper and the TV news: Nikolai had taken his sister-in-law and her teenaged daughter to the shore for the afternoon. A madman had attacked the teen and tried to drown her. Nikolai had shot him dead and saved her.

"I bet Nikolai went there to kill him anyway," Franz said. "The Dunkers had been making trouble for him anyway, and he was sick of it."

The body guards had all lied to the police, and Nikolai was rather hailed as a hero for saving the girl from being drowned by a maniac. If anyone spoke out in defense of the dead man, that quote never made it into the newspapers.

37

Torstein was blue about the Dunker. He went off by himself for a while. Not long, a few days. We carried on same as always... which is to say, we went to Story Hour in the park in the afternoons, then sat around shooting the breeze with some of the regulars. Without Torstein floating from group to group like a shimmering green dragonfly, though, it wasn't the same.

That detective, Waverling, came around. He sat and listened to Story Hour, looked everybody there up and down like a cop would. Wondering who was armed, maybe, or who was high? I don't know. One thing we'd all learned from Torstein was armed, or high, or sober, or whatever, every person was a human being with dignity and value. We weren't as quick to size each other up anymore. But I guessed I had sized up Waverling. I figured he was there because Nikolai had sent him.

He recognized me and Pete from that time he tried to arrest us, and after story time he came and sat down with us and a few old bums who always came to hear the stories. Franz wasn't far away, but he managed to look like one of the homeless rather than like one of us...and it wasn't how he dressed; he was dressed OK. He just had that ability to blend in.

"Where's your boss?" Waverling asked us.

Pete and I looked at each other, shrugged. "No boss," Pete said.

"The green jacket," Waverling said.

"Torstein took some time off," I said.

"Where'd he go?"

Another shrug. I really didn't know. He'd just said he'd be away a few days.

The old guys we'd been sitting with started to drift away. They could recognize a cop, I guess. They liked the chance to chew the fat with somebody besides each other, but they sensed there was no advantage in their conversing with a police officer. He watched them go with an expression somewhere between boredom and contempt. It wasn't an expression we saw often here.

"You guys bankroll Torstein's operation here?" Waverling asked.

Again Pete and I shot a glance to one another, but there was no way to answer that, really. "No operation," Pete said.

"Whatever," Waverling said. "You give money to Torstein?"

Pete was smooth. He said, "If you want to join us, there's no fee. You don't have to fill out any forms or make a deposit. Friendship's free."

Waverling wrinkled his nose as if the idea of our friendship—or Torstein's—was repugnant.

"I'm just trying to warn you, buddy, about giving money to a con man, okay?"

We both laughed at this. It had never occurred to us anyone might think of Torstein as a con man. If he was one, he was the worst ever, as he gave away any money anyone might actually give to him.

"You think it's funny? This Torstein character, he takes your money, and he doesn't mind putting you guys crossways with Nikolai."

"None of us is crossways of Nikolai," Pete said. "I don't know what you're talking about."

"Fine. Right now it's *your* money he's throwing away. If you don't mind that, that's your business. But when he starts taking money out of a mobster's pocket, you gotta watch out for your own safety."

"What are you talking about?" I asked. "None of us has anything to do with Nikolai, and Torstein certainly isn't stealing from him."

Waverling shrugged. "Whatever you say. But you got two story ladies who used to be big attractions at one of Nikolai's clubs. You got a muscle-head who used to do collections for him."

"Why are you delivering Nikolai's messages, anyway?" I asked. "Aren't you a police detective?"

"I'm here to protect and to serve," Waverling said. "I'm trying to protect you idiots. You don't want to listen, that's your business."

38

Franz went snooping and came back with the report that Nikolai was uneasy about what he heard was happening downtown. People giving money to Torstein to give away. People making homes for runaway strippers to get real jobs. People arranging for crack addicts to go into charity rehab programs. All of this, in Nikolai's opinion, stunk. Crack addicts fueled his drug operations. Strippers filled his nightclubs. If Torstein somehow started getting people to throw away guns, he would be biting into Nikolai's final cash cow: arms dealing. The mobster had been only too happy to have an excuse to get rid of the Dunker. He wouldn't balk at taking Torstein out, too, if *his* followers became a problem.

When Torstein came back, we told him what Waverling had said, and what Franz had discovered. He didn't care. He said:

"That night Sig came, with Tartan's broken leg, he accused us of doing nothing to combat evil. But in that little laundry list of things Nikolai is mad about, you can see what we're doing to combat evil. We're opening our hearts to people ensnared in evil. It's bound to make someone mad."

"Someone evil," Franz said.

"Someone else entangled in evil. Someone else who could be set free."

Franz cocked his head to look at Torstein in disbelief and said, "You still think Nikolai could stop being evil? After your cousin and all?"

Torstein laughed then, the last thing we'd expected, a ringing laugh.

"Franz, if I didn't think that Nikolai could change, I wouldn't even bother. If I didn't know that love is the most powerful agent for change we have or could ever have, I wouldn't keep on doing what I'm doing. We wouldn't keep doing what we're doing."

"What *are* we doing?" Franz said.

It was late afternoon. Sully had come from school to Story Hour, and now he was sitting with Tawny, Mari, Maggie, Bruiser and some of the old homeless guys who'd come for the story. They were telling more stories, I supposed.

"We're raising one boy who sees value and dignity in every human being," Torstein said. "Maybe that's all it takes."

"What, Sully's gonna be the Messiah?"

"No," Torstein said. "Sully's going to be a husband, and a father, and his children will know that love is their strength, and that all people are worthy of respect. And that it's more blessed to give than receive."

"You're talking 30, 40 years down the road," Franz said.

"What's the difference?" Torstein asked.

"Well, Nikolai might come gunning for you any time."

"If he does, if anything happens to me, I expect you guys to carry on. And if I can, I'll come back to you."

"No coming back from where the Dunker went," Franz said flatly.

Torstein laughed again. "I'll find you," he said. "Here's the thing, boys. Evil can't stamp out good. Good is older, and stronger. Nikolai might snuff out one of us, but the rest of us will keep shining."

Pete didn't like the thread of this conversation at all. He was a cool guy, but he was sort of a man of action type, my brother. Strength and loyalty were character traits he prized, and he felt he had them in abundance. He didn't see how Torstein could talk about being snuffed so easily.

"Look here," he said. "There's no reason Nikolai should come after you. What have you done to him? Nothing. And if he did come, well, there's a few of us here who aren't any too easily intimidated. I guess we could stand him off. We can knock a few heads together, anyway."

"You're missing the point, Pete," Torstein said. "Violence can't stop violence. Violence can only escalate violence. If they come gunning for me, no one is to try to save me. If you fight them, you feed the evil. I don't want that. Don't choose evil, Pete."

39

"It's the Dunkers."

Jack had seen them getting off the bus, and tumbling out of some busted-up little mini-vans and off a couple of little Japanese motorbikes. You could tell them because of the shirts they wore. The t-shirts used to say things like "The end is near," but now they said, "The End is Here." They had the line drawings of the Dunker, but now they were more iconic, like the faces of Elvis and Selena on the black velvet walls of true believers. The Dunkers were mostly young guys, Jack's age, late teens and early 20's, but there were some grown-ups, too. They had crew cuts and tans, baggy pants. We hadn't heard anything about them since the Dunker had been killed. We assumed they'd been terrified by what happened to him and quietly disbanded. But that did not appear to be the case. They came to our park one day.

They had maneuvered their p.o.s. vehicles into metered parking, seemed to have packed about 10 of them into every mini-van so they kept pouring out like clowns at the circus. The overflow was on the city bus, which had arrived at the same time; like a caravan, and some of them were pulling their bicycles off the bus' front rack. They trooped over to the park, and when they saw me and Pete, Bruiser, Jack and Jazz, the ones in the lead came over to us.

"We're looking for Duncan's cousin," said one of the older ones, one of the grown-ups. He had the crazy eyes. You know, you could tell, looking at the Dunker when he was alive, that he was some kind of madman. With the camo and the wild hair, and the flashing eyes. This guy had the flashing eyes but he lacked the Dunker's bulk and power. He seemed nervous, that was the flash in his eyes, nervous energy, anxiety, but defiance, too.

"He's here," Jack said, "over there." He pointed out the green jacket on the other side of the park, sitting with some of our bum friends. "You guys ok? Did Nikolai come after you?"

The rest of the Dunkers had followed the leaders to us and were surrounding us. I saw Torstein had noticed and was coming to meet them.

"I don't know," the leader answered Jack. "We all split. We were scared when it came down to it. He was so brave...and we...we ran out on him."

"No use you're getting killed, too," Bruiser said. "Look, Torstein's coming."

"Gentlemen!" Torstein was calling. "Welcome! You're welcome here. You're just the guys I'm looking for."

Since when, I wondered? I had never heard him mention the Dunkers at all.

"We're looking for you, too," said Crazy Eyes. "We don't know what to do now."

"Yeah," said another Dunker. "We need to *do something,* for Duncan."

"And Duncan always said you were the one with the answers," said Crazy Eyes. "You were the one."

There really seemed to be a lot of these guys, 50 or 60, maybe 70. They all crowded around Torstein, jostling each other to get a look at him, staring at him with this ridiculous intensity. It was as if Duncan had been their head, and it was cut off, so they were desperate for a new head.

"Duncan was the greatest of men," Torstein said. "He was always honest and didn't pull any punches. He prized integrity, prized the truth. He would have wanted you to pursue the truth. He doesn't need you to avenge him, and he wouldn't want you to forget him, but he would want you to seek out the truth, and defend it. Right?"

The Dunkers nodded their heads.

"Stay here with us in the park this afternoon. Take a look at what we're doing here. What's unfolding here, before your eyes, is no less than the kingdom that Duncan told you was coming. Walk around, talk to my friends, discover the truth here…and then tonight, I'll tell you what you can do for Duncan, and for me, and for the kingdom."

The Dunkers appeared ready to do whatever Torstein commanded, so they dispersed throughout the park. They listened to Story Hour and talked to Tawny and Mari, to Maggie and to the rest of the guys. They sat beside the homeless and argued with some of them about their alcoholism. They all had some sunflower seeds and applauded Sully's obstacle course routine with the little dog, Tartan. They listened as Torstein comforted a grieving dad whose wife had taken the kids and left, and they bit their tongues when Torstein told a crack addict she could still be a good mother…They didn't understand his method, but they respected that Duncan had loved and admired him.

At the end of the day, he gathered them around and told them:

"Here's the truth: love is the answer. The kingdom of God, the one Duncan told you was coming, it is nothing more than the kingdom where love rules…and it's here. Now. Whenever someone takes a risk for love, the kingdom has arrived. This is what I want you to do, for Duncan's memory, and for me. I want you to sort yourselves out into pairs, fan out across the city, and go tell this truth to everyone—and not just in this city. Go north, south, east, west, and preach it."

"Repent and be saved?" asked Crazy Eyes.

"No, just what I told you: The kingdom of God is the kingdom where love rules, and so whenever someone risks everything for love, the kingdom has arrived. If anyone accepts your message and wants to buy you a beer or a soda, you sit down with them and tell them what you've witnessed here, and how love can transform a life, a park, a city. You have your bikes and vans, and the rest of you can take the buses. Just go tell people the facts. The truth."

They looked dubious, but they agreed to do it.

They felt they hadn't been brave when the Dunker was killed, but really, they were way braver than me. I would never have stood on a street corner and preached like they did about criminals and gangs and drugs. I would have died from embarrassment, but they had done that for the Dunker. Now they had a new message, and they were going to preach it for Torstein. They may have been afraid of Nikolai's bullets in the heat of the moment...but they weren't afraid of this much more dangerous thing: trying to tell hateful people that love is the answer.

40

The days were cool now. It wasn't too cold to be outdoors, but we were all wearing jackets, and we didn't linger as long in the evenings as we might have done. Torstein, he didn't have a home. He stayed with Jack and Jazz a lot of the time, and sometimes he would stay with me or Ferdy. Maggie had offered him a room in the second condo, but I don't think he ever stayed there. Sometimes he stayed outdoors with the homeless people. They were always glad to have him, and they tried to do something special for him…but it usually ended up that he bought their dinner.

He had never been to my brother's house. Pete's marriage was… rocky, maybe you could say? I don't know if his wife was manic-depressive or just a sort of mean woman, or what the problem was. They'd had two nice children, a boy and a girl, twins. They were red-headed kids, cute as could be, and right form the start they loved each other more than anyone else. They tolerated their mom somehow, and they were fond of Pete, but they were each others' best friends. They'd gone off to college together two years ago. They were both studying marine biology.

They'd grown up in the fish market and already knew everything about fish. I don't know what they were learning at college, but they were good at it and got good grades. Pete's wife, since they'd been gone, she traveled a lot. Pete didn't go with her much, at first, because we were running the fish market. And because he didn't really like spending that much time with her. Since we'd sold the fish market, he'd had plenty of time to travel with her…but he'd met Torstein and started hanging out with us on the streets or in the park. I don't know what his wife thought of it. I don't even know if Pete told her. It was almost like they were leading separate lives.

So I was surprised one day when he called and told me Phyllis was sick, and he was going to stay home with her. We almost always met for coffee late in the morning and then went looking for Torstein and our crowd. (Unless we needed money, in which case we'd meet Jack and Jazz really early and go out fishing.) I asked Pete was there anything I could do for him—run to the pharmacy or something? He said no; he thought maybe it was just the flu, but he wasn't comfortable to leave her, and he'd call me if he needed anything.

Since I wasn't meeting Pete for coffee, I just brewed some at home. I had a nice apartment with two bedrooms and some very nice modern appliances back in the day. I hardly ever used them. I only cooked occasionally and then it was only to grill fish and toss salads; I didn't know how to do much else in the kitchen. So I got my coffee machine going, lingered over the newspaper, and never went out to find Torstein until about noon. We had lunch, visited some of his homeless friends, and went to the park for Story Hour about three in the afternoon ...

Mari and Tawny were really great at this by now. Actual adults with jobs would come and listen if they had the chance, people taking a break from their work in the downtown high-rises. You could tell the girls practiced, and they did these great character voices. Little kids, homeless people, old drunks, everybody loved it. So we watched the performance, then Torstein went off and started visiting with all the folks, the way he would. It was routine now. He floated from little group to little group and spoke to everyone and sometimes whistled for Ferdy and gave someone a hand-out.

Around six p.m. he said to me, "Let's take Ferdy and Franz and go to Pete's for dinner."

This was wrong and so may levels. First, I'd told Torstein the reason Pete wasn't here was that his wife was home sick. Second, Phyllis never liked people coming to her house without advance clearance of at least a day, or preferably a week. She liked to steam clean everything before anyone walked in the door! Third, I wasn't even sure if Pete would have any dinner for us if he'd been tending his wife all day. I explained to Torstein that I didn't think this was a good idea, but he said, "Sure it is! Come on, I'm hungry."

In the car on the way, I called Pete to try to give him some warning, but he didn't pick up his phone. I had to leave a message. When we got there, he looked at me as if I were crazy, but he let us in the door. The house looked great, as always. Phyllis was an awesome housekeeper. She was the only one who would have thought she needed to have the maids in before we came. We all thought the place looked super.

Pete said, "Come on in, guys. Go into the kitchen there, I'll see what I've got to feed you."

But Torstein said, "I heard your wife is sick. I came to visit her."

Another bombshell! The last thing Phyllis would want if she were laid up in bed without make-up and a peignoir would be anyone coming into her room!

"Oh, ah, that's not a good idea," Pete said. "She doesn't look her best and she wouldn't want to —"

"I don't mind," Torstein said. "I'm sure she won't either." Before anyone could stop him, he was up the stairs calling, "How are you, Phyllis?"

"Really, Torstein," Pete was saying, doggedly running along behind him, "she's not gonna like —"

But Torstein brushed past him into the master bedroom. I had run up to the landing to try to stop him, but I figured Phyllis wouldn't want me there, too, so I stopped, in agony about what would happen next. The last thing you want to do to a manic-depressive person who's obsessed with appearances is drop in on her when she's sick.

I heard muffled voices coming from the sick room; apparently Phyllis was too sick to blow up, or else she was restraining herself for appearance's sake and would blow up at Pete after we left. I held my breath…and in a moment, Pete came out of the room, looking a little dazed. Torstein followed him in just a few seconds, calling back over his shoulder, "That would be wonderful, Phyllis, thank you!"

To me Torstein said, "She feels much better now and said she'd be happy to make us dinner. She'll be down in a few minutes."

The next day, when I met Pete for coffee, Phyllis was with him.

Jaxn Hill

She said she hadn't had anything planned, and she wanted to see what we boys did all day. After that, she came most days. She and Maggie became quite good friends. And once a week or so, we all went to Pete's for dinner. Phyllis was a really good cook.

41

Torstein did that to people, the unlikeliest people. He would turn on the Irresistible Charm, and suddenly they wanted to be the people he believed they could be. Mostly the transformations were amazing. The stripper, Tawny, when Franz had brought her to us, she'd been so sorely lacking in self-esteem, she'd thought the only reason anybody would ever care for her was her rocking body. Now, though, she still knew she had a rocking body, but she carried herself differently, and saw herself and others differently. It was a heartache for Franz. He still wanted her. I don't know if he loved her. I don't know if he was sure what love was. But he knew now that he wasn't getting anything from that girl until he put a ring on her finger—and he wasn't sure if she would say yes, even if he asked.

Franz had been transformed in his own way, too. He'd believed his greatest strength was that he could ferret out facts, sell the information, or use what he learned to manipulate people. It was a good ability, to be able to get the truth out of a twisted situation, but it was a small thing on which to stake your existence. He was learning, maybe not as quickly as Tawny was, that he could be valued for the sake of his heart, which was a good one, all things considered. He hadn't gone back to work for Nikolai since he'd made his initial report on Torstein. And he'd helped Tawny get that kid Marigold out of the strip club, despite that he was afraid what might happen to him because of it. And that day we'd given out the coats in the projects, he'd been like a kid himself, clowning with the little boys and girls.

Bruiser, of course, had changed a lot. He was about as far now from a mob guy as he could be. He'd made friends with several of the business owners he used to threaten. He'd become like a big teddy bear for the kids at Story Hour. Where once he had seemed thoroughly menacing, now he seemed like the Jolly Green Giant. Albeit not green. Pete and I, and Jack and Jazz, I suppose we had changed in our own ways, too, although I didn't notice it as much.

Jack seemed to *get* Torstein more and better than the rest of us did. We all loved him, but I think we were just amazed by him, and didn't really understand what he was trying to tell us in those days. Jack, he seemed to know. He hepped right away to the idea that love had to be stronger than hate; that you couldn't stop somebody hitting you by hitting him back…for my brother Pete, in particular, it was a foreign idea. He'd always been quick tempered and able to take care of himself in a fight. The notion of "not fighting" being stronger than fighting was crazy to him.

But I think in those days, "crazy" was what we lived and breathed. If you took yourself out of it and looked back in like a stranger, the way we were living and what we were doing *was* crazy. Who sells their business so they can spend their days on the street with a homeless guy who gives away sunflower seeds to strangers? Who invites strippers to live in their home, or takes in the child of a crack whore? When you looked at it that way, it was crazy.

The crazier thing was, we didn't care. We felt like the little bit of good that was being done was bigger and longer-lasting than the craziness. Angel was getting off crack. Sully was going to school. Some poor kids had coats before the winter started. And Phyllis was actually enjoying life (and I guess, enjoying her marriage, too)—something I would never have believed possible.

Jack was the only one who didn't, at some time or other, deem what we were doing madness. He seemed to sense, intuitively, that what we were doing was really the only way to live, and the rest of the world was mad. And he was a kid, maybe he was turning 20 that year. He, his brother Jazz, and my brother Pete, they were like Torstein's inner circle. If he were going off on his own, sometimes he would say, "You, you and you!" to them, and they'd go with him.

One of those days, they went to visit Torstein's father.

42

Pete told me about it. Torstein had asked him, Jack and Jazz to meet him early one morning, and they drove toward the coast—but not toward the shore where we'd gone, and not toward the docks where Jack and Jazz's father had his boat moored, but toward the mountains in the north that looked out on the water. This was a very prestigious area—the homes were built into the mountainsides, perched up there like aeries, looking out at the endless ocean.

They'd come to a big gate that opened onto a winding private drive, then Torstein had made them leave the car at a turn-off and go ahead on foot. The way wound through a thick pine forest. It was still early morning, and fog had rolled in the night before, so they could only see so far ahead of them as they went, they were sort of isolated in this blanket of mist and shadow, surrounded by these thick trees.

The birds were just waking up and starting to chirp, otherwise it was very still, and a little cool. "So this is your dad's place?" Pete asked, more to hear himself speak than for any other reason.

Torstein nodded, but he didn't speak, and everyone fell silent again.

Then, suddenly, they broke out of the fog, and they were on a huge, green lawn, with the morning sun shining out cheerily on them from where it had risen over the ocean almost parallel to the lawn, and in the distance, one of those huge slate-front houses, looking out toward the sea, all windows across the front of the top floor, the sun reflected in all that glass.

"It was like stepping out of a closet into a big banquet room that's all

117

lit up and a fire roaring," Pete told me. "It was shocking to suddenly be in all that light, that green lawn with the dew sparkling on it, and those windows with the sun shining on them, and of course, looking out at the sea where the sun beams were dancing on every little ripple in the water. The impression was all light, light, light, almost too much light. It was hard to focus on anything because it was suddenly so bright."

"Did you go in the house?" I asked. "Did you meet his dad?"

But Pete seemed reluctant to go on.

"It wasn't like that," he told me. "Torstein had stepped out into the sunlight first, and where he was standing, with the sun behind him, he was suddenly too bright to look at. It was like he was all light, standing there, made from light."

"Didn't he block the sun though, if the sun was behind him?"

"You'd think so ..." Pete mused. "And then, I think Jack and Jazz and I ran into each other. We'd been following Torstein pretty close, and when we stepped out of the fog and into all that light, I think we piled up against each other. Jazz and Jack and I ended up on the ground, on our hands and knees. Torstein was laughing. But then he was talking to these men."

"What men? Where did these men come from?"

"I don't know," Pete said. "It was strange. They were all bright like he was, maybe not as bright as he was, but still, it was hard to look at them. There were two of them, big guys, powerful looking, and they were holding onto Torstein, slapping him on the back. They were glad to see him, you could tell that, and they were encouraging him."

"Encouraging him to do what? Did he introduce them?"

"No, it was almost like he'd forgotten we were even there. And keep in mind, it was so bright, all of a sudden, it was really hard to focus on anything. So I maybe got the wrong impression of what was happening ..."

"What was happening?"

Pete shrugged. "You know how weird stuff happens to Torstein. That seagull that bit him, and the two marlins tail walking toward him out on the boat. This was like that, only it made even less sense. These guys, they were warning Torstein about trouble that was coming, but they were telling him to stay the course, and he would prevail, he would suffer, but he would win."

Dragonfly

I'd noticed when Torstein, Jazz, Jack and my brother had come back from this little jaunt, Pete, Jack and Jazz had seemed a little dazed, like maybe they'd got up too early or needed to go back to sleep...I'd certainly not expected to hear this story!

"I was beside myself," Pete said. "When I heard them telling Torstein what was going to happen to him—it was scary. They think he's going to die, and soon. So I thought, and I was dazzled, you know, that these guys looked big and powerful, and maybe they could prevent this happening. So I blurted out something like, 'You could just stay here. We'd stay here with you. You'd be safe.' I felt like an idiot. They all just stared at me. Jack and Jazz were no help. They didn't say anything."

"Did they know who these guys were? Did they understand what was happening?"

Pete shook his head. "Who knows what Jack understands? Sometimes he's miles ahead of me. But I don't think he knew any better than I did. He was just staring at them, shielding his eyes, his mouth hanging open. Finally the light got so strong, we had to close our eyes, or look away. And then, the light went out. Not out, like dark, but all that brightness disappeared, and it was just a normal sunny morning looking out over the sea. The men were gone."

"What happened then? Did you go in the house?"

"No," Pete said. "Torstein came over and helped us up, and slapped us on the back. He said we looked like we needed to get out of the sun, and we started walking back down the drive to the car. We asked him if we weren't going to meet his father, and he said, 'Oh, well, you've met me. That's enough for now.' No idea what he was talking about. No explanation about who those guys were. If they were really even there. It felt like a dream."

"Did you talk to Jack and Jazz about it?"

"Later. They saw what I saw. They heard what I said. They didn't know what had happened."

"Did they hear these men telling Torstein he was going to die?"

"Yah, they heard. But it wasn't news to Torstein. It was like they were coaches telling him he was 10 yards from the goal line."

"Criminy."

"Yah."

43

Jack, Jazz and Pete didn't tell anyone else about that Visit. I didn't blame them. That was weird, even for Torstein. But the worst of it was this idea that he was going to die. He hadn't seemed afraid when we'd told him what Waverling said about Nikolai. But now I was scared.

We got a letter, or I should say Maggie got a letter, from Angel, at the rehab. She said the program was working really well, and she had found Jesus and He was helping her stay off crack. I was glad for whatever would help her stay off crack. She hoped to be back in the spring, to be ready to graduate in the spring.

Winter was coming fast. The nights had turned cold, though it was only November. Another one of Bruiser's contacts in the business world had come up with blankets for the homeless, and everyone got a great buzz handing them out. But we had to be careful, too. The city didn't like having homeless people on the streets or in the parks. There were shelters, and the authorities would have preferred people went there. For whatever reason, some homeless people didn't want to go to a shelter. Maybe because they couldn't drink or use drugs there. A lot of homeless people had a problem that way.

I guess someone besides Nikolai had noticed what we were doing downtown...coats for kids and blankets for the homeless...Story Hour... there wasn't really a lot else we were doing. A TV news lady, a really good-looking one, came to interview Torstein. She was called Ariel Prince, and she had this shiny dark hair and deep blue eyes. She also had a mellifluous voice, and she dressed really well. The whole package. She came by herself, and stayed with us one day; we weren't doing anything very special, just Story Hour and then visiting with whoever happened to be in the park. Because of the cooler weather, there weren't as many people as usual. Only the most die-hard drunks and pan-handlers stayed in the park in the evenings.

Ariel sat with them and asked them all about what went on here, and asked all of us about Torstein, and asked Torstein what he was thinking and why he spent his days this way when the rest of the world was working for a living. She was really good at her job because she made you think she was terribly interested in your answer. Even some of the loopy drunks, she listened to them just as if they made good sense.

She watched Torstein moving around visiting with different people, and she smiled. I thought maybe she was succumbing to his Irresistible Charm, but that wasn't it. He told me about it later. She invited him to come to dinner with her. Wow. I thought that was a pretty cool thing, dinner with that beautiful TV news lady with the lovely voice. I guess I was a bit jealous of Torstein. He walked off with her, and waved at us over his shoulder. She was taking him to The Top. It was this revolving restaurant downtown that looked out over the city. Spectacular view, pricey food. It was exceptional by all accounts.

So they got to The Top, and fortunately Torstein was wearing his sport coat. Dress code and all. Unfortunately it was his usual iridescent green one, but they let him in anyway. Half of being able to pull off a wacky style is acting as if you're at home in it, and Torstein always seemed right at home. So they were seated at a table by the window, of course, and the whole room was gently turning to show a different view of the city, every moment. And Torstein said to Ariel, "Did you enjoy the afternoon? Aren't they a great bunch of people?" She said yes they were, and she did enjoy it, and she had an idea how to take Torstein's message to even more people, through TV.

"You have an amazing personality for television," she told him. "I think I could get you a regular spot on the nightly news to begin with, at least weekly. But I think once more people see you on TV, they're going to want you every night. They're going to want you round the clock."

Torstein told her he was flattered, but he didn't see TV as a very personal medium, and besides, what would he say on TV?

"Just what you say in the park or on the streets, to begin with," she said. "But once we get an audience for you, then we can begin scripting other, bigger messages. You've already got this great little movement going on downtown, but we can paint it with broad strokes all across the city. And then, I believe, across the nation! Think about that. You're going to be a big star."

Torstein told me he thought about it, but big stardom wasn't what he wanted, and he told her so.

"It's not just that," Ariel said. "It's big money. Right now, you can get winter coats for a few dozen kids in the projects, and you can get blankets for a hundred homeless people. But once you're on TV, making the major money, think about what you could do, about the good you could do. They were telling me about the crack addict you sent to rehab. You'd have money to help so many more people like that. You could do a lot of good with the kind of money I'm talking about."

He said she gestured toward the city lights below, as if they were hers to offer him, and said, "You can do whatever you want to do once you're a star. You and me, I think we'll be an unbeatable team. This city is at your feet right now. What do you say?"

"Here's what I say. Feeding the hungry and getting blankets to the homeless and coats to cold children, that's all great. But the real hunger out there right now is a soul hunger. When we nourish our souls with God's love and human kindness, then nobody needs a million dollars to feed the hungry. Everyone will be feeding his neighbor with the extra $20 in his pocket, and no one will go hungry."

"OK," Ariel said. "You can nourish a lot more souls through TV than you can by handing out sunflower seeds on the street corner. If that's your vision, I can give you the means."

But Torstein told her, "You can't nourish a soul through a soul-less mechanism. When someone takes some sunflower seeds from me, I'm right there looking into their eyes, and they're able to walk away from the experience with something in their hands. That personal connection can't happen through TV. It's got to happen face to face."

"Get serious, Torstein," she said. "Dr. Phil, Deepak Chopra and

Dragonfly

Eckhart Tolle are nourishing souls through the TV airwaves every day. I know you've got what it takes. Show me you can fly with those eagles! Show me your message has wings that theirs don't."

When Torstein was telling me the story, he just sighed. "She didn't get it at all, Andy. I had to tell her I had nothing against any TV guru, but that I wasn't going to risk what we have here for all that glitters."

Frankly, I was disappointed. I had hoped Ariel would join us here. Torstein said he didn't see it happening. "I don't think she liked my coat," he said.

He was weird like that. His coat.

44

It was late November, and now it felt like winter. Once there had even been a snow flurry!

Thanksgiving was just a week away. I figured, the way Torstein got such a charge out of helping people, we'd all be working at the charity dinner serving turkey and mashed potatoes. But he said a lot of good-hearted people would be doing that. What we could do, any of us who wanted to, was run down to the casinos. The casinos for Thanksgiving!

There were several Indian casinos about 40 miles north of the city, on the river. They were riverboat casinos, and they all ran together like one big gambling complex.

"Who needs company on Thanksgiving more than some poor soul who has nowhere better to spend the holiday than a casino?" Torstein asked us.

"Maybe they're at the casino because they like to gamble," Franz said. "Maybe they won't want our company."

"And probably the casinos are serving some kind of turkey buffet," Maggie said. "What would we do?"

"Give away money," Torstein said. "We'll pay people to come and eat at our Thanksgiving dinner. The worst most casino-addicted souls who've lost all their money and can't stop gambling will come in and eat with us."

"How are we going to pay them?" Ferdy asked. "And who's going to pay for the dinner?"

Dragonfly

"Those are excellent questions my friend," Torstein said. "Will you get on it right away? Andy and Pete's step-mom would be a good resource. Umm, Maggie, maybe you could contribute? Bruiser, would any of your friends...?"

"Wait a minute now," Phyllis said. "You're going to feed their gambling addiction? They come in to get money so they can go gambling after they've lost everything? How's that helping them?"

"Well, my hope is, during the Thanksgiving dinner, we'll get a chance to talk to them, and maybe convince them that their best option is to give up the gambling and go home to their family, or stick with us. What do you think?"

"I think we're gonna lose our shirt," Ferdy said. "There might be 10,000 people at those casinos, and everyone of them will want free money."

"I bet those casinos can't hold 5,000 people all together. It's not Las Vegas. And I imagine only the poorest and hungriest will come to our dinner. Let's say we offer them $10 each."

"Five," Ferdy said automatically. "They're getting dinner, too."

"All right, five. Here's the deal though, we don't tell anyone what we're up to, except that we'll be serving a dinner. I don't want anyone just showing up there for the free money. I want the real gamblers, the really lonely folks who just don't have any other place to be on Thanksgiving."

"Quality folks," Ferdy said.

"Exactly!" Torstein said. "They'll be our honored guests. Now, who knows anyone at the casinos? How can we set up a tent or something where people can find us at dinner time? And who can cook the turkeys?"

We had one week to throw this all together. And no idea how it would turn out.

45

"Who are you, and what do you think you're doing?"

That's what the cocktail waitress was asking Torstein as our tent filled up with honored guests, each clutching their ticket for a $5 bill after dinner.

Torstein laughed, offered her some sunflower seeds and said:

"I'm Torstein, and I think I'm paying people to have Thanksgiving dinner with me."

Then the girl laughed, took a handful of sunflower seeds and said, "I like you, Torstein. I get off work at one a.m. Will you still be here?"

"Heavens, no, I turn into a pumpkin at 10 o'clock," he said. "But if you get into the city, come and find us. We're usually at Patriots Park about 3 in the afternoon."

"OK," she said. "I just might." She had a little wallet on a string around her neck, and she reached into it and pulled out a five dollar bill. "Here," she said, putting it into Torstein's hand. One of these guys you're paying to eat with you probably gave his last fiver to me." She grinned, and started on her way.

"Aren't you going to eat?" Torstein called.

"Gotta get back to work!" she called back, and she waved as she clicked away on her high heels. She was already dressed in her cocktail waitress outfit, and she looked good walking away.

If Torstein had been a different guy, he could have had the women. They all liked him. And why? Like I say, he was built kind of like a gymnast, short and sort of muscular, but he just had straight black hair and a kind of prominent nose. He wasn't so handsome, but he had that electric smile. Not to mention his electric coat.

We'd been setting up for hours. Sully had come along with us. He couldn't go in the casinos, so he'd been put to work in the kitchen, and he was really pretty helpful for a small child. They had one of those safety can openers, and after Maggie showed him how to use it, he'd opened dozens of cans of corn and green beans. Phyllis had cooked up the green beans with bacon, and man, it smelled awesome. I think she'd cayenne'd up the corn because it had little red glints in it and it smelled spicy, too.

The turkeys had been donated whole and frozen. Pete and I, with Jack and Jazz, and both our dads, had fried dozens of them. It was a blast! Frying a turkey—you get this peanut oil heated up to 325, then lower the turkey in, and it cooks *fast*. Man, they were good, too. We'd none of us done this before, so we had to try the first one we did. It was delicious. Then we'd brought them all here to the mobile kitchen set up in the back of our tent, and we'd torn them to bits, taken all the meat off the bones and put it into huge chafing dishes to keep it warm.

The gravy we had to get canned. Frying a turkey doesn't generate any grease you could use to make gravy, and even so there weren't enough turkeys to make the gallons of gravy we anticipated needing. Again, Phyllis had thought up some ways to spice it up, including a bit of red wine and a little of the bacon fat from the green beans mixed in with it.

Bruiser had been able to borrow some of those outdoor heaters that people use on their patios, and we'd stationed them around the tent. They were doing a nice job, and it was pretty warm considering the cool night. We'd also set up a lot of lighting so everyone would be able to see each other and see what they were eating. I thought the place looked nice; for amateurs, we'd done a fine job.

Any adult who wasn't working in the kitchen or getting the tables set, Torstein had sent into the casinos with tickets to our dinner.

"Don't just hand them out willy-nilly," he advised. "I want you to look for the sorriest, loneliest, most desperate people, and make sure they get a ticket. After that, if you have tickets left over, you can give them to whoever you want. And make sure you tell them, there's no catch, OK? They eat dinner with me, they get five dollars."

The ticket wasn't a ticket to get into the tent; it was the ticket to get your five dollars. Ferdy was nervous as could be. He was pacing around the tent, doing absolutely no good to anyone. He had the cash box locked up in a little safe he'd brought with him, but he was certain this evening could only end in disaster.

Pete's and my step-mom had made a big cash donation to this venture, and she was there in the kitchen helping prepare the meal. I was floored because she had family, and I thought for sure she and Dad would be tied up with them. But she had this soft spot for Torstein, and I think she thought this whole idea was a gas.

We'd decided to have our dinner at 8 p.m. We figured all the worst gamblers would be broke and desperate about then. They started straggling in about 7:30. Torstein was greeting people at the door— well, at the opening to the tent. Marigold and Tawny were the hostesses, they showed people to their seats at a table. Torstein wanted one of us to be responsible for every six or eight people, so when the ladies had seated a whole table, they would wave one of us over to come and welcome the guests. We didn't actually have to take orders—except for drinks—because we only had one menu. The drinks were easy, just iced tea, water or Kool-Aid. Even those of us who had never been waiters could handle that.

The folks who came in were a little uneasy. I think they still thought there was some catch. Some were a bit tipsy, too. The casino had been feeding them free drinks all day, I imagine. Some were in little groups, but a lot of them were alone. Those were the people I think Torstein had in mind when he dreamed all this up, really. Most were guys, but there were a few ladies on their own, too. Nobody looked desperately poor or homeless. What would a desperately poor person be doing at a casino? But a lot of them looked depressed, and a few looked shell-shocked.

I saw my dad sit down with the bunch at his table, and put his arm around an old guy who seemed to be crying. He was probably a little drunk. But I was proud of my pop. He was always like Pete, a strong guy, an action figure. For him to sit down and put his arm around some stranger's shoulders, that was pretty cool.

Dragonfly

We waited until about 10 after 8. We'd set up the tent to accommodate 500 people. We really had no idea how many would come. I would say it was half full. There were 250 desperate gamblers with nowhere to be on Thanksgiving Day. Torstein stepped up to the little dais we'd made for him with a podium and a microphone.

"I don't usually make speeches, and I will make this one short," he said. "My name is Torstein, and I don't have much family. I didn't want to be alone on Thanksgiving Day, and I thought, how can I get some people to have Thanksgiving dinner with me? I'm not proud, so I decided I'd pay people to have dinner with me. So, you're my honored guest. After you enjoy your meal, you can just take your ticket over to Ferdy there by the door, and he'll give you your five dollars for joining me. Thank you for coming! Enjoy your food." Then he showed his hands like a retiring dealer, clapped them together and called, "Good luck!"

46

There was a round of polite applause when Torstein finished his speech. Then those of us who were acting as waiters jumped up and trooped over to the kitchen window to pick up the trays of food and serve our honored guests. After everyone was served, we sat down with them to eat dinner and chat.

Torstein didn't have a table to look after. He began to move among the various tables, shake people's hands, learn their names, and talk to them. He was at his dragonfly best, flitting here and there in that crazy green coat, and getting people to smile, or cry, or tell him their stories.

I don't know how to describe what he did, or how he did it. It wasn't as if any of us could have put on the coat and become the dragonfly. There was something in him so bright, so electric, something that made him float above it all, and yet alight with you and be fully present in your personal drama.

That's what he was doing. When he came to my table, I stood up so he could sit in my chair, which he did, grabbing my arm and holding onto it for a moment, letting me know he wouldn't stay long, wouldn't interrupt my dinner—and I gave his shoulder a squeeze to let him know I didn't care. He started asking everyone's name and shaking hands.

There were four guys together at my table; young guys who'd come to the casino together and were a little bit drunk and enjoying their dinner. There was a couple there, a middle-class looking guy and his wife. From what I gathered, he'd lost rather more than they'd agreed they would spend that day, and she was pretty peeved about it. She expected him to recoup their losses with the $10 they'd get for eating with us. Then there were two singles at my table: a middle-aged guy and a younger woman. The guy, I think he was a divorced dad whose wife had the kids on Thanksgiving, and he was at wit's end what to do with himself. He warmed to Torstein right away, showed him pictures of his kids. The woman, she just seemed really sad.

Torstein said to her, "No family expecting you tonight?"

"No," she said quietly.

"Me neither," he said. "I'm free as a bird."

She looked up at him and smiled a little.

"Have you been winning?" Torstein asked.

She shook her head. "No, breaking even, maybe losing a little."

"Well, look," he said. "When you're done eating and you get your five bucks, if you don't want to lose it, we could use you here. There will be a major clean-up to do. We'd be happy to have the help."

"Really?" she said, just as if he'd offered to buy her a new pair of shoes or something.

"Sure. Just find me after dinner, and I'll get one of the ladies to show you what to do."

"Great," she said. "Great. Thanks"

Torstein turned to the couple arguing over their plans for how to win back the money they'd lost, and he said, "Same goes for you two. We'll have a job of cleaning up to do after dinner, and if you want to stay and help you're welcome. You could still go home with $10 cash tonight ..."

I thought they were less likely than the woman to stay. But the divorced dad said he'd stay.

"Super," Torstein said. He introduced the divorced dad to the young woman and told them to come find him after dinner, and he'd put them to work. I figured he was doing the same thing at every table—telling people they didn't have to go back to the casino if they didn't want to. They could stay here and have the pleasure of our company. It was weird how many people accepted!

By half past nine everyone was done eating. We still had a ton of food left over, so Torstein sent a lot of people out to tell the casino employees if they wanted to come on their break, they could eat here for free. We cut the kitchen in half, put the left-over food into warmers in one half, and started the tear-down and clean up on the other half.

Bruiser, Pete and I started turning off and tearing down the column heaters and lighting, leaving one area lit and heated for the casino employees who began to turn up in shifts. Half our wait staff took care of them while the rest of us organized teams to do tear-down and clean-up. It went fast because of how many gamblers had stayed to help out.

By 11 p.m., only one small area of our big tent was still lit, and warm, and we were all gathered there, sitting at the tables, talking and laughing together, drinking tea and Kool-Aid, and eating leftover pie. We'd had to buy the pies at a bakery; no one had enough time to home-make dozens of pies. They were really good though. About 30 of us had come with Torstein to make this dinner happen. I would say there were another 50 diners still sitting with us. When some casino employees showed up for their free dinner, sometimes it was one of the previous diners who jumped up and ran to get a plate for them.

It was nice, and kind of homey. And fluttering through it all, Torstein was still talking to people, touching them, offering them sunflower seeds, telling them to come and visit us downtown sometime.

Sully, who'd worked really hard all afternoon, had fallen asleep right after dinner. Now he was sitting slumped against Bruiser, who was being very quiet so as not to wake him. Maggie came and said, "I better take him home, you guys."

Torstein heard and called, "Yeah, anybody who needs to get going should go. Some of us will stay here until the food's gone, and then we'll pack it in."

Bruiser got up and carried Sully to Maggie's car. She waved at me on her way out the tent flap, and for a minute I remembered the first time I'd seen her, flanked by her seven assistants, caught up in whatever they thought it was so critical she had to be doing. Now she had such a lovely smile on her pale face, and though she looked tired, her eyes were bright. And no assistants. Just our Bruiser carrying Sully for her. She was a pretty picture.

47

"It's the Dunkers."

They were back! We had not seen any of them since that early fall day when Torstein told them they were to go north, south, east and west and tell people that love is the answer and the kingdom of God arrived whenever people dared to love.

We'd *heard* about them, of course. And we'd seen evidence of where they'd been. They were controversial before, when they were preaching at Nikolai's goons down by the shore, and when they were canvassing the inner city and telling people to "turn or burn." But this new message, this message of *love,* it seemed to spark even more publicity! The Dunkers were fanatics. They couldn't do anything halfway. They were prone to sharing their message with big gatherings in public areas where maybe they weren't supposed to be the main attraction. They caused a commotion wherever they went—and they were guerrilla marketing geniuses.

Crazy Eyes started a blog and a Facebook page about the Dunkers' new message. He organized the teams of two and sent them out in strategic blocs to various communities. Who knew he was an art school graduate? (Then again, I probably should have known his eyes were crazy from the inside out, too.) He created a fantastic poster with the Dunker's face, and Torstein's, in that new icon style they'd adopted. It showed the two idols, and was emblazoned with the words, "Where is love?" The background of it was all muted rainbow colors, like those old playbills from the 70's. Somehow, he had the thing enlarged and printed by the hundreds.

The Dunkers would go into their assigned area in the middle of the night and slap these posters up, but everywhere! Three, four, five posters in a row on the side of every building. Crazy Eyes had also created the art for new t-shirts for them, dragonfly green shirts of course, with bold fuchsia lettering and line drawings of the Dunker and Torstein and the same tag line: "Where is love?"

They'd come into the streets in their bright green t's the next morning after the posters went up, and over the next few days they'd literally stop traffic with little dramas they'd created based on what they saw that day in the park and what they knew of Torstein's life. After a few days of this, they'd swoop down under cover of darkness and replace all the "Where is love?" posters with new ones that said, "Love is here!" Then the poster would give a schedule and locations where more information could be had—places like Starbucks and bookstores and any large events, but with strange little directions like "under the third lamp pole from the front gate." They'd station themselves at these places, and tell people exactly what Torstein had told them to say. Crazy Eyes had even made up bright green business cards with the gist of the message printed on them, to hand out to people.

Their efforts had always been bold, but now their effectiveness was also quite extraordinary. Several new people had joined us in the park because of what they'd heard from the Dunkers, plus they'd been covered in the newspapers and TV news. Crazy Eyes' blog was popular—not just in our city or region, but worldwide. He'd report on where some Dunkers might be and what they were doing; remember they'd gone out in teams of two (then Crazy Eyes would send two or three or four teams to each neighborhood), so this was happening in various communities all simultaneously.

It was, frankly, astounding what they'd accomplished. They were used to publicity from their days with the Dunker, but this new message had legs they'd never imagined. Naturally their return to the park that winter afternoon was quite triumphant. Crazy Eyes led the pack, and they ran to Torstein calling out to him, "It worked! People listened! They love this message!"

Dragonfly

After our usual afternoon of Story Hour and visiting with the folks in the park, Torstein got all the Dunkers to sit down with us and tell us about their adventures. Their main theme was that, while not *everyone* listened, those who did were often times quite taken with the idea.

"Tell us, tell us," Torstein encouraged them.

One by one, the teams reported on what they'd seen and done.

48

"We met a woman named Shayla," began one of the kids, the surfer punks. "She's the one you maybe saw on the news—her baby was crawling down the street at two in the morning."

Yes, we had all seen Shayla's story on the news. There was a party in her grandma's house where she lived, and grandma was out of town, and Shayla's one-year-old baby had somehow made her way out of the house, down the sidewalk and into the street. The motorist who almost ran over her stopped and shot video of her toddling down the street before he called 911. He wasn't sure where the baby belonged; she had actually managed to get several houses down from her own home. It was this amateur video they played on the news: the dark tarmac, the white stripe down which the baby in the white t-shirt and diaper was hastening on hands and knees. It was awful, there was no doubt of that. Pretty awful.

Shayla's defense had been: "None of you think something like this can happen to you if you're a good parent, but it can. Sh-t happens." This did not endear her to the public.

As soon as the Dunker punk told us he had met Shayla, mother of the runaway baby, the walls went up. None of us would ever have let a toddler crawl down the street at night! But Torstein's look of excited expectation never changed. He nodded and encouraged the boy to go on.

"She's had a terrible time since that video. Child Protective Services is making her go to classes and have inspectors in her home at all hours of the day and night, plus they actually gave custody of the baby to the grandma, so unless Shayla completes the classes, she can't get her daughter back, legally. And everyone who saw her on the news comes down on her hard. Bad mother, you're a bad mother, that's what everyone tells her. How do you think that feels?"

"She *is* a bad mother." Ferdy said. But all of us were thinking it. Of course she's a bad mother!

"Well, yeah," the kid said. "But if you've got a big nose and everyone keeps telling you that, does it make you feel any better just because it's the truth? She knows she's a bad mother, but she doesn't need everyone telling her that."

"She never admitted she was a bad mother!" Franz said. "She basically said it was just one of those things. Could happen to anyone."

"It's all right," Torstein said. "She doesn't have to *say* she's a bad mother. Go on, Kurt."

The Dunker punk nodded.

"What she said, to us, was: there's no love in this neighborhood for me anymore. I want to move, but unless I finish all the classes, I can't take my daughter with me. I'm stuck here unless I leave her."

"What did you say?" Torstein asked.

"I told her that somehow, love was the answer to her equation." He smiled. "She said, 'My what?!' And so I told her the answer to her problem. All we had to do was figure out how love was the answer."

"Perfect!" said Torstein, clapping his hands, his eyes shining.

49

Shayla really was in a fix, the Dunker punk, Kurt explained. She lived with her grandma who was 60 years old and worked every day as a teacher's aid so she could provide for her grand-kids, their mama having left long ago. Shayla herself was only 17; she had the baby at 16, and there was no daddy in the picture—not hers, nor her baby's. As Kurt asked her about her life, this was the picture she painted: she wanted designer clothes for her little girl (and herself) plus the attentions of a man named Zeke, or the equally ghetto fabulous Mtrane. Was that so much to ask?

"Let me get this straight," Kurt had said. "Your whole plan for your future is to dress nice, and dress your baby nice, and get with one of these two men?" Shayla admitted, these were the things that would make her happy; and maybe a car.

Kurt, wise beyond his punk years, told her, "Shayla, I think I see how the wheels came off. Your life is about shallow things. Really, it's about nothing. We need to make your life *about something*. We need to make your life about love. Now, who in your life is really deserving of your love?"

"My baby and Zeke or Mtrane," she responded readily.

"How about your baby and your grandma?" Kurt responded. "The baby, because you brought her into this world, you're the only one she has, and she's the only one that's fully yours. And your grandma, because she has taken care of you, all your life. Zeke and Mtrane are certainly worthy of being loved, but I think you have to start closer to home, and build out from there."

Wasn't that what Torstein had told us? To love everyone, you had to start by loving the people closest to you, and then work outward.

"The problem you're facing right now, that everyone's dissing you because you're a bad mama, that isn't the *real* problem," Kurt informed Shayla. "That's just a symptom of what's really wrong. What's really wrong is that you're wasting your passions where they're not doing any good, you follow?" He could tell Shayla didn't really follow; her whole mindset had been geared toward the clothes, the boys, and maybe a car, to impress all her friends. Now all her friends were laughing at her, uploading the awful video of her baby in the street to You Tube, and telling her she was an unfit mother.

"Even if you get the clothes and the man and the car at this point, you're still facing a world of persecution," Kurt said.

"Say what?"

"Your friends are still going to hold this against you. You've got to repair that breach, devote yourself to your baby, and helping your grandma, and then, when everyone can see you're a good mother, and a good grand-daughter, then we'll look back and see whether the things you think are important now are really so important to you."

As Kurt was telling the story, he smiled, and I wondered: what made a girl like Shayla, who lived in a whole different world than the surfer punk Kurt, listen to him? And the only answer I could come up with was: love. She must have sensed that he'd been touched by Torstein's love, and now he was showing her the way to put that love in action. He had nothing to gain from her transformation...he just loved, and he wanted to share love.

He turned to us now, as he told the story, turned to Torstein, and, smiling, said:

"It worked. It's working. She agreed to try it, for 90 days, to give up the party life, to stay out of the hunt for those two guys, to help her grandma around the house, maybe look for a job...I mean, we can't expect miracles, but this *is* kind of a miracle. Maybe that video of her baby in the street is just what she needed to open her eyes to the power of love, you know?"

Kurt's partner, another surfer punk just as tan and blond, said, "We sent her to a pregnancy assistance center. I mean, she already has the baby, but they have continuing education and stuff. She's going to try it, at least for three months. I know it's going to work."

"Love never fails," Torstein said, grinning. "Tell us more."

50

A nother Dunker punk stood up.

"Kurt and Joe were in the inner city," he said. "And maybe poor people seem more needy than others…but Ernie and I were getting run out of places like Wood Forest and Sawmill Run." He mentioned a couple of the tonier areas pretty far to the north. "But I figure the more they try to run you out, probably the more they need you, right?"

I couldn't too well imagine the "town centers" of Wood Forest or Sawmill Run enjoying the site of the psychedelic playbills pasted up on the sides of their stylized centers of commerce. These were suburban enclaves where the Town Associations strictly controlled everything about the retail centers from the brick of the buildings to the color of the blinds…I could see why Ernie and pal would get chased out. Lucky they weren't arrested—except the rent-a-cops hired to police these areas weren't real tough guys. They didn't have too many real criminals to come after.

"And think about it. What do the people in those places find their security in? Their money, right?" the Dunker punk was saying. "They think they get behind the fence of their gated community, park their Beamer and close the automatic garage door, they got no troubles because the money's there. But this economy? Even the rich guys are starting to sweat it."

Ernie and his partner, Vinnie, they'd created their own take on the whole "Where is love?" theme. Their posters and publicity proclaimed, "Can't buy me love?" This seemed to resonate better with their audience. They played out their dramas at outdoor malls and parks, and they planned their information sessions for places like Starbucks, outside Barnes and Noble and Pottery Barn—places the families of Wood Forest and Sawmill Run would eventually turn up.

"At first, we figured they'd run us off because, well, can you imagine the Dunker bellowing outside a Starbucks in Sawmill Run?" Vinnie laughed. I had to laugh, too. No, I couldn't imagine it. But the Dunkers, they didn't bellow. Maybe they did, when Duncan was alive, but their new message, Torstein's message, didn't demand it. Instead, they handed out their little cards and talked to people about what was really important in life.

"I want to tell you about J. Clayton Berger," Vinnie said. "We'd been outside the Barnes and Noble all afternoon, talked to a lot of kids, and a few adults, and now it was getting on toward 10 o'clock. The bookstore there is open until 11. And J. Clayton Berger walks up. We'd seen him hand off his Land Rover to the valet. There's a buncha restaurants around the bookstore, and a mall with valet parking that's open until midnight. We figured he was going to dinner, but he came to the bookstore. And he stopped when he saw us."

Ernie stepped up beside Vinnie now, and continued the story. He was an Hispanic kid, early 20's, his black hair bleached almost blond from the sun, his dark skin tanned almost black.

"He said, 'Voy aprender español,' you know, *I'm learning Spanish*. So I started talking to him in Spanish. He's using that Rosetta Stone system, and he's pretty good. I was impressed. He told me about his wife and kids, their names and ages, and his job, a little bit, *abogado*, he's a lawyer. Then, after a while, we couldn't talk in Spanish anymore, because he ran out of words to tell me about the hours he worked, the things he planned to do for his kids, and the things he wanted to get for his wife and himself. The *reasons* for his work, he said, *razon de ser*, his reason to be. He said, *Ernesto, mis niños van recibir mas de mis padres mi dan*. My kids are going to get more than my parents give me."

Ernie stopped and smiled. "It was so easy then to ask him, what did your parents give you? Wasn't it enough? Why do your kids need more? What is this *razon de ser* that you're living?"

51

"He told me a story, to show what he meant."

Young J. Clayton Berger had been raised in a nice middle-class home with a dad who was a nice mid-level manager at a K-Mart store. Dad had doted on his boy and made sure Clay got a job at the store when he was just 16. While to Dad this seemed like a great gift for a teenager—a way to make his own money to buy his own clothes and car—to Clay it seemed like a huge humiliation. If any friends from school happened to dash into the K-Mart to buy big boxes of candy to smuggle into the cinema, who did they see setting up the Blue Light Special but their schoolmate Clay?!

Already saddled with the reputation as K-Mart boy, Clay had to struggle to keep up appearances. He refused to buy the reasonably-priced clothes at K-Mart, but couldn't afford to buy the more expensive designer ones he wanted, so he took the bus to the other end of town to shop at thrift stores where he wouldn't run into anyone. Usually he could find something trendy and not too used. One day he found exactly what he wanted, the height of cool at the time, pipe-stem jeans. They were straight-leg, wide-leg jeans all the guys were wearing. He bought them at the thrift store, had them cleaned, and wore them to the next school dance. He knew he would be the coolest one there!

His passion at the time was acting—singing, dancing, *performing*—and he felt he was very good at it. So of course, when he arrived at the dance in his new finery, he went out of his way to get everyone's attention. He put himself front and center on the dance floor, he stood on stage and lip-synched several of the songs the d.j. was playing (these were the days before karaoke). He had a ball showing off and shaking his groove thing in his new jeans.

And at first he was thrilled that people were overly exuberant in commenting on his new jeans; in fact, some of them seemed on the verge of hysteria about them. Finally, one of his friends let him in on the joke: they were women's jeans! He rushed to the restroom, whipped off the pants, looked at the label, and sure enough: there was the leather patch embossed with the cowboy hat and lasso: Lady Wranglers.

As he told the story, Ernie did not laugh, but looked him straight in the eye. "What'd you do?"

"What could I do?" J. Clayton Berger, 20 years later, groaned. "I stayed in the bathroom until the dance ended and everyone was gone. Then I walked home in my lady pants."

This, and many other embarrassments associated with having a father who worked at K-Mart and being forced into a job at K-Mart himself, and living in a subdivision and never being able to afford a car until college, had crystallized in J. Clayton's mind the plan to give his own children far more then he'd ever had. None of his children would be working at K-Mart or buying their clothes in a thrift store. All of his children would receive cars for their 16th birthday. And they would have a dad who was a lawyer and a money-maker. He managed to come back from the embarrassment of wearing lady jeans and continued to pursue his acting in high school and college but he got serious about law school, gave up the stage, and had pursued his deeper goal of making money and giving his kids everything they wanted.

"But here's the hell of it," he said, rueful. "They don't know any different. They'll never understand what a gift I'm giving them."

Vinnie, who'd been letting Ernie tell the story, stood up now.

"We told him, any risk you take for love means the kingdom of God is here. You love our kids, you're sacrificing for them. But he told us...He said the hardest thing he gave up, to become a lawyer, was the stage. Every now and then, not often, because he's too busy to have daydreams and he doesn't believe in second thoughts, but every now and then...he feels like his heart is breaking because he wonders if he could have made it. *I wouldn't even have to be a movie star or a stage great—I just wonder if I could have been a local celebrity in a community theater, or a guy in the chorus at the opera house,* that's what he told us."

Torstein, sitting near me, sighed. "Unfulfilled dreams," he said. "Dreams deferred."

"But what can you tell a guy like this?" Ernie asked. "He can't quit his job and look for work as an actor. So we told him again what we were telling everyone: love is the answer to your secret longing. You just have to figure out how love is the answer in this case."

He reached into his backpack, then, and pulled out a battered ToughBook laptop computer, which he seemed to be booting up. He handed it to Torstein and said, "Here, you can see J. Clayton Berger now."

Because I was close to Torstein in the crowd, I could look over his shoulder. The internet browser was open to a You Tube video, and the little recording was of one of the Dunker dramas, the crazy outdoor sketches they did when they were preparing to blitz a new community. I could tell Ernie and Vinnie, and an older guy in a bright green t-shirt whose dramatic flair outshined both of theirs.

"He joined us!" Vinnie said, laughing, calling it out so everyone in the crowd could hear. "And he was right, he *is* a great actor."

"He doesn't go with us all the time, but he's been meeting up with different teams on the weekends or evenings and doing the dramas with them—he's awesome. And he's loving it. He brought his kids a few times on the weekends—they're amazed. They can't believe it's their dad...They go to some mega-church, and the kids are begging him to get on the drama team there."

Torstein was laughing. "That's terrific. That's a start, see, look at him, filled with joy. Tell me more."

Every team had a Shayla, or a J. Clayton Berger to tell us about.

Somehow, this message just reached out and grabbed some people. And they were transformed by it.

Not everyone, of course. Some of the Dunkers told about being laughed at, spit on, roughed up. They'd all been called freaks, losers, and worse. They didn't seem to mind—I guess they'd been used to it when they worked for Duncan. They seemed to value the joy of the few people who *did* respond to their message far above whatever they'd suffered. It was pretty impressive, to tell you the truth. I remembered thinking how brave they were just to stand up and shout their message… something about coming into contact with a Duncan, or a Torstein, it seemed to empower people to forget themselves, and their dignity…yet I didn't feel like I was there yet.

52

Christmas came barreling down on us pretty fast after the Dunkers' return. I figured since we'd spent Thanksgiving at the casinos, Torstein would want us to have Christmas Eve at Sharky's Bar or something. But he didn't. In fact, he said, he would like very much if just a few of us could get away from everyone else for a bit. He was tired, he said. And lonely. How he could be lonely, I'm not sure. He was always surrounded by a lot of people.

He liked them; he wanted them to seek him out and share their stories with him. He always had time to stop and listen. And touch. There was this little autistic girl, Cyd, who came often to Story Hour with her dad. She didn't care much about the stories, but she loved Torstein. She would latch onto him and hold onto him until her dad had to pry her away. One day after story hour, her dad had come running up to us and said Cyd was having a seizure—this was something new. She had a lot of troubles with the autism: poor eyesight, a speech impediment, poor social skills, but no seizures before.

We started hurrying to where she was; Maggie was phoning 911 on her cell phone—but people kept crowding around Torstein. They didn't realize what was happening, and they wanted him to stop and talk. Some were reaching out for him…and in the middle of all this, he came to a complete standstill and said, "Wait now, who just touched me?"

Who just touched me?! About a dozen people were trying to touch him! But he's looking all around, high and low, and just behind us, between Maggie and Tawny, was a little old lady. *The* little old lady—the one whose groceries Torstein had carried back in the summer when we went to the shore! She had somehow pushed her way through this crowd…and I guess she had *touched* him. And he had noticed! He was weird that way.

He reached out and hugged her, and said, "There you are. I thought it was you!"

She said, "You told me I'd be seeing a lot of you…but I didn't see you again. I had to find you."

"I know," he said. "And I still mean it, you will be seeing a lot of me. Very soon. Did they tell you when, how long you have?"

"Just a few weeks," she said. "I just wanted to see you again. I thought if I could just grab hold of that crazy green coat…"

At this, he laughed, a deep, rumbling laugh. He was still holding onto her, his arms were still around her shoulders. "It's all right," he said. "I promise, you'll be seeing me again, very soon. Maybe in just a few weeks." He kissed her forehead, and her face lit up. Then he looked around and called out, "Ferdy! Can you make sure she gets a cab home? Be careful with her."

Ferdy came and took the little old lady's arm, and escorted her back toward the street. Meanwhile, Cyd's dad had run ahead to where she was having the seizure, but when we got there, he looked up with tears in his eyes and said she was dead!

We could hear the wail of the ambulance in the distance now, but when he said those words…I think our hearts dropped right to our feet. Maggie stumbled and grabbed onto me. Jack grabbed Torstein's arm and dragged him forward toward where the little girl was lying so still on the ground, her daddy kneeling over her.

"Dead?" Torstein said. "I don't think she's dead."

He and Jack knelt down beside her, and Torstein reached out and shook her by the shoulder. "Cyd," he said. "Cyd, wake up."

Her big green eyes fluttered open, and she was looking myopically up at Torstein. Her glasses had flown off, I guess while she was having a seizure, but she lifted her head and got a better look at his face, and a big smile came out on hers. She sat up and gave him a hug.

"Atta girl," he said. "How are you, Cyd? You OK?"

Dragonfly

She made a little purring noise which was about all she ever really said, and she sat in his lap until the paramedics came.

I don't want to say stuff like that happened regularly, but it wasn't unusual, either. And I think it was wearing Torstein out. He told Jack, Jazz and Pete that he wanted to spend Christmas with just us and the ladies, and maybe Franz and Bruiser—and of course, Ferdy. Ferdy would have to be there to pay for it. But Pete said Ferdy wouldn't have to pay for anything, we could all come to his house. Phyllis would be glad to have us, he said. Ferdy would be welcome, of course, but it would be Pete's pleasure to have us all for Christmas.

Ferdy was delighted, but he said, "Aren't you going to do anything for your homeless friends or feed the hungry or something for Christmas?"

Torstein sighed and said, "I'm homeless. And I'm hungry. I think a lot of charities are doing nice things for the poor this time of year. They'll be there waiting for us to serve them when the holiday is over. Maybe I'd like somebody to look after me for a day or two."

53

Phyllis, Pete's wife, had changed a lot since she met Torstein. For one thing, Pete said, she started actually taking the drugs her doctor had prescribed for the manic-depressive symptoms, and that helped a lot. For another thing, she seemed to genuinely like helping people. It gave her the same kind of lift it gave Torstein—and the rest of us I guess. She'd been a mom for many years, but the kids preferred each other to her, and now even they were gone. She'd been shopping and travelling, and somehow as fun as it was, it hadn't made her happy. Actually doing something for someone who needed something done, that seemed to make her happy.

But she was still Phyllis. She had the maids in to go over her house top to bottom, even after she and Pete had cleaned it all up. She had made up each of the twins' rooms into guest rooms, plus her sewing room and the regular guest room. She wanted to make sure each bedroom and bathroom had clean matching linens and little hotel bars of soap and bottles of shampoo. She made it like a spa for us! It was an awesome gift for everyone, like going to a nice—but homey—hotel.

Maggie and Sully got one of the twins' old rooms to share, with a cot for Sully, but Phyllis made it up with bolsters and cushions so he looked like a little rajah propped on it. Tawny and Marigold got the other twin's bedroom—it had a double bed in it they were happy to share. Bruiser and Franz got the sewing room with futons to sleep on, but they said they'd be perfectly comfortable there. Torstein got the guestroom to himself! I told Pete and Phyllis I would stay at my place.

It was only a 20-minute drive away, and their house was packed now. But Torstein wanted me and Ferdy to stay, too, and Jack and Jazz. So Pete made places for us to sleep in the basement—his billiards room! The four of us were set up down there.

So on Christmas Eve we all moved in. Phyllis was planning a terrific banquet for us that night, and the smells coming out of the kitchen were insane. Pete had gotten a big live Christmas tree, and he'd somehow persuaded Phyllis not to decorate it with all her matching designer ornaments, but to set out boxes of decorations from when the twins were small, so Sully could decorate it. Actually, everyone fell in to decorate it, because it was so tall. Bruiser got assigned the top level, and then he lifted Sully up to put the star on top ...Tawny and Marigold were as delighted as Sully to be decorating the tree. Christmas carols were playing, and Torstein was just sitting in a big easy chair, with Maggie sitting on the floor beside him. She was holding his hand.

Torstein, he looked...relaxed, I suppose, but tired. And...subdued? Frightened? I wasn't sure.

It was getting dark out by the time we finished with the tree, and then Tawny and Marigold went to help Phyllis. Pete and Phyllis had a big dining room table, and the girls were laying out plates and glasses while Phyllis had her blender and food processor whirring and her timers dinging and the stove-top hissing with sausages in a pan...but she was also still trying to be the hostess, and she would bound through the family room every few minutes to see if anyone needed a drink or a snack. Once as she glanced in, Torstein looked up and said, "Phyllis, why don't you sit down here with me for a minute?"

She smiled at him, but she said, "I've got stuff on the stove top—I just wanted to see if anyone needed anything —"

"I do," he said. "I need you to sit down here a minute." He motioned to the arm of the overstuffed easy chair where he was sitting. "I don't have a wife or a sister. I spend my time with a bunch of rough guys like your husband...Can you just stay a few minutes?"

She looked toward the kitchen where we could hear the sausages sizzling. "Maggie," she said, "could you just —"

"No, no," Torstein said, grasping Maggie's hand harder. "I need you both."

I was no cook, but I could stop a sausage from burning. I jumped up and said, "Don't sweat it, Phyllis. I got the stove-top."

As I was rushing into the kitchen, Phyllis blew me a kiss, something I could never remember her doing my whole life, and she and Pete had been married for almost as long as I'd been alive...Then she sat down on the arm of the chair next to Torstein, and put her arm around his shoulder. I heard her talking to him as if she were speaking to her own son back in the day. "What's wrong, honey? It's Christmas. Are you sad?"

"No, well, maybe a little," I heard Torstein saying. "I'm grateful for all you've done for me, Phyllis, and for having everyone over. But your sitting here with me, and Maggie sitting here with me...that means more than anything. Thank you."

Then I was turning sausages and juggling frying pans and asking Tawny and Mari if they knew what Phyllis had been planning to do with this sausage—they didn't but they said they'd find out, and they went into the family room and didn't come back! I figure they were sitting at Torstein's feet, too, so I called Pete in. He said the sausage was for the stuffing, and he knew exactly what to do with it. He and I put the last touches on the dinner! And it turned out really good.

54

Jack and Jazz's parents, and my dad and step-mom came on Christmas morning for breakfast —a big country breakfast with bacon and eggs and biscuits and gravy and oatmeal, ham and cheesy grits. Sully, the only kid we had, had never experienced an actual *Christmas* Christmas before...he must have been the only kid in the nation who did not realize there was supposed to be an orgy of gift-giving at the crack of dawn on Christmas. He believed it was Christmas because of all the amazing *food* we were getting...He'd never even heard of a grit before.

As we were all shoving away from the table, about to burst, Maggie said to Sully, "Well, do you want to open presents?"

He gave her a round-eyed look that reflected pure amazement at such a question. He had just turned six years old the week before, and he had received actual birthday presents from Maggie and Tawny and Marigold, and a birthday cake and candles shared with the rest of us... it was clear he could hardly believe there were *more* presents associated with this time of year. It was sweet, in a way, that he wasn't expecting anything and was astonished just by the bounty of the table here at Pete's house...but it was also sad that he'd never supposed there might be a gift for him on Christmas day.

Angel had sent him some things. She had progressed so far in her program, she had now joined a choir that visited churches and schools to sing and tell about drug and alcohol abuse prevention. On one of those outings, she'd been allowed to visit a shelter for abused women and children—when they heard she had a little boy, they gave her a backpack full of Crayons and coloring books and a few little school supplies. She had wrapped it all up and sent it, the backpack for his birthday, and the rest of the stuff for Christmas. I'm pretty sure these were the first birthday and Christmas gifts she'd ever given Sully. What's more, one of the program directors from the rehab had also sent Sully a present, some kind of Transformer that was a car and a robot.

And my step-mom had brought him a couple of sweaters and a pair of shoes, and Jack and Jazz's mom had brought him a pair of jeans and a polo shirt. And Maggie and the Story Ladies had bought him some of his favorite books from Story Hour, to keep as his own, since he was learning to read.

He was overwhelmed by it all. He tore through all the wrapping and kept running around to various gift-givers to say thank you and give them big hugs. Then he passed out. Not literally. I think the combination of the big breakfast and all the excitement was too much. He piled all his new things in a corner around him and sat down to read his books, and in about 10 minutes, he was asleep.

The rest of us...we hadn't gotten each other any gifts. There was this unspoken but very powerful idea that what we had together was enough; that gifts would have been superfluous. All Sully's presents had made a nice pile under the tree, and now it was just empty wrappers and bits of ribbon and crushed bows. But it was perfect.

"Pete, Phyllis, thank you," Torstein said. He seemed more relaxed, and happier, than he had been the night before. "I know this was a lot of trouble for you."

"Not at all," Phyllis said. "And you could stay, Torstein, you're welcome here."

She didn't include the rest of us who were sleeping in her basement and sewing room and children's rooms! But we all had our own places.

"Thanks," he said. "I know you mean that, and I appreciate it."

Franz was sitting on the big chair—Pete and Phyllis had this big chair that looked like an easy chair but was just big enough for two people to snuggle into if they weren't too big. Franz was small, and

Dragonfly

Tawny had consented to sit in the big chair with him. Now he pointed to the tree and said:

"There's one more present under there still wrapped up."

Tawny sat forward to see where he was pointing and said, "Oh, too bad. Sully missed it. Should we wake him up?"

"I don't think it's for Sully. Can you see the tag on it, Marigold?"

Mari had been sitting in the floor with Sully, helping him sort out which presents came from who so he could make his thank-you's. She reached for the small box in its red and white striped paper and said, "Tawny—it's for you. From Franz." She stopped and looked up at Tawny, wrinkled up her nose like a kid and stuck her tongue out as she said, "*With love* from Franz!"

We hooted at that, and Tawny blushed.

It was amazing, really, how far Tawny and Mari had come. Mari had been so determined to appear grown-up and tough as nails when she joined us. Now she was sticking her tongue out like a little kid. Tawny had been so afraid and unsure about everything except her ability to excite men…and now she blushed at a "With love."

She glanced at Franz as she took the box, and opened it, revealing, of course, a diamond solitaire set in a slim gold band. "Franz!" she said, in a choked little voice.

"Will you marry me?" he said, trying to get a glance under the hair that had fallen over her face when she ducked her head.

"OK," she said, "OK, but not for a while, all right? Not until the spring maybe?"

"Whenever you say," he said, and then she did look up, and they kissed, and the rest of us cheered, and Maggie cried, and Mari pouted. "Who's gonna be my room-mate now?"

And Torstein looked happy, but, I don't want to say, *pained* as well. He was happy for them, clearly, but it looked like he also feared for them, too.

55

New Year's Eve seems like another prime holiday for freaks and losers. No, I don't mean it that way. You know how Torstein wanted to be at the casino on Thanksgiving because he figured desperate people would be there, and they would be glad to eat with us? New Year's Eve strikes me as a time when people are desperate, too, desperate to have a good time, to be at some crazy blow-out, to make a memory they can cling to all through the coming year…and of course it never works out. For me it never had, anyway. New Year's Eve, to me, is overrated.

Torstein had gotten over whatever melancholy had possessed him at Christmas, and the day after, we were back in the park for Story Hour and mingling with all our old friends. He was back on the street, handing out sunflower seeds to passersby, inviting them to stop and chat if they had a mind to. Toward evening, most of his "regulars" had gathered around. He said, "Here's what we're going to do. We're going to make this a real New Year's Eve to remember."

As I say, I was not that wild about New Year's Eve to begin with. I was only 30 years old, roughly Torstein's age I guess, but I was over New Year's. The past few years I'd gone home from the fish market and gone to bed early, didn't even watch the ball drop or anything on TV. I don't know. It was always a disappointment. It kind of cheesed my dad off because he and my step-mom usually had a party. But even their parties were stupid. It was a bunch of older couples, the country club set. What was I supposed to do? If I brought a date, she was bored.

Dragonfly

If I came alone, I was bored. So, yeah, Torstein's pronouncement about a New Year's Eve to remember just didn't hold any promise for me.

But I didn't say anything…I mean…it was Torstein.

He said, "We have five days. Here's what we do. Everybody go home and invite your friends, from your neighborhood, people who wouldn't normally hang out here with us. Tell them it's going to be the worst New Year's Eve party, ever. No Alcohol. Bring the kids. What else makes for a terrible party?"

"Karaoke!" Franz called out.

Torstein laughed. "You're right, you're right, that's awful. But no, people still think that's fun. No food. There won't be anything to eat. And it's only going to be 20 minutes long. A 20-minute New Year's Eve party from quarter to 12 until 5 after. With no food, no drinks, and no noisemakers and no party hats."

"*Why* would anyone come?" Marigold asked.

"Because I promise, if they come and they want to make a new friend, they will. It's going to be the most intense 20 minutes of the year. If they want to see and hear and do something meaningful with the last 15 minutes of this year and the first 5 minutes of the new year, then there is no other place to be." He grinned. "Yeah, it's going to be so sober and so meaningful, it's not even enough of a party to be called a bad party. It's the anti-party. An Anti-New Year's Eve party."

"If it doesn't start until 11:45, a bunch of people are going to come already drunk," Bruiser said.

Torstein nodded. "You're right. OK, there's a condition for getting into this party. You have to be sober."

"What are we going to do, breathalyze people?" Ferdy asked.

"Yes!" Torstein said. "We are. We're going to hire some off-duty policemen with breathalyzers, and they're going to check. If you're over the limit, then you get sent to the fireworks show in Patriots Park. If you're ok, you can come to our anti-party."

"Any music?"

"No, of course not. No music."

"Where is it going to be?" I asked. I had assumed we'd be in Patriot's Park. The city put on a musical show and fireworks in our park on New Year's Eve.

Torstein looked at Ferdy, who held his hands out, palms up. "We've been broke since Thanksgiving," he said.

"It has to be close by here so we can send the people who aren't sober over to the fireworks show," Torstein said.

"Look, if there aren't going to be any drunks, and there's not going to be any food, music or dancing or anything like that, maybe I can get the lecture hall in the museum," Bruiser said.

A dozen heads whipped around in his direction. The lecture hall in the museum?! The civic art museum was just down the block from Patriots Park, in the opposite direction from Sharky's. It had a big lecture hall, or concert hall, where they sometimes had lectures (or concerts). But if we'd been broke since Thanksgiving, I didn't see how we could rent the place.

"How can you do that?" Torstein asked.

"The physical plant manager, he's a friend of mine."

"The janitor?" Franz asked.

"The maintenance man."

"And he's going to let us into the lecture hall?"

"No, but there's a gala there from 7 to 10 on New Year's Eve. They wanted to make sure the guests could get away in time to celebrate or go home or to the show in the park, whatever they wanted to do by midnight. So my friend, he has to hire a team to clean up after the gala. If some of us will go help him, I'm pretty sure he'd let us stay in the hall until midnight. As long as, you know, no one is drunk, tearing up the place or wandering through the museum. It'll be blocked off after the gala, anyway."

"I love it!" Torstein called. "Perfect. So, I'll definitely help clean up after the gala. Now, I wonder how many people will come?"

"Who wouldn't want to come to the worst New Year's Eve party ever?" Franz said.

Torstein laughed again. "Right, if all of you invite about 30 people ..."

"I don't know 30 people," I protested.

"The people in your apartment building. Just put flyers in their mailbox or something. I've got to try to find Sig and see about hiring some policemen with breathalyzers ..."

56

We spent the next five days telling people about our Anti-New Year's Eve party. The Dunkers, of course, took to the streets with natty business-card sized invitations that were very mysterious and yet very alluring, promising, as they did "World's Worst New Year's Eve." But honestly, once you got past the no drinks, no food, no music, no noise-makers, no party hats, it was surprising how many people were still interested. And this time, it wasn't people who worked downtown or, for some reason, came downtown or to the park. It was people who didn't know Torstein and would have to make an effort to come downtown on New Year's Eve to meet him.

We couldn't find Sig to ask him about the off-duty policemen, but Franz managed to connect with several who all said the rate on New Years Eve was sky-high, and they couldn't afford *not* to work regular gigs that would last all evening instead of coming over to the museum for half an hour's work. He didn't give up, though. He found out who was working security at the big show in Patriots Park, promised them each $50 cash if they would just *take their breaks* over at the museum using their breathalyzers, and organized it so there were three guys at the side entrance to the museum every minute from 11:30 to midnight. It was a lot of money to pay them for about 10 minutes work each, but at least it got them there.

Ferdy was appalled.

But other than this, the evening was costing us nothing. Bruiser was right, the physical plant manager was glad to have our help in cleaning up after the gala, and thanks in huge part to the Dunkers' industriousness, by 11:30 everything was cleared away and the hall was set up as a hall again, with about 500 chairs facing the front where there were built-in carpeted risers and a low dais with a podium. Whatever the entertainment was to be, it would take place up there.

We'd invited people and told them to come the museum's side entrance, so no one on the street would think there was an event inside and try to come in—and so no one otherwise connected with the museum would notice our party was taking place inside. Or our Anti-Party.

There was a lobby in front of the lecture hall, and Torstein had asked us to keep people in the lobby until 11:45, and then open the doors to the hall. There was nothing in the hall that would surprise anyone, but he thought it would be friendlier beforehand if everyone were standing in the lobby chatting rather than taking seats in the hall.

Torstein was standing beside the door starting at 11:30 when people began showing up. I couldn't believe it! People had come when invited to the worst New Year's Eve party ever! And they were submitting to the breathalyzer! (We had all done it, as a matter of fact—even Sully who could barely blow hard enough to make it work. He didn't want to be left out.)

"Welcome to this terrible party!" Torstein would exclaim, shaking hands with someone coming through the door. "I guarantee it will be the worst New Year's Eve ever."

People would laugh and hurry inside. I saw some residents from my building and went to say hello to them. "Hey, you made it. Thanks. I don't really know what's going to happen,"

"It's cool," said the guy from a few doors down. "I wasn't going to do anything tonight, anyway, and I figured, how could I resist the worst New Year's Eve party ever? And the shortest."

We laughed, and then the old lesbians who lived on the floor above me came and joined us. They gave me a hug, and I apologized for inviting them to such a dreary party, and they laughed. "Can't be any drearier than getting blitzed in a gay bar," one of them said.

"Yeah, I bet it could be," I said. And they laughed again.

The funny thing was, for people who had come to the advertised worst party ever, they all seemed pretty happy. It occurred to me, at other New Year's Eve do's, people were dressed to impress and forcefully determined to have a good time. Here everyone just seemed curious and a bit friendlier than they might have been on the street... but no one seemed self-conscious or nervous ...

Except me! Because I'd invited these people, and I had no idea what Torstein was up to!

At 11:45, the doors to the lecture hall opened, and in we went. True to our word, we'd provided no food, no drinks, no hats, no noise-makers. Everyone just sort of bustled in and took their seats. As it happened, no one had turned up tipsy. Everyone who'd wanted to come had been admitted.

Torstein walked up to the dais, then across it to the risers, and climbed up a couple of steps, so he was rather looking down at everyone, then sat down. Bruiser's friend had provided him with a one of those near-invisible microphones and had turned the sound system on for him, so everyone would be able to hear him.

"Thank you for coming!" he called. "And happy new year to you. And thank you for coming here sober. I know that may have been a trial for some of us."

It was only then I noticed Sully was sitting up in front with his back against the dais, with Sig's dog Tartan in his lap. I looked around, and there was Sig standing at the back of the hall. Our eyes met, and he nodded. He looked about 30 years older than when we'd seen him back in the summer. His eyes looked red and wet, but he had passed the breathalyzer too. I waved to him, then turned back to Torstein.

The next few moments would tell if this were, indeed, the worst New Year's Eve Party ever.

57

orstein continued with his speech ...
"There are two kinds of people in the world outside tonight.
People who are desperate to make these final few minutes of this
year memorable, and people who have given up on ever having any
memorable moments in their lives. But in here, tonight, I think there
are people who are ready to discover the secret that every moment can
be memorable. But that it doesn't take cold beer, hot sex, a big bank
account, a fast car or TV fame to make moments matter.

"Right now, I'm challenging you to make the final moments of this
year memorable by looking inside, at what really matters, and deciding
whether the year to come is going to be different than the year that's
passing. I'm challenging anyone who has ever heard *Auld Lang Sine*
playing and wondered, 'Is that all there is?' I'm talking to anyone who
has ever thrown up or passed out in a place you never saw before on
any long ago New Year's Eve and started your new year with a crushing
hangover. I'm talking to everyone who spent last New Year's Eve asleep
on the sofa or staring at the TV ...

"And I'm telling you: you were right. Those moments weren't
memorable. Those moments don't matter. What those people outside
here think they're doing—either to seize the final minutes of the year
and *force* them to be fun, or to steadfastly ignore that this night is any
different from any other night—they're both wrong! The real truth
is: this night *is* different, but not because it's the last night of the year
and we're all in a frenzy to have a hubba-hey good time. It's different

because this is the night you're hearing something that can change everything for you.

"I don't want anything from you. If you want to be friends, I want that too. If you don't, that's okay. But I promised you something intense, and here it is, take it or leave it."

The audience was hanging on every word. I was hanging on every word! It was as if he knew what I'd been thinking about New Year's Eve—and how stupid it is—all along.

"Everything you've ever heard about how the world works is wrong. Here's the truth: if you're poor, you're happy, because the kingdom of God is yours. If you're hungry, you're happy, because you will have the greatest satisfaction in being filled. If you're crying now, you're happy—because your inheritance is laughter, eternally. If you're hated, you're happy; if you're outcast, you're happy. Because God's best business is with the hated, the outcast, the marginalized.

"I know it doesn't make sense. But this can be your awakening moment, here, in the heart of the city, on the last night of the year. Because while what I'm saying doesn't make sense, it *is* the truth. And here's the greatest truth:

"You are made in the image of God. And God is love. So your image is *love.* And love is older and stronger than hate. Good is older and stronger than evil. When you meet evil and you meet hatred, you have the very thing that can whip them—and it isn't more hatred, and it isn't more evil. It's love."

58

⚜

orstein looked out at the audience and said. "What time is it? Is it midnight yet?"

"A couple minutes," Ferdy called back.

"We didn't miss it then." He stood up. "Stand up, everyone, let's ring in the new year. If you want to, join hands. Take the hand of someone next to you. Doesn't matter if you know them or like them or dislike them, just reach out."

Everyone stood, and hands were stretched out to one another. Sully and Tartan had fallen asleep, but otherwise everyone seemed to be holding on to someone. I'm pretty sure I even saw J. Clayton Berger standing with the Dunkers, with his wife and kids there beside him.

"I won't always be here," Torstein said. "My journey could be over very soon, and perhaps even very violently, and my best friends might be so terrified they'll want to forget they even knew me. But that won't matter, because what I've told you here is still true, and it will work, whether I am here or not—as long as you remember it, and practice it, and love one another.

"Happy new year, my friends. Choose to make this year count. Not by the money you make, the clothes you wear, the vacations you take, the awards you win…but by the way you choose to spend your time and share your treasures. By the way you choose to treat the people least able to help or reward you. Show your quality. Show your love! Happy new year!"

The entire audience called back enthusiastically, "Happy new year!"

Then they let go of each others' hands and cheered, applauded, for several minutes.

Torstein grinned, and sat back down. People started to file out, chatting with each other, hugging each other. A few came forward to speak with Torstein. I heard Sig whistle for Tartan, who immediately jumped up and bounded through the crowd to him, and they slipped away. I wondered what had been happening with Sig's case. Clearly Tartan's leg had healed all right.

Torstein stood and started moving the people who'd come to meet him toward the back of the hall and then through the side door. We'd told Bruiser's friend our party would end at five after midnight, and he was anxious to lock up. He thanked us for helping him clean up after the gala. Then he said to Bruiser, "You buy all that?" Obviously he meant "all that" talk about love being stronger than hate.

"Sure," Bruiser said. "Look at me. You know what I was before."

"Guy making a living, same as me."

"Not quite the same. But yes, I believe it. Any time you want to know more, we're always on the street, or in the park in the afternoons. Come on by sometime."

We thanked him for the use of the hall, then stepped out onto the street. In the park now they were setting off the big finale of fireworks, and Sully was jumping up and down and shouting at every new burst of color in the sky. Torstein still had a crowd of people around him, but they were all standing and staring up at the display.

When the final thunder rolled and we were left blinking at the chalky residue of the rockets carried on the black night, Maggie picked up Sully and said it was time for him to be home in bed. Tawny and Marigold had arrived in Maggie's car, so they began to leave with her. Franz managed to catch a quick kiss before they started on their way, and held Tawny's hand as he walked them to their car.

Bruiser called to Torstein, "We're heading home. Thanks for the terrible party!"

Torstein's laugh rang out, and I looked at him, at the streetlights glinting off his electric green coat, at the new friends eager to have a word with him, at his rag-tag band of followers that included me and my brother...and I knew: I would never forget this New Year's

Eve. With the worst party in the world, Torstein had created the most memorable of New Year's Eves.

Suddenly I started laughing, too, and I grabbed Torstein around his shoulders from behind, to hug him, lifting him off his feet by pressing him back against me.

"Hey get off!" he hollered, laughing still.

"You can do the impossible, my friend," I said when I put him down. "Happy new year!"

"Happy new year, Andy," he said, and he motioned to the people around him that I was a crazy man and should be humored. "See ya tomorrow."

59

I went home that night and put some music on. I rang in the new year listening to a bunch of opera CD's. It's not something you'd expect a fisherman or a fish market guy to do. But I had a soft spot for grand opera...and it seemed like the only thing that matched my mood. What Torstein had said was just what he said all along...except for the part about how something might happen to him that would leave the rest of us shattered and terrorized...but it was easy, with *"Ah! Mes Amis"* playing, to forget that part, and only to feel the joy of the moment. The joy of letting go of everything that ever claimed to be important and embracing the only thing that really was.

On New Year's Day, all the downtown businesses were closed, but there were still a few families in Patriots Park for Story Hour, and the usual bums and drunks. Torstein had his bag of sunflower seeds, and Tawny and Mari had a picture book between them. In a way, everything was exactly the same as it had been last year. But in another way, everything was new. It was like a declaration that Torstein had made last night, and all of us felt that now there was no turning back.

Sig came to the park with Tartan. I hadn't imagined the change in him that I'd noticed last night. The skin on his face hung more haggard than ever, and his eyes were as bloodshot as I'd ever seen them. Torstein embraced him and wished him a happy new year. Tartan sprang up onto Sully's shoulder and slid down his back like they used to do in the summer, the trick they used to do. With a parting glance at Sig, Tartan ran off with Sully to do their obstacle course around the playground. And Sig sat down with us.

"I don't know who handed out the invitations to your party," Sig said. "But you had two of Nikolai's show girls and one prostitute there last night who say they aren't going back to work."

"And you know this, how?" Torstein asked.

"Wire taps," Sig said. "Nikolai's already calling his associates at my department, telling them they gotta shut you down before you ruin his investment."

"What about the women?" Maggie asked. "What about the women who want to get out of that kind of work?"

"Nikolai will have someone convince them they're mistaken about that," Sig said. "The point is, Nikolai's actively trying to get the law after you now."

"Torstein?" Tawny said softly.

"Yes?"

"It was Mari and me, we invited those girls. You told everyone to go and invite their neighbors, and really, the people at Maggie's complex are *her* neighbors. So we thought we'd invite our old friends ..."

Sig snorted a little, a sort of "that explains it" sound. But Torstein said, "That's perfectly fine, Tawny. That was the whole point."

Maggie said, "Do you remember who you invited?"

"We invited all the girls in the club where we used to work," Mari said. "Of course most of them had to work, but because it was such a short party, a few of them were able to come in and hurry right back out."

"Here's the thing," Maggie said. "When you girls moved in with me, it was great for me, and it's been great for Sully, too. If you think these women really want to get out of stripping and, um, prostitution, that's why I bought the condo next door. So there would be a safe place for anyone that needed to get away."

"It's not safe!" Sig said. "Did you hear what I said? Nikolai's coming after Torstein with the law if he can, but if that doesn't work, he'll come at you another way. And you don't have a dog he can get to, to warn you."

Torstein grinned at Maggie. "You're really something," he said. To Sig, he said, "Sig, I appreciate your coming here to tell me this."

60

"That's not the worst of it," said Sig. "There was someone else at your party, and she matters a lot more to Nikolai. A lady named Caroline."

"Was Caroline there?" said Tawny. "I never saw her."

"Who is it?" Maggie asked.

"You could say, Nikolai's administrative assistant," Tawny said.

"She hired me," Marigold said.

"Administrative assistant!" Sig snorted. "She's the mother of one of Nikolai's children, and she manages the talent in his clubs. I don't know what happened, exactly, between them. But she apparently told Nikolai to let those women go if they wanted to, and not to bother you. They had a pretty vocal dust-up about it."

Torstein whistled, a sort of speculative two-note tone. "I must have impressed her!" he said, and grinned.

"It's not funny," Sig said. "Nikolai doesn't like being crossed, he doesn't like losing his girls to you, and he definitely would not like losing Caroline. She started with him years ago as a stripper, and she's a good businesswoman—and quite a favorite of his, I hear."

"I thought that sister-in-law was his favorite," I said, remembering Franz's story from the shore the day Nikolai killed the Dunker. "And the niece."

"He has a lot of women," Sig said. "But Caroline's the only one who's also a business partner. I think he loves her, if that guy can love anyone. So it's not like you're coming between him and a few strippers.

It's like you're coming between him and a wife, or close as he has to one. You gotta make sure that doesn't happen."

Torstein refused to show the shock Sig had hoped to inspire. Instead he said, "We've missed you around here, Sig. Any chance you'll give up that internal affairs business, and come join us now?"

"I told my wife last night I'd try to get off the booze," Sig said softly. "I got AA meetings to go to now. She already found me one, for today. I guess alcoholics have it rough on New Year's Eve. I don't know if I *can* do my job and not drink. I don't know how I can keep it together."

"We'll help you," Jack said. He was such a good kid. And he always had been hoping Sig would get off the sauce. He thought everybody should be a teetotaler and jog. In a lot a ways, he was an idiot. But he always led with his heart. "You just come here after work instead of Sharky's. We'll help you."

"Thanks," Sig said. "I'll come when I can. Look, one reason I don't wanna leave the job right now, I wanna try to keep tabs on what Nikolai's thinking about you," he said to Torstein. "Someone has to look after you."

Torstein laughed. "No, no one has to. It's not going to make any difference to me what you find out about Nikolai's plans for me. I'm going to do what I do, regardless. You might as well retire, and do it with me."

Sig shrugged. He turned to Maggie and said, "If I were you, I wouldn't take those women in."

"I hear you," she said. "But I don't think anyone should be forced into that kind of life if they don't want it."

"Your call," Sig said. He looked at his watch, whistled for his dog, and said it was getting near time for his meeting.

61

The one woman, the prostitute, she didn't leave that life. I think she probably wanted to, when she heard Torstein's speech, but then the reality of it was: she was a junkie, and she couldn't stop. Maggie invited her to come and see us in the park, but she lived a lot further away than Angel had, and I doubted we'd ever see her. One of the strippers, she just packed up and went back where she came from, which I think was Idaho or Iowa or Maine, something like that.

But the one thing Sig had warned us about seemed to be happening: the "administrative assistant" of Nikolai, Caroline, she came to find us. And brought her son. Nikolai's son. He was called Van, but his name was Ivan Nikolayevich, the Russian way of saying "Ivan, son of Nikolai." Caroline was a nice looking woman, probably 40 or 45 years old, short dark hair, big blue eyes. She didn't look like a stripper at all; she dressed conservatively and if she was wearing makeup it looked natural enough. You wouldn't have suspected she was a *madam* or whatever you might want to all her...and her little boy was nice, too; not at all what you'd expect from a mobster's kid.

They were leaving Nikolai, she said, and leaving the business. She'd heard something she couldn't forget on New Year's Eve, and she wanted that something for herself and her boy.

"Don't you think it's something Nikolai wants, too?" Torstein asked. He liked the kid, and I think he didn't like for a kid to be separated from his father.

"I tried to tell him," Caroline said. "He won't listen."

"Won't he come after you?" Ferdy asked.

"He thinks I'll change my mind and come back," she said. "I don't think he'll bother you, if that's what you're worried about."

"Of course I'm worried about it," Ferdy said, as if she were crazy.

"I'm not," Torstein said. "If he comes after you, maybe he'll stay and talk and decide he'd like to join us, too."

"I'd like that," Caroline said.

They moved into the condo next door to Maggie, and Caroline went to work in a department store. She worked the morning shift, though, so she'd be home when her son came home from school. After doing his homework, they would come and find us on the street, or more often in the park, after Story Hour. Sully was happy to have a friend next door, and was impressed with Van's superior third-grade knowledge of many aspects of reading and math. It seemed like the boys were always together.

One of our regular drunks in the park left one day. He went to live in a shelter, and he started going to AA meetings. Just like Sig! He would come back from time to time, sit with us, and encourage the other drunks to come with him to the meetings, and the shelter. The Salvation Army had given him a suit of clothes and helped him get a job at the dry cleaners. Not the best job in the world, but he was making some money, staying off the booze, and he looked about 200% better than we'd ever seen him. He was shaving and bathing regularly, which was an improvement.

Suddenly it seemed like whatever Torstein had been trying to do was beginning to happen. J. Clayton Berger and a few of the most talented Dunkers started a little drama workshop for kids and teenagers to practice performing and music at that mega-church Berger and his family attended. A few of the other Dunkers who had been playing games of touch football and pick-up basketball games in the park organized a intramural league for kids and adults. In my building, where my apartment was, a few of the folks who had come to the worst New Year's Eve party ever had joined Torstein's movement. They would come and visit with us in the park, but they had also started doing great things right there in our neighborhood. They adopted a nursing home down the way and started visiting with the old and sick folks and giving them things that their insurance didn't supply like toiletries—the patients who were there on state funding with no families to help had no one to buy things like that for them. Who knew?

It was little stuff people were doing, but it was awesome. And it wasn't just my building. I guess everyone who had invited neighbors to the party now had a little nucleus of born-again do-gooders in their community, and lots of good was being done. Including some wonderful mercy and forgiveness. Victims of crimes were coming to court when restitution was being decided and telling the judge they forgave the evildoer and hoped to see him go and sin no more.

62

Caroline, the former brothel and strip club administrator, started a new community service, too. She'd visit the girls she'd hired, and invite them to come visit with her, and Torstein, in the park. She was so sure Nikolai would not bother us…but she was sort of "recruiting" women from his clubs!

Granted she didn't go in and tell them they had to quit stripping. She went and told them to come and visit us in the park and learn about the power of love. A lot of them seemed to have children to provide for and no real belief that they could possibly take care of their families if they didn't work in the clubs. A few of them were addicted to drugs and couldn't imagine not being able to get their fix. She didn't have much luck with them—if her objective were to get them out of dancing and stripping and whatever else they did for a living.

But she did have some luck at getting them at least to come out to the park now and then, bring their children, sit for an hour, and listen to Torstein, or talk with him. They liked him. I guess they felt like he didn't judge them…or maybe it was just his Irresistible Charm. I suppose Caroline felt like she got these women into that life, and she owed it to them to try to get them out. Aside from Tawny and Marigold, and the one stripper who'd gone back to Maine or Idaho or wherever, none of them quit dancing. Whether they quit anything else they were doing, I don't know.

Maybe they did. Or maybe they just talked about it. The word got back to Nikolai what Caroline was doing. And the strangest thing happened. He came to see us.

Dragonfly

It was sort of early in the day, not the time you'd expect a mob guy to be out doing business. We'd just finished our morning coffee and were making our way to the park. Franz was walking with me and Pete and Torstein. Bruiser, he was off on his walkabout visiting all the businesses where he used to do extortions, making amends and chatting with the business owners. But Franz recognized Nikolai half a black away. He grabbed Torstein by the arm and said, "Let's go another way. That's Nikolai up there."

But Torstein was delighted. "Nikolai?" he said. "Really? Introduce me."

Only Franz didn't want to. "No man, this is bad medicine. Let's just go another way, down another street."

"You go," Torstein said. "All of you go. I'll talk to him alone." Pete didn't want to leave him, but Torstein said, "Look he's looking for me, there's no doubt of that. Whatever he means to say is intended for me. I'll meet you guys in the park later." Torstein could see Pete was getting ruffled. "Just go over there into the Starbucks. You can watch through the window and come to my rescue if anything happens."

We did what he said. It didn't occur to me until later that Torstein was trying to protect us, not even let Nikolai get a good look at us.

He strolled up to Nikolai, they shook hands, and they sat down at a bus stop.

We couldn't hear what they were saying, of course, but later Torstein told us.

"He said he liked me. He really did. He thought it was nice what we were doing to help people in need, and all that. And he said he'd hate for what happened to Duncan to happen to me," Torstein said.

"He'd hate to have to *kill you?*" Pete said, flabbergasted.

"Yes, I guess he meant he'd hate to have to kill me," Torstein replied, as if just now thinking about it, his eyes twinkling a little. "He wanted to know what I was doing, what we were trying to accomplish. So I told him, and I told him how excited Van and Caroline are to be part of it, and how great it would be if he could come join us, too."

"What'd he say to that?" Franz asked.

"He said he wasn't going to join us, but he would be happy to support us with a big cash contribution."

"Mob money," Franz said. "I hope you didn't take it."

"I told him I'm not in the money end of things, and he could talk to Ferdy if he wanted, but that the really important thing, the really critical thing for him, for everyone, is to meet face to face like this and learn to love. That's what I was inviting him to come and do."

He shook his head and went on, "That part didn't *seem* to interest him too much. Although I know deep down he would like to join us. He just said he would rather we didn't focus our efforts so much on his investments. That's what caused the tragedy with Duncan."

"The tragedy?" Pete said. "Did he mean that time he murdered your cousin, *that* tragedy?"

"Yes," Torstein said, "that was it. I told him that we weren't focusing our efforts on anything except loving and giving, forgiving and showing mercy. And I even told him I thought those were the very things that would help him find the peace he was looking for."

"Bet that went over big," Franz said.

"He denied that he was looking for peace," Torstein said sadly. "I told him, you know, how much Caroline and Van love him, and how all of us would be more than happy to have him with us, that he could start a new life, start all over. I really thought I was getting through to him, but in the end he just said it's impossible for a grown man to go back and start over, especially himself, after the life he's led. And then he told me to stop screwing with his clubs and to send Caroline and Van home, or something bad would happen."

"You gotta send them back," Franz said. "He don't make threats."

"I'm not sending them anywhere, and I would appreciate if none of you mentioned this to Caroline. She, at least, has found some peace with us, and I won't let anyone take it away."

"He ain't kidding, Torstein," Franz said. "Ask Bruiser, ok?"

"No, look, don't mention this to anyone. I think Nikolai felt the truth of what I was saying to him, and I think he may change his mind. I don't want Caroline worried about it."

None of us told her about it.

We all went about this new business of making the world a better place by loving each other and practicing mercy. It got to be quite a buzz, to tell you the truth, finding new ways to help the people who needed it the most. Everyone was talking about it, about the green coat, the sunflower seeds, the way he'd started a revolution on new year's eve.

63

Our old friend Ariel Prince was interested in what had happened since New Years, and she came back, looking for Torstein. "I told you your ideas had legs!" she said. "I've been all over the city, and talked to dozens of people who claim you gave them the idea to feed the hungry, visit the sick and elderly, rescue dogs and cats, give more generously. It's great what's happening! I've got amazing footage of so much good work being done. I'd love to at least do a feature on it, for the news."

"You can put whatever you like on the news," Torstein said. "I just don't care about being on television myself."

"One interview," she said. "I mean, why not, you're not wanted in another state or something are you?"

He laughed. Torstein had been doing his dragonfly thing around the park, fluttering from group to group to meet with all his friends. I'd been walking with him, but at this moment, across the way, I saw some guys I hadn't seen in five or six years, fraternity brothers from the couple years before I dropped out of college. Greeks! I ran over to them, shook hands, asked what they were doing there.

One of them said, "C'mon, Andy, we want to meet Torstein."

"How do you even *know* about him?" I asked.

It turned out, they both worked at a law firm in the Rurhs building, several blocks away. They were first-year grunts, and they were both trying to date this same paralegal, a babe a couple years older than us who had been showing them the ropes around the firm. After the world's worst New Year's Eve party, this babe had turned in her resignation and said she was taking a job with that Food for the Poor charity Torstein liked so much—they didn't know, she might even be going to Haiti where he was helping feed a hundred kids for a nickel or whatever it was.

"She's going to be working in some hell-hole for peanuts," my frat brah Conny told me. "And she's all happy, like it's the best decision of her life, like it's a promotion!"

They were both mystified, and when they pressed her for details, she told them about this amazing guy in the green coat who was starting a new way of doing things downtown.

"So, you know, we thought we better check this out for ourselves."

"Yeah, c'mon," I said. "I'll introduce you."

They followed me to where Torstein was still talking to Ms. Prince.

"Torstein, I have some people I want you to meet—couple old fraternity brothers of mine."

Torstein turned to us briefly, then turned back to the TV news lady and suddenly said, "OK, yeah. The time is right. This is it. Let's do it. Bring your cameras. Let's get this ball rolling."

"You'll do it?" she said.

"Now or never," he said.

"Tomorrow," she said, "in the daylight, what time will you get here?"

"Two," he said. "After lunch. See you then."

He turned to me, shook hands with my friends, and then said, "Listen boys, you've come at an important time. Tomorrow, or the next day at the latest, this whole city is going to hear about what's been going on in this park and all over downtown—it's going to be crazy here for the next little while. But the timing is right. I'm glad you're here now."

"What—like we're getting in on the ground floor?" Conny said, laughing, shaking Torstein's hand.

"No," he said, "no, you're getting in on the very tail-end. Or maybe a new beginning, depends how you look at it."

He was shaking hands with Robert, my other frat brother now, and he said to me, "Your frat brothers, right? Greeks?"

"Yah," I said. "And Conny is *Greek* Greek, too." He was some kind of Greek extraction, had the curly black hair and swarthy skin.

"Perfect," Torstein said. "That was the sign. The Greeks. Perfect."

Then he went flying off to shake hands with some other folks, and left me and my buddies standing there mystified. "I don't know," I told them. "No idea what he was talking about. That happens a lot. But I'd say you better stick around."

64

After Ariel Prince's feature on Torstein aired on the TV news, our park went up for grabs.

People came streaming downtown to see Torstein—lots of folks just looking for a hand-out, but lots of people who really wanted to be part of a movement that was doing some good, too. My frat brothers would sneak out of their offices and come check in from time to time throughout the day, it was like a carnival now.

Torstein couldn't actually visit with everyone who poured into the park anymore, the crowds were too big. But it was never a mob. People would gather around him, and listen to him, and his theme was always the same: you want to make this the world you always wanted, start by loving the people around you and move out from there, and keep loving.

It had been a nice, warm message for winter, but it really began to bloom in the spring. The park was coming out in flowers again, and the weather began to warm up, people kept reaching out to anyone with a need to offer a helping hand…and I started to be less afraid that anything bad was going to happen to Torstein, or us. We'd heard nothing more from Sig, and the law had not come after us as he'd feared.

And Angel came home!

You would hardly have known it was the same person…she was still rail thin, but not emaciated like a crack addict. And she was dressed nicely, with her hair clean and combed out. I think she even had a little make-up on. She looked, now, like somebody's mother. Maggie had picked her up at the bus station when she came back, and of course Sully had gone, too. Maggie said Angel held onto her son and cried, for a long time. She kept telling him she loved him, and she'd missed him, and she was going to make everything up to him.

She had other news for us, too: the program coordinator who had sent that Transformer toy at Christmas for Sully had proposed to her! He was a Jesus freak, too, and he had fallen in love with Angel while she was in the program. She wanted him to come to the city and marry her in a church where all her friends could come. She counted Maggie, Tawny, Mari—and all of us guys—as her friends! She wanted Torstein to give her away.

Tawny excitedly told her that she and Franz were engaged, too, and Angel begged them to make it a double ceremony with her. Tawny was delighted with the idea, and Franz agreed, saying: "The sooner the better now." Only Marigold was sad about it, but Maggie promised *she'd* always be there for her, and Tawny promised that although she would be living with Franz she would remain Mari's best friend. And Caroline told Marigold she could move over to her condo with her and Van. It was all very high school, but it was sweet in a way, too.

I think that's what Torstein gave us: a way back to innocence, a way to value sweetness. We were tough guys, and we had to make fun of the tears the girls seemed inclined to shed at the drop of a hat. But in a way we valued it, too. He'd given us permission to believe in something perfectly good, perfectly right, perfectly honorable. He believed in it, so we had to believe, too.

It was like the sunflowers—they came up again in March, as Torstein had predicted, little green shoots where Sully had cleared away last year's dead plants. He was so delighted with the new blooms, we had to be, too. We were grown men who had stopped caring about flowers a long time ago. But Torstein made something new blossom inside us, resurrected the wonder you think only kids can feel.

The wedding would be in March, which would make it during Lent, but none of the bridal parties cared about that because there was to be no booze at the wedding anyway on account of Angel's being a recovering addict. It would be on a Sunday in March, and there would be pizza in the park afterward.

Dragonfly

Bruiser, of course, was friends with the man who owned the pizzeria, and he could get us all the pizzas we wanted at a low discount price. Franz came up with the money for the pizzas. Angel's fiancé Len came up with the money for the sodas. Maggie bought both the wedding dresses and two nice suits so Sully and his new best friend Van could each be ring-bearers. (It was lucky there were two sets of rings to be borne.)

So on a Sunday afternoon in March, Torstein walked two brides down the aisle to their nervous husbands-to-be who both appeared elated and a little bit awestruck by the women in white and the gravity of the occasion. Torstein wore his crazy green coat, and walked between the ladies, lending an arm to each, as the wedding march played... and when the minister asked who gave these women in marriage, he said, "Their families, our family, and I do" in such a pleased and ringing voice, I got a lump in my throat, and Maggie and Phyllis started crying.

It was one of those perfectly good, perfectly right, perfectly honorable things that Torstein had made it possible to believe in again.

65

I know I've mentioned a time or two how weird things always happened to Torstein. At the wedding reception in the park…it happened again.

For one thing, too many people showed up. There were no formal invitations to the wedding. Everyone who was part of our crowd just knew when and where it was going to be and about the reception. But all these new people who just kept turning up in Patriots Park every day, they didn't know this particular Sunday was anything unusual. They turned up, and they started eating all the pizza and drinking all the sodas.

It wasn't a huge deal. Those of us who actually knew the happy couples had sort of formed our own little group off to one side of the park with a cooler and a few pizzas. But the bigger group of people we didn't know particularly well, they ran out of pizza. And things got ugly. As I said, many of these folks turned up looking for a hand-out. I guess some of them had no idea at all what Torstein was all about; they just heard that there was a guy who gave away sunflower seeds—and sometimes money or food—and they happened to have come down on this Sunday afternoon and felt like they missed out on the pizza party.

It was *not* a Torstein kind of scene at all: several low-lifes were facing off against some of our own bums and drunks who, honestly, probably hadn't liked the way the park was filling up with *other* free-loaders these days. There was a nasty shouting match going on.

Torstein, instead of going over there and trying to set things straight, just called Jack, Jazz and Pete to go with him for more pizzas and sodas. He and Pete headed for the pizzeria, Jack and Jazz to the bodega for more drinks. It happened that as they came back with the boxes of pizza and crates of sodas, a bunch of little kids from the projects came running along with them, screaming about the pizza, pizza, pizza! At the same time, Ariel Prince and her camera team had arrived. She'd been at the wedding—she told us if she did a follow-up story on Torstein, the wedding footage would be a nice touch, particularly considering how the brides' lives had changed since they met him.

So, here comes Torstein, and Pete behind him, with his arms just full of pizza boxes. They must have bought every one the pizza man had ready. And behind them, Jack and Jazz with more colas. And around them, these little kids shrieking about pizza. So the crowd in the park started parting to make way for them, and what with the little kids running along cheering about the free food, it started to be like a parade. Everyone who had been so het up about the disappearing pizza started cheering like mad as Torstein came walking through the park.

And Ariel was getting it all recorded. It couldn't have been any more perfect if we had choreographed it: the scene looked amazingly like a scene from days gone by, a conquering hero being hailed by vassals, or a new prince approaching the throne where he'd be crowned king—this huge crowd of people parted as Torstein strolled through, flanked by his men in waiting, and everyone cheering and screaming his name. It was unbelievable.

Ariel Prince put the feature together that afternoon, and it was on the news Sunday night. How Torstein had transformed the lives of two ladies of the night, and there they were, being married in white to decent men who were dying with love for them—and then how Torstein had attracted hundreds of people to Patriots Park to celebrate a new way of bringing hope and compassion to the mean streets of the city. The way her crew had taped that march of his through the park, it looked like a crowd of thousands cheering for him rather then just a couple hundred.

I'd been there in person, and I was impressed!

Torstein watched the news with me, at my place. He'd come back to my house after the reception. He shook his head after Ariel's feature was over, and he said, "My coat really looks good on television, don't you think? The whole key to that piece was the coat." Then he laughed.

We didn't know it then, but Ferdy had gone out with Ariel Prince that night. They'd made arrangements to meet after the news broadcast...I don't know what all they spoke about, but I learned the gist of it in the next few days, when Ferdy explained the plan to us... basically it was the same plan Ariel had proposed to Torstein back in the winter, but in Ferdy she'd found a more willing listener.

66

"You have to listen to me, Torstein," Ferdy said. "This woman knows what she's talking about. They're getting more calls and more hits on the website about those two features she's done on you than any other human interest stories. You're going to be wasting all this great publicity if you don't get on board."

"Ferdy, I don't care."

"I thought you wanted to be a great philanthropist. You're always giving away $5 here and $10 there. Don't you want to be able to give away millions?"

Torstein wrinkled his nose, rolled his shoulders, shook his head slightly. "I guess not," he said slowly. "My idea is, instead of one man giving away millions, maybe every man could give away 5's and 10's and 100's. It's more of a face-to-face and heart-to-heart thing."

Ferdy looked to the rest of us for support. We were huddled in a Starbucks at the far reaches of our usual stomping grounds that Thursday morning, to try to avoid the crowds that were now stalking Torstein because of the TV news. And maybe just because they liked his message and wanted to be near him. Pete and Phyllis, Jack and Jazz were there; Ferdy, Bruiser, Maggie and Mari.

I had to admit, I'd been really astonished by the news report about the wedding reception. Torstein looked good on TV, not just his coat, he was one of those people like John F. Kennedy whose personal charm seemed to be carried equally well on the airwaves. But I also shared his thought that television was sort of phony. If Torstein deserted the park for a TV studio…I didn't know whether his message would be the same. He was a people person. How did that work on TV? I couldn't give Ferdy any help.

Marigold said if she and Tawny could do Story Hour on TV, she would. Torstein said if they got an offer, they should do it, because they were really good, and Mari beamed at him.

"But they aren't getting an offer," Ferdy said. "*You* are, Torstein, and I think you'd be crazy to turn it down. There's no risk at all. Just give a few messages on the news once a week for the next few weeks. Ariel's got a real feeling that your popularity is only going to grow from here on out."

Torstein smiled at Ferdy, a really genuine, warm, smile, the way I might smile at Pete or my dad. There was a lot of love in that smile. But then, in his eyes, there was sadness, too. It caught me off-guard, because Torstein's eyes were always sort of sparkling, twinkling, like his dragonfly wings. Now there was this deep, gray well of…I don't know any other way to say it…sadness.

"No, Ferdy," he said softly. "My popularity is not going to grow any more. This is the end of my popularity." He turned then, and looked around this circle of friends, looking each of us in the eyes, if only for a brief moment. And he said:

"My popularity is about to come to a screeching halt. I'm not only going to be unpopular, I'm probably going to be downright contagious. If it happens—no, listen to me."

Pete had begun to protest, "There's no way you could become contagious to us, Torstein —"

But Torstein waved the objection aside. "Listen, really. Listen, and remember this. And you'll have to tell Franz and Tawny, and Angel and Caroline."

Caroline, Nikolai's ex, she was at work now. Franz and Tawny, and Angel and Len, had gone away for a couple of days to the shore. A sort of honeymoon.

"Something's going to happen, soon now. I don't want any of you to get hurt. If it looks to you like a good idea to come rushing to my rescue, I don't want you to try it."

"What are you talking about?" Pete demanded. "We're not going to let anything happen to you."

"Hush, Peter," Phyllis said, putting her hand on my brother's arm.

"Nothing is going to happen to me but what I let happen," Torstein said. "Nothing is going to happen except what is meant to happen. Nobody takes my life from me, unless I lay it down. But if and when I do, you're not to interfere."

"If anyone comes at you, they'll have to get through me first," Pete said. Good ol' Pete. He had changed a lot since we started this journey with Torstein, but under all he was still the man of action. I envied it, I really did. I'm no coward, but I was scared of what Torstein was saying. Not scared for me, but for him, and for Mari, and for Sully and for everyone who had put their dreams in his hands.

"Pete, you're strong, but that's not who you are. You can't build your life on your idea of yourself as this strong man. You've got to build your life on the foundation I've given you, the foundation of love."

"I don't understand you, man!" Ferdy said suddenly, angrily. "I've bought into your vision all the way, gave up my job, spent a year on the streets with you basically working and sweating to make this great plan, this great movement of ours happen—and now what? Now that the door is open for you to start making it happen, you're saying, you're saying this is the end? Not the beginning?"

Torstein's brow wrinkled across his forehead. He grimaced a little, then said, "Oh Ferdy. No, this is the beginning. But it's an end, too. What I want to do, this great movement, it has to happen *inside* people. It can't happen on TV. It can't happen with piles of money. It can only happen like this," he motioned to all of us. "Like this." He reached out and grabbed Ferdy's hand, but Ferdy jerked it back.

He was steamed.

"You can't just try it Ariel's way?" Ferdy asked. "This is what I can contribute to your vision. This is how I can see it happening, and you can't even try it? This is what we've been waiting for—this is our chance, Torstein!"

"My dear friend," Torstein said softly, to Ferdy. Then he turned and glanced around to the rest of us. "My dear friends. My heart's heavy. I don't know how to say what I need to say, and there's so little time left."

Again, that fear, that fear that Pete seemed able to shake off and bluster through, it clamped down on me. Hard.

67

Jack was sitting beside Torstein, and now he leaned over, and put his arm around Torstein's shoulder, and his head against his chest. Jack was so young. Maybe he'd turned 20 when I wasn't looking, but he was still, to me, a kid. His hair was brown and softly curly, and he closed his dark eyes as he leaned on Torstein's chest, and he murmured, "What is it? What's wrong, Torstein? What's happened?"

Jazz was sitting next to Jack, and he reached over and gripped the back of his kid brother's neck. Maggie was sitting beside Torstein on his other side, staring at him with a soulful expression which was equal parts confusion and despair.

Pete and Phyllis were next to me. He was still fuming. He didn't like this talk of sadness and loss and laying down lives, and he wasn't going to cry about it like Jack. He was going to fight it. Phyllis still held onto his arm from when she'd tried to shush him, but she was looking at Torstein, too. Marigold, beside Maggie, had been so happy when Torstein had complimented her about Story Hour...now she just looked bewildered. Bruiser had almost an identical expression.

"What's it all been for then?" Ferdy asked. "It was all just a lark to you, and this is the end? That's rubbish. Some of us invested our lives in you, Torstein. For you to throw it away now—that's an insult. Don't you get it? Don't you get that there could be a gold mine at the end of this road? We gave up our jobs and our ambitions to stick by you, don't we deserve something better than this?"

Torstein looked up at him, his deep, clear blue eyes seeming gray and infinite, and said, "Do what you have to do, Ferdy. Do it now."

Dragonfly

"Do what?!" Ferdy said, standing up, shrugging, looking at all of us as if we'd all betrayed him. "What's left to do if you won't move forward? What was it all for, anyway?"

He turned around and stormed out of the Starbucks.

Jack had sat up straight again, but he was still looking at Torstein with deep concern.

"What's going on?" he said again.

"Things are changing," Torstein said. "It's important, for what I've been trying to do, to teach you, that this movement doesn't get focused on one person, here, in Patriots Park. It needs to come alive inside each one of you. And it needs to be clear that what's inside me, is inside you. In order for what I've been trying to do here to live on, inside you, and the people whose lives you touch, I have to get out of the way."

"No," Pete said. I thought he was going to get as mad as Ferdy. "That's like saying for a dog to live on you have to chop off its head! That doesn't make any sense."

"Oh, Pete, Pete," Torstein sighed. "Don't talk back for once, OK? I'm talking about a seed—a seed can't come to life unless it gets stuck in the ground, planted. It has to die a little before it springs into amazing life. Don't tempt me to see this your way, because it can't be your way. I can't be everywhere at once, but all of you, with a little seed of me inside you, you *can* be everywhere. You, and the people you raise up after you. I only have one life while I'm sitting here with you...but when each of you takes on this life, then I'll have 12 lives, 15, a hundred, a thousand—more even.

"Now listen, there's not much time, and there are some things I want you to know, and remember, and share. But first I want you all to be clear: when the time comes, I'm going down, alone. Nobody else needs to get hurt. Everyone agreed?"

"No!" Pete said again. "I'm not going to desert you."

"Yes, you will," Torstein said. He reached out with one hand to grasp Jack's forearm, reached out with the other to grip Maggie's hand. He looked into Pete's eyes, glanced around at all of us. "You'll all desert me. Pete, you think your strength and your loyalty are the foundation of all you are, and they'll never fail you, but they *will* fail. You'll desert me. You'll deny me. You'll run away. But it's OK. It's what has to be. And when I come back, it won't matter. Just trust me now."

"Come back?" Pete said. "Come back, how?"

"I will come back. But here's what's important, starting now. You all have to *be me*, to each other. You *have to love* one another. I know I've been *saying* this, and you've been agreeing with me. But this is a new mandate, friends, and I mean you have to love one another the way I love you, and cling to one another, and no matter what happens, live for one another. You're going to need each other, now more than ever. Because I won't be there. But *inside you* I'll be there."

I was getting the fidgets now. Things had been going so well! We'd heard nothing from Nikolai in ages, despite we were harboring his son and his son's mother. The TV news features had been *good* publicity. That detective, Waverling, all his threats had been empty. Just when I'd been prepared to declare victory, now Torstein was prophesying defeat, and a huge defeat, the worst possible kind.

"That's where your strength is, in love," Torstein was saying. "When you remain in this love, when you act with the absolute best interest of each other ahead of your own interests, then you're following in my footsteps and you're shaping this world into the place it was meant to be. So, remember all what I've told you, let it live in you, and always, always, let love be first place."

He glanced around, and I guess he saw bewilderment and fear in every face looking back at his. He laughed, and his blue eyes sparked with a bit of their iridescent shine. "Don't be afraid," he said. "We'll be together again. I'm not letting any of you go. Except Ferdy. I don't know what will happen to Ferdy." He stood up suddenly. "Come on. Let's go," he said. We fell in line behind him and followed him out of Starbucks. As we went, he began to chant this reggae song ...

"Woke up this morning, smile with the rising sun—three little birds, perch on my doorstep. Singing a sweet song, in melody pure and true. This is my message for you ..."

Jack and Jazz, relieved that Torstein sounded more like himself, had taken up the tune, and we wandered down the street singing together..."Baby don't worry about thing, 'cause every little thing is gonna be all right…said don't worry about a thing—'cause every little thing is gonna be all right …"

By the time we arrived at the park, Torstein was dancing at the front of the line, his green coat shimmering as it always did. He was doing some soca steps that he must have thought matched the calypso tune, and I thought:

Every little thing is going to be all right.

68

We thought Nikolai didn't care what had happened to Caroline and Van. He'd told Torstein to send them back or something bad would happen...and nothing bad had happened. Lots of great stuff had happened. As far as I knew, Torstein had never told Caroline that Nikolai had come to see him.

She'd told us he believed she'd come crawling back...but she also told us he had never actually acknowledged the boy as his own; Van's last name was Caroline's last name, not Nikolai's. He'd never paid child support (of course, up until then, Caroline had worked for him and lived with him, more or less). We were hoping he'd given up and wasn't going to try to get his son back. And that was a huge relief to us, honestly. Okay, it was probably very wrong to hope that a man would just forget about his child. But that man...we would all have rather he forgot us entirely.

I don't know what goes on in the head of a mob guy. I don't know what was going on in Nikolai's head at this time. Maybe he realized Caroline wasn't coming back...maybe he didn't understand the new way of living that being with Torstein inspired—how you found yourself needing less and less for yourself and giving more and more away...maybe that's hard for a mob guy to grasp. Maybe he thought once Caroline was poor and tired of making an *honest* living, she'd come back. But she didn't.

Here's what we could piece together later. Nikolai saw the TV news feature with footage from the double wedding. Ariel Prince was right about one thing: on TV Torstein looked just great. He looked eccentric because of the green coat and glowing eyes, but he looked endearing. The Irresistible Charm just seemed to radiate from the TV. He looked like a charming crazy man who just might know more than he was telling, Big Secrets might be locked up in a crazy man's mind. A modern-day Rasputin or Zoroaster.

That much made it a cinch that the video would be uploaded to You Tube as well as replayed a couple times on the news throughout the day. People were liking to see a sentimental wedding, and bright new face, a dazzling display of all kinds of people swept up in enthusiasm for Torstein…and the little snippets of hope and joy that Ariel had edited together from interviews with various people whose lives had been touched by Torstein.

It was this whole feel-good thing, in a three-minute package. I guess Nikolai didn't get "charm" from Torstein. What he got, apparently, from watching the video, was the idea that his son was now being raised more or less by a bunch of homeless bums with a crazy ring leader. He saw his son on the TV news, ring-bearer in a wedding of a crack whore and a stripper, and he must have decided this had gone far enough. It was time for the "something bad" to happen.

Thugs busted onto the school playground at recess and grabbed Van, who immediately grabbed onto his best friend, Sully, who immediately grabbed him back. They told us later, the two boys wrapped their arms around each other and would not let go. God bless the teachers, they came running to try to help, and they got the crap kicked out of them while the thugs jerked at the two boys and tried to pull them apart. Failing that, they sped away with both boys still wound tight around each other.

The police were called. Caroline was called. Maggie was called. She had to call Angel.

Detective Waverling came to the school to take statements. He immediately took the view that Caroline and Angel were a stripper and a crack whore who had not taken proper care of their children, and that if in fact the boy's father had come for him, that was not a crime. Angel and her new husband Len insisted that the way the boys had been snatched *was* a crime, and the fact that their boy had also been taken was definitely a crime. Waverling said they should file a missing persons report once Sully had been missing for 24 hours, but until then, they should stay out of his sight. Maggie was there, too. In fact she was still Sully's guardian because Angel had given her temporary guardianship for him while she was in rehab, and they had not had a chance to annul this before the wedding.

Maggie doesn't take any crap, and Caroline was a tough woman, too—I guess she'd had to be tough working for Nikolai. She and Maggie told Waverling none of them were strippers or crack-heads and they were not going to wait for Sully to go missing 24 hours before they got his sorry ass fired, and at this point Waverling had Maggie, Angel, Len and Caroline handcuffed and taken away! They were deprived of their cell phones, jailed, but not charged with any crime. Waverling said they were disrupting an investigation and maybe once they cooled off he would deal with them.

69

This much we learned from Sig Scarr. He came and found us in the park, and dragged Torstein away from the crowds that now followed him everywhere.

He told us what had happened and said:

"Waverling's out of control. He can't go up against Nikolai."

"Are Angel and the others in any danger? Would he hurt them?"

"No, I don't think so," Sig said. "I think he just wants to keep them quiet until he can get Sully back. Of course the other boy, Van, he'll leave him with Nikolai."

"All right," Torstein said. "Then there's no reason to panic. We just let Waverling do his job. He gets Sully back, he lets our friends out of jail, and then we work on how to get Van back once we've got his mom out of jail."

Tartan, of course, had come with Sig. He was nosing all around us, looking for Sully. He knew someone was missing. He was a smart little dog.

Sig looked the same as he had at New Year's Eve, tired and run down, with bloodshot eyes and hair that looked as if he ran his hands through it a lot. "You take a lot for granted, Torstein," he said. "*Best case scenario*, Waverling gets Sully back and lets your friends out of jail. Worst case…Nikolai decides to get back at whoever helped Caroline get away from him with his son and make sure it can never happen again."

Torstein nodded.

"I understand," he said. "Thank you, Sig." He reached down and picked up Tartan, who licked his face. "I think you ought to take Tartan, go home and get your wife and daughter, and leave on vacation. Once you're out of town, phone in your resignation. In a few days time, come back. My friends will be waiting for you."

"Look, I can stay," Sig said. "I can help you. You don't know how this might play out."

Torstein reached out and gripped Sig's shoulder. "We love you, Sig, but you've never been one of us, you've never joined us, really. I can't, I don't want, to put you in danger."

"I'll join you now," Sig said. "You're going to need me."

"Oh, yes," Torstein said. "We're going to need you. But not now, not in this. Do what I say. Disappear for a while."

"And you?" Sig said.

"I'll find you. Or my friends will, if I'm not here. Don't worry." He grabbed Sig's face with his hand, pulled him close and kissed his forehead. "You're maybe not convinced now, maybe you think I'm an idealist, or an idiot, I don't know. But later, all will be well. Thank you, Sig."

Sig shook his head, and turned to go, whistling for Tartan who jumped out of Torstein's arms and ran along beside him.

70

Pete, Jazz and Jack were standing there looking stunned. Even Torstein looked a little pale. The crowd of people who'd come to see Torstein was restlessly looking for him, turning our way, starting to move our way. We wouldn't be alone for long. It occurred to me that if Nikolai sent his friends on the police force or his own thugs, either one, our best chance for escape was in the crowd.

"Let's go back into the park," I said. "If there's nothing we can do for Maggie and Angel, we can sit tight here."

Pete looked at me as if I were speaking Chinese. I don't know what he thought he could do, maybe storm the jail, call Waverling out? That would be Pete's style, and clearly, it would accomplish *nothing*. But in a huge crowd of people, we had a good chance of protecting Torstein. Nobody would try anything with all these people around us.

Torstein nodded. "All right. Let's do what we can with the time we have," he said.

At this moment, Ferdy came running toward us. We hadn't seen him since he stormed out of the Starbucks hours earlier. He'd been angry then, but now he looked scared, and alarmed. "Torstein," he called, as he ran up, and threw his arms around Torstein, giving him a hug. "Come on, you've got to come with me quickly. Sully's in trouble, and he needs you." He released Torstein, then turned and started running toward a side street that led out of the downtown and toward the projects. It ran behind a big bank building, and there was a side entrance to a multi-level parking garage, which he turned into and sped out of sight.

We all ran after him. I don't guess we tried to figure out why Sully might be down a garage—or if we thought about it at all, I suppose we thought Ferdy's car was down there. Inside the garage we followed Ferdy down one level. It was dark in there; we'd been in spring-time sunlight out on the street, and our eyes were having trouble adjusting. We almost ran smack into the thugs Ferdy had led us to.

To paraphrase the "drunk in New York" comedian, I didn't know how many of them it would have taken to kick our backside, but I knew how many they were going to use. And that's good information to have. There were at least 15 Bruiser-size guys down there waiting for us. I saw in an instant when Pete's hackles went up—and how they drooped when he counted our opponents. There were four of us. We'd be slaughtered. Before we could even react, two big guys had seized Torstein by his arms. I could tell Pete could sense the futility of it, but he launched himself at them, anyway, and punched one of the guys solid on his ear. The guy crumpled to his knees and let go of Torstein, who reached down and touched the guy on the side of his head, saying to Pete, "No, Pete. Remember what I told you. Violence can't end violence. Only love conquers —"

At that moment another guy smacked Torstein so hard on the back of the head that he pitched forward, and two other guys grabbed him.

They were dragging him toward a big black panel van they'd had waiting. Torstein turned to Ferdy and said, "You didn't have to do it this way. I was on the street or in the park every day. You didn't have to —" But then his words were cut off as they threw him into the van and slammed the doors.

The remaining guys started in on us, but they weren't figuring to kill us. They punched our faces and left us dazed and leaning crazy against the back wall of the garage while they peeled out with Torstein in the van...I guess they took Ferdy with them, too. He was gone, anyway.

Pete helped me stand up straight, and we picked Jack and Jazz up and started staggering out of the garage. We could hear a lot of commotion coming from our street...but I was so dizzy, I couldn't run up the way and see what it was. Jack was younger and fitter than me. He held onto his bloody nose with his hand and ran up the pavement toward the park. The police were there. They weren't busting heads or anything, but they were telling people they were assembled illegally and had to disperse. Anyone who gave them any back-talk they were loading into a police van.

As the rest of us caught up to Jack, we saw Bruiser shepherding Marigold out of the park. Jack waved toward them, and then we faded back down the side street. We didn't want the police to notice our beat-up faces. Marigold stared at us in horror. "What happened?" she said. "Did the police —?"

"No," Jack said. "It wasn't the police. It was Nikolai's guys. They took Torstein."

We quickly told them what had happened, what Sig had told us about Van and Caroline...and how Ferdy had led us to the thugs.

"No," Marigold said. "That can't be right ..."

"Are there any of the Dunkers in the park?" Jazz asked. "If we can get them together, maybe we could find out where they've taken Torstein and go get him back."

But we all knew the answer: the Dunkers were gone again. They'd developed some new dramas and planned some new publicity stunts, then they'd formed into teams and left again. They were techno-savvy and kept in touch with each other through text messages and Facebook...but none of us had ever bothered to get into their grid. Jazz might have been right; with all of them behind us, maybe we could have taken some *action* to get Torstein back...but just then, with the police chasing all our friends away, and with Torstein gone who knew where—it felt like there was nothing we could do.

Then we heard, above the sirens, shrieking from the park. We all knew that scream. It was Cyd, the little autistic girl. Sometimes when someone touched her, or a worm or something walked on her foot, or her dad tried to get her to let go of Torstein, she would have a screaming fit. It was a really awful scream. No one could make her stop it, either, except Torstein. She'd fling herself on the ground, totally stiff like a board, and shriek. She couldn't help it. She wasn't like kids that just have a fit because they're spoiled. She couldn't control it, I don't think.

"Cydney!" Marigold shouted, and she took off running back toward the park. Bruiser followed her, and Jack and Jazz followed them.

71

Pete was just standing with his back against the wall of the bank that fronted our street and the side street we'd come up. His eyes were a bit glazed, and his shoulders slumped, his hands hanging loose at his sides.

"Pete, you okay?" I asked.

"I don't know," he said. He slid down the wall until he was sitting on the sidewalk, his knees pulled up toward him. "Will you go look for Phyllis?" he said.

I didn't want to leave him, but I knew he'd want to make sure his wife was all right. I ran off after the others. The park was in chaos. Some of the people in the crowd were giving the police a hard time, shouting at them that it was a public park and they had a right to be there. Cydney was flat on her back on the ground, wailing like a siren. Her dad and Marigold were stooped beside her and Bruiser was desperately trying to tell the officers that they had to leave her alone so she could get calmed down. Phyllis, too, had run to Cydney. She was all right.

"Bob, just pick Cyd up and let's get out of here," I said to Cydney's dad.

"If I touch her you know she's going to get crazy," he said.

"Let's risk it. Come on, now."

Bob stooped down and picked Cyd up, and she did go wild. She was a difficult one to touch at the best of times, but when she was in a state like that, it was crazy. I think maybe her wild thrashing scared the policemen who'd been telling us to get out of the park, and they backed off. Bruiser helped Cyd's dad hold onto her, and we made our way out of the park toward where I'd left Pete.

The detective, Waverling, had arrived here with the officers sent to break up the unlawful assembly in the park. He was standing out on the street, and he'd noticed Pete sitting by the bank with his bloody face. I saw him walking that direction and ran out ahead of our little shrieking party to get there first. The last thing I wanted was Waverling confronting Pete. I wasn't even sure what was wrong with Pete.

I saw the detective call over his shoulder for a couple of uniforms. This could not be good.

I was still dizzy. I didn't think those guys had broken my jaw, but it hurt like the devil. With every thud of my footsteps as I ran, the side of my head felt like a little explosion. But I didn't want Pete to mouth off to those cops and get arrested, so I kept running.

I was close enough to hear Waverling saying to him, "Hey, you been in a fight? You're one of Torstein's guys, aren't you?"

"No," Pete said to his hands which were propped on his knees in front of him. "Not hardly." He didn't even look up, and he sounded as if he could barely speak.

"I know you are," Waverling said. "You got arrested with him before."

"Never been arrested," Pete said.

The uniformed officers were advancing.

Pete looked up and started to push himself to his feet.

"Look, I told you, dammit, I've got nothing to do with Torstein," he said.

I finally got close enough at that moment to help Pete up and said to him, "C'mon, Pete. We've got Phyllis. Let's go."

"Yeah, get out of here," Waverling said. "Torstein's days in the park are over."

I steered Pete back toward Bruiser and Mari and Phyllis. He had a black eye, but otherwise I think he was okay. Just...deflated.

Cyd had finally stopped screaming and thrashing, and her dad said he would take her home. He asked if we'd seen Torstein, if Torstein had been arrested...but what could we tell him? We said we didn't know what had happened to him.

Back at Pete's house, Phyllis and Marigold made ice packs for our various aching jaws, eyes and noses. Bruiser made some phone calls to old friends in Nikolai's organization. Marigold called Tawny and told her what had happened. Angel and her new husband Len had gone away with Tawny and Franz for a few day's honeymoon. They knew that Angel had been called home because Sully had gone missing, and they'd just been packing up their things, and Angel's, to come home themselves. Franz said he would drop Tawny off with us, then go try to find out what he could about Torstein.

I called Vic Mondino, the lawyer who'd come for us when we'd been detained for taking Sully to the shore, and told him about Caroline, Angel and Len being in jail. He said he'd see what he could do.

Then there was nothing to do.

72

It was midnight before Franz turned up again. But he had no information. For once he'd failed—no one in Nikolai's organization was talking about Torstein. And that, in itself, was a bad sign, he said. If it were anything but murder, someone somewhere would be talking about it. A hit was the only thing they kept absolutely silent. Bruiser had run into the same wall...none of his old friends knew, or said, anything about Torstein.

Pete had not rebounded as well as I'd hoped he would. He went up to bed after Franz came and made his report. The rest of us just sat in his living room, but we had nothing to say. It was all so grim. Around one a.m. Maggie called. She and the others had been released from jail. They'd left Angel and Len to continue trying to pressure the police to take action to get Sully and Van back, but Maggie and Caroline were on their way to Nikolai's.

"You're what?" I asked, dazed. "Do you think that's a good idea?"

"Caroline knows him," Maggie said. "She thinks she can get the kids back. I'll be there with her. What's he gonna do?"

"Kill you!" I said, for the moment forgetting about Torstein who was probably there, too.

"We'll be okay," Maggie said. "But I heard there was a big commotion in the park after we were detained," she said. "Are you guys all right?"

"Ah, no, Torstein's missing," I finally told her. "Some of Nikolai's thugs came and took him away. We don't know where he is or what they want with him. I really think you and Caroline shouldn't go there."

"No," she sighed. "Look, did you call the police when they took Torstein?"

It was like a slap in the face. No, we had not called the police. We had been scared when the police started busting people in the park, and we'd run away from them. It hadn't occurred to us to try to report Torstein's kidnapping.

"Idiot," Maggie said brusquely. "Get down there, now. Waverling's gone, and I've threatened this lieutenant enough where I think he's going to help us. Anyone who witnessed the kidnapping, get down here and report it."

I went to wake Pete, but he wouldn't get up and come. He said there was no point. Jack, Jazz and I went alone. Maggie's lieutenant was very nice and took our statements, and gave every evidence of believing we'd been the victims of a crime and that our friend was missing...but then he said:

"Now, do you have anything that links the kidnappers to Nikolai? Did you get a license plate number on the van, or anything?"

Of course we didn't. We were all beat up. And the thugs had not spoken to us in Russian or worn any kind of "Nikolai's Knights" t-shirts or anything. It simply stood to reason ...

"We can't assume it was Nikolai's men, but we're going to investigate and see if we can find Torstein. Meanwhile I've already sent men over to Nikolai's to get the little boy back."

"Boys!" Angel said. "He's got Caroline's son, too."

"That may be more difficult. She admits Nikolai is the boy's father, I'm not sure there's anything we can do about that ..."

The lawyer, Vic, was still there. He'd had a hard time getting confirmation from the police earlier in the day that Maggie, Caroline, Angel and Len were even there because Waverling hadn't filed any paperwork. He'd just locked them up. Vic had persevered, but it had taken until Waverling went off duty before he could get our people out of jail. Then he had forced the lieutenant to listen to him and take action. I'm assuming he was embarrassed that one of his officers had locked people up without any charges and seemed to be protecting a known mob guy.

73

Angel was sitting quietly, holding hands with her new husband, Len. He seemed like a nice guy, and seemed very fond of Angel. I was wondering if he were wishing he'd put off the wedding for another week or so. This was no way to spend your honeymoon! But he just whispered to Angel that Sully was going to be fine, and he occasionally got up to get her a cup of coffee or walk with her to the door of the ladies' room. It was kind of strange to see Angel in plain street clothes, with her hair combed out and pulled back. Her eyes were a little bloodshot still, but it was pretty clear she'd been crying. I was wondering, too, if she wished she had put off giving up crack until this crisis were over...if anything was going to test your resolve about kicking the habit, I would think it would be having your child kidnapped.

We were sitting in a conference room or something like it, where we could all be together while our statements had been taken. It wasn't the most comfortable place in the world, but none of us felt like leaving.

"Does anybody know how to pray?" Angel said suddenly.

"I know some prayers," I offered. "You know, Catholic prayers."

"I know the Serenity Prayer," Vic said. He'd been in AA even before we met him.

"No, pray to Jesus," she said. I forgot she'd found Jesus in rehab.

"I can pray, you know that," Len said. "Here, everybody, let's join hands around this table, and I'll pray."

We drew in close—Jack, Jazz, me, Angel and Len—and we joined hands. "Do you want me to pray just for Sully and Van, or for Torstein too?" Len asked.

"Torstein, too," Angel said. She was actually quite a nice person when not high on crack. I would have snapped at Len that *of course* I wanted him to pray for Torstein, what did he think, that Torstein wasn't worth the trouble?! But Angel just said that, and bowed her head. So we all did.

I know all the parts of the Rosary, from growing up Catholic—the "Our Father," "Hail Mary," the "Glory Be." I guess I never thought about them as being prayers, to People, you know...they were just... what you said when you prayed the Rosary. Len just let loose with this long, rambling prayer to Jesus, as if Jesus were standing there in the room with us, asking him to bring the boys and Torstein back to us, safe and sound. It was pretty weird, but it was nice, too, and it seemed to make Angel feel better.

When he said Amen, Angel asked me to do a Catholic prayer. I didn't think Hail Mary or Our Father was very apropos, but my patron saint is Michael, and I had memorized his prayer for my confirmation. I prayed could remember it now. "This is a prayer to St. Michael, the archangel," I said. Thankfully the prayer came back to me as I recited:

> *St. Michael the Archangel,*
> *defend us in battle.*
> *Be our defense against the wickedness and snares of the Devil.*
> *May God rebuke him, we humbly pray,*
> *and do thou,*
> *O Prince of the heavenly hosts,*
> *by the power of God,*
> *thrust into hell Satan,*
> *and all the evil spirits,*
> *who prowl about the world*
> *seeking the ruin of souls. Amen.*

I had only just finished when the lieutenant came back into the conference room, and cleared his throat. I guess he probably thought we were nuts. Good thing he didn't come in during Len's prayer if he thought mine was weird.

"Why don't you all go home?" he said. "I'm sure we'll have Sully back very soon..."

As if we'd go home.

74

Later Maggie told me what happened with Nikolai, Caroline, and the boys.

They went to Nikolai's house outside the city, which Maggie said was a very nice house with a big fence around it and floodlights that illuminated everything outside like daylight. Caroline knew the gate code to enter the property, and the soldiers outside all knew her, so there was no trouble to get in. It was the middle of the night, but the boys were sitting up with Nikolai playing video games and eating ice cream. The boys were delighted to see Caroline and Maggie and immediately began telling them all the fun they'd been having, sailing on a sugar high.

Nikolai also seemed delighted to see them, told Maggie she could have a job in one of his clubs any time, told Caroline he'd missed her and was glad she'd come back.

"I'm not *back*, Niki," she said. "I'm taking Sully to his mother, and taking Van home. You've put everyone through hell with this little prank."

"Carolinitzchca," he said. "There's nothing to go back to in the city for you and Van now. I'm putting an end to all that green coat madness tonight."

Maggie said it sent a shiver down her spine—all that green coat madness?

"Niki, you don't know what you're talking about," Caroline said. "It's not madness."

"It's madness if it makes you think you can take my boy and leave me," he said. "It's madness when my collections men quit and start *giving* instead of *taking*. It's a cancer growing in Patriot's Park, and it's making my whole empire sick. I've had enough of it. I won't let it destroy my business, or my son."

Maggie said she could see Caroline was scared now, for the first time. Not for herself, and not for her son, but for Torstein. And that scared Maggie. Clearly Caroline knew Nikolai well enough to understand how serious his words were.

"Niki, it's nothing to do with you," she said. "Why do you care what's happening in Patriot's Park?"

"I care because that green-coated jack-ass has stolen you away from me, Carolinitzchca," Nikolai said. "I care because what he's asking people to do—this loving and forgiving and caring, it's ruining my investment. I won't have it."

"Oh, Niki," Caroline said, softly, almost a sigh. "Don't do anything to Torstein. You don't understand what he is. Don't lay a hand on him. Do you have him here? Let us see him."

"Have him here?" Nikolai laughed. "Of course I don't have him here. Mateo has him in the city."

"Niki, don't do anything to him!" she said, quick and urgent not yelling for the sake of the boys, but obviously scared. "For your own sake, Nik, don't do it. You don't know what you're doing, you don't know what he is."

"I *do* know what he is. He's a bastard cousin of that bastard Dunker. Did *you* know that? Madness must run in their family."

"If it's madness it's no threat to you," Caroline said. "Torstein's a good man. Let him be."

The police arrived then. Maggie said they seemed embarrassed to be there in Nikolai's plush home, and ask him to return the children he'd kidnapped, as if *they* were an imposition to *him*. But Nikolai turned the kids over to them without the slightest resistance. He told them he'd merely wanted to have the boys over to watch movies and play games, and he was sorry it had all gotten so fouled up.

"I haven't seen my son in two or three months," he told the relieved policemen. "I just wanted him and his friend to have some fun this afternoon. We lost track of the time. Isn't that right boys?"

Jaxn Hill

The boys affirmed that they'd been having fun and had no idea what time it was.

As for sending thugs to kidnap them from school, Nikolai assured the officers that this had been a terrible mistake. He'd only meant to sign Van out from school for the day, as any father might do. Of course if Caroline wanted to take him home with her, that was fine, that was what he'd intended all along. Maggie said it was obvious to everyone (except the boys) that Nikolai was telling one ingratiating lie after another, but by this time she and Caroline didn't care. All they wanted to do was get away from him and get the officers hunting for Torstein.

Sully and Van both hugged Nikolai when they said goodbye, and everyone was walking down the beautifully paved curving driveway to their cars when Nikolai called out, "Caroline, if you want Torstein back, I imagine they're dropping him off in the park about now!"

Maggie said it *ought* to have sounded like good news—but to her and Caroline, it had an instantly chilling effect.

"Oh, God," Caroline shuddered.

She pushed Van toward Maggie, and turned back to Nikolai.

"Niki, my God," she said. "I hope you haven't, you haven't..." For the first time, Maggie said, Nikolai's jovial mask seemed to slip.

"What, Carolinitzcha?" he asked. "You know what I am. You know what I do."

"But Niki, this man, this innocent man ..."

Maggie said she could hear in Caroline's voice that she loved Nikolai, loved him as a wife and the mother of his child. And if her heart were breaking for Torstein, it was breaking for Nikolai, too. "Tell me you didn't do this, Niki."

Then Nikolai reached out for her, took her hand, said softly, "I wanted you and Van back, Carolinitzchca. How could I get you back?"

"You could have come and joined us...You don't know what you're doing, Niki. Tell me you can stop it, save him ..."

"What's done is done," he said, suddenly granite-faced. "It's my business, Caroline, and you know that. Just my business."

Dragonfly

And Maggie said she knew, at that moment, even if she didn't have the strength to face it.

They trundled the boys into her car and she sped off toward the Park.

75

aggie called me on her cell phone and told me they had the boys. She told me what Nikolai had said, and that she and Caroline were on the way to the park. I hung up, told Angel that they were bringing the boys to the park, and then my phone rang again—this time it was Franz. Someone had called Pete's house and told him if we wanted Torstein back, we'd find him in the park this morning. The downtown police station was only a few blocks from Patriots Park, maybe a mile. We told Franz we'd meet him, Tawny and Bruiser there, and we piled into my car and into the car of our lawyer, Vic Mondino, then raced the empty streets to Patriots Park. We left the cars on the street and ran into the park. It was strangely deserted. Usually a few drunks or homeless were lounging on the benches first thing in the morning, having slept there all night. I guess the big bust yesterday had discouraged them from coming back here.

But we didn't see Torstein, either.

We ran past the little playground, followed the concrete trail that wound into the park itself, felt stupid about calling out his name, but did it anyway—and there was no answer.

We were all looking for any sight of that electric green coat; I know that's what I was looking for as my eyes scanned the park in the early morning: the iridescent shimmer of the dragonfly. In desperation I was looking back across the park, toward the street, in case the kidnappers were just now dropping him off. But again, I didn't see the green coat.

Dragonfly

I saw a red one. A burgundy jacket.

When I dared to let my brain interpret what I'd seen, I was afraid to go to it...but afraid not to. I didn't want anyone else to get there first, to see it before I did, to prove me right.

They had dumped him from the street, just flung him into the park, probably from a moving vehicle. Even as I stood there, staring at the red jacket heaped on the ground, I saw Pete's car pull up, Franz and Tawny, Pete and Phyllis, and Bruiser piling out. They were on the other side of that wretched red jacket and what it contained.

I couldn't take a step toward them. I couldn't call out. I just watched as Phyllis sort of collapsed beside the jacket, and Tawny flung herself into Franz's arms, and Pete knelt down beside his wife, and Bruiser knelt down beside them. It was like watching people in a movie, like watching something that had nothing to do with me. That red jacket couldn't mean anything to me, or to Torstein. He wore green. That wasn't his jacket.

Then Jack and Jazz were running past me, Angel and Len were running past me.

I stood there, it seemed, a long time. I could see the reactions of horror taking place as one after another our friends drew close and saw what we were afraid to go see. The jacket was so stained with blood, it was entirely red. There wasn't a speck of green visible on his whole electric coat.

I saw Caroline and Maggie arrive, saw the boys bouncing out of the car and toward their friends...only to stare in curiosity at the red coat... they had no frame of reference for what they were seeing. Angel ran to her son, embraced him—so glad that he was alive, but so horrified by that awful red jacket. Len put his arms around both of them and moved himself between them and the coat. Caroline had gotten hold of Van's hand, and pulled him away as well.

Finally I began to pull myself toward them, leaden step by leaden step. Maggie came to me and took my hand. She was trembling. "Andy," she said softly. "Remember what he said...he said he would come back, he would find us ..."

"How can he come back, Maggie? If that's him, how can he come back?"

Sully had broken free from Angel and Len. He was standing beside Van who had got way from his mother somehow. They were standing together, their arms around each others' shoulders, looking down at Torstein's newly red jacket and the awful truth it contained.

Ivan Nikolayevich and our Sully. Son of Nikolai and Son of Nobody. Torstein was dead. But maybe what he'd started was not.

76

The police came. I don't know what else happened. A lawyer came from Torstein's family, told the authorities that they were Orthodox Jews, and an autopsy was not permitted. In fact, he needed to take the body for burial immediately. Orthodox Jews! I'd never seen any indication of it...I wondered if this lawyer really even came from their family...but then I got to looking at him, and I knew I'd seen him a time or two in the park, maybe even on New Year's Eve. Torstein knew him. His name was Joseph. That was all I'd ever known about him, up until now.

The Medical Examiner wouldn't give the body to Joseph, but he seemed pretty certain that before the day was over he would have it, and the family would bury it. What family? None of us had ever seen any of Torstein's family. *We* were his family.

"That's right," Joseph said. "You are. So you'd best come to the funeral tonight."

"Tonight?" I said numbly.

"This afternoon," Joseph said. "The family has a crypt at Green Lawn."

"You can't get him ready to bury in a day," I said, looking at the rusty red jacket, unable to see anything there that looked like Torstein.

"It has to be this afternoon or Sunday. The Sabbath begins at sundown. If you want to be there for the funeral, come this afternoon."

I didn't want to be there for the funeral. I didn't know anything about Jewish funerals. I didn't know Torstein was Jewish. I didn't want it to be his funeral. Everything was hideously unreal.

But at three o'clock everything was hideously *too* real. There was no funeral. There was no family. We were there, and Joseph, and the cemetery people who slid the coffin into the crypt and pushed the marble door closed to lock it. Where was Torstein's father, who supposedly lived up the hill, and where were the two gleaming men— the ones Pete, Jack and Jazz had met when they drove up to that family home? If he really had a dad who lived up there, where was he? Why were the only mourners by the crypt a bunch of shell-shocked losers who hadn't even stood by Torstein when he needed us most?

That really got to Pete. He'd always thought he'd fight his way out of anything. He'd always prided himself on his strength and loyalty. And in the end he'd done nothing to save Torstein. He was like a man without a center now. He stood staring at the sturdy marble door of the crypt with lifeless eyes and slumped shoulders. We were all heart-broken. But Pete was just broken.

The Dunkers had turned up. Someone had gotten a text out to one of them. They were like a hive mind, I swear. The word had passed around from their cell phones and laptops, their FaceBook pages and blogs. They came to the funeral, such as it was, but they weren't the exuberant bunch who had reported on the success of their "love is the answer" campaign all those months ago. They were, once again, deprived of a leader, just as they had been when Duncan was killed. They were like an elite fighting unit, or a Borg collective, that took its instructions from one head, and if that head were gone, they were lifeless droids. They tried to talk, to say it would have gone differently if they'd been around. I didn't know what to say to them. I didn't know anything. They drifted away in pairs, bereft.

Joseph disappeared as soon as the crypt was sealed. I'd wanted to ask him where the hell Torstein's father was, but I wasn't thinking clearly enough. If he was really the family's lawyer—and I guess he was because he'd got the body released from the M.E. so fast—he maybe would know where this rich dad of Torstein's was, the one with the house on the side of the mountain and the beautiful view of the sea…but Joseph was gone, and I couldn't ask him anything.

Dragonfly

The rest of us started to drift away, too. Franz said he would take Tawny home. They'd just been married on Sunday. The first week of their life together had ended in tragedy. Maggie said she would take Mari, Caroline and Van home. But Caroline was already planning to leave town. She wanted to take her son and get away. Len and Angel went home with Maggie and Caroline—they would be moving away, to live in the little mountain town where Len worked at the rehab. But they didn't want to take Sully and leave so soon when he'd been living with Maggie all these months. They would stay another week with her.

Jack and Jazz said they would go home; they wanted to tell their parents what had happened.

I don't think any of us really knew what we were doing or saying. It was like the world had shifted out from under us, and we were desperate to get our feet back on the ground. Bruiser and I were standing there with Pete and Phyllis, when Ferdy came. I thought for sure Pete would clock him. But Pete, he didn't really seem to see him.

"I didn't want this to happen," Ferdy said. He was staring at the crypt, same as Pete was.

"What *did* you want to happen?" Bruiser asked.

"I wanted Torstein to take my advice, to do the TV gig. Nikolai was supposed to rough him up, get him scared. He was never supposed to kill him. Then we were going to get the TV news on the story. Ariel told me if Torstein came to her after he got away from Nikolai, with a black eye and broken nose and whatnot, she'd put the whole thing on the news. I was just trying to get his message out. I was trying to get him to be a hero...to help get the media and law enforcement after Nikolai and draw attention to our cause ..."

"That's the stupidest thing I ever heard," Bruiser said. "Torstein didn't want to be on TV. Why would getting roughed up by a mobster change that?"

"Don't you see?" Ferdy said. "Once he realized how evil Nikolai was, he'd *want* to go on TV and expose him. That's what Ariel said... And once he saw what a powerful difference he could make on TV, he'd *want* to keep doing it, keep spreading his message. It was supposed to jar him into taking action."

I didn't want to feel sorry for Ferdy, because he'd done this to all of us. But if you could hear the desperation in his voice, the way he really seemed to have convinced himself that somehow this was a good plan… it was pitiful. It was painful. It added another horrible layer of heartache to an already horrendous situation.

I didn't want to feel sorry for him…but I didn't want to forgive him, either. I just threw my arm around Pete's shoulders and turned him away from the crypt, then took Phyllis' hand and started walking back out of the cemetery. We were done.

Bruiser came with us.

We left Ferdy standing there, his hands held out to us, wanting something none of us could give. Forgiveness, absolution. Maybe, someday, but not then.

77

Friday night was like a bad dream. Only, you *wished* it could be a bad dream, so you could wake up. Only, I couldn't really sleep, so there was no waking up. On Saturday morning, I called my dad. I thought none of us had thought to call him and our step-mom the day before, but Phyllis had. Dad told me to come to his place, that they were just fixing breakfast, and I could join them. But I didn't feel like it. I'd told Bruiser I'd meet him for coffee later…only I didn't want to go back to the Starbucks where we'd been Thursday morning. I didn't really want to go back downtown at all. So we met at De Caf Bar about 11 a.m. He didn't look like he'd slept anymore than I had.

He told me he'd talked to Jazz earlier, and they were going fishing the next morning, if Pete and I wanted to go. I didn't know…fishing is a mindless thing you can do to keep your mind off your troubles… unless once upon a time you'd been on an extraordinary fishing trip with a guy who has now been murdered.

It was like that with everything—for the past year or so, everything I'd done had revolved around Torstein, and now there was nothing I knew to do that didn't bring up vivid memories of him, just at the moment when I least wanted to think about him. What had he been trying to tell us? Ferdy's question from Thursday morning was more real to me on Saturday than it had been then…"What's it all been for?" What had it all been for? We'd been enchanted by Torstein, and while he was with us, we felt our lives were worth something, that we were doing something worthwhile, maybe for the first time in our lives! Now he was dead.

Maggie called me around noon. She was crying on the phone. As best I could understand her, she said:

"Oh, Andy, Andy. Ferdy's dead."

"Ferdy's dead?" I said, and the whole phrase really was in italics, I mean, Ferdy? "Why would Nikolai—"

"Not Nikolai," she said, trying to speak more clearly now, and more loudly, although I could tell she was still crying. "He killed himself! He's dead, and he killed himself."

God, that wasn't what I wanted. I couldn't forgive him, not so soon…but I hadn't wanted him dead.

I thought about what Torstein had told us, and I knew we'd failed already. He'd always said *love*. He'd always said *forgive*. What if any one of us had been strong enough to say to Ferdy, "It's okay, man. You didn't mean for this to happen"?

Would he still be dead? One dead guy had been enough. Had our failure to love just added to the body count?

I hung up the phone with Maggie, and told Bruiser what she'd said. He shrugged. I think maybe after losing Torstein, he was numb. I told Maggie where we were, and she said she would come, but she wanted to go by the park first. People were leaving memorials at the park, she said.

I know these days, when a celebrity dies, it's the thing for the adoring public to leave memorials at his front door or wherever they think it's appropriate—like all the wreaths and roses and teddy bears at Windsor Castle when Princess Diana passed away, or all the glitter and gloves people heaped in front of Michael Jackson's rental home. I know it's how people share their grief and pay tribute to the one they feel they've lost. But I could only think of a handful of people who had really, meaningfully lost Torstein, and I didn't think any of them had been in the park this morning leaving a cross or a sympathy card or some kind of green doll's coat as a tribute. I didn't want to see that. I didn't want anyone who had just followed Torstein around—or worse, just seen him on TV—acting as if they were grieving with me.

Looking back on that now, my irrational anger that other people actually felt bereaved (or acted bereaved!), I don't even recognize myself. How could I have been so narrow-minded as to think that Torstein had to have stayed at your house or gone on a fishing trip with you in order for him to mean something to you? He hadn't been *mine,* just *my* friend. What he'd had, what he'd said, it had touched people all over the city, certainly all over downtown. But at the moment it seemed to me another Selena scenario: now that he was dead, everyone was going to claim they'd been his biggest fans.

Everything had turned to rubbish for me.

When Maggie came, she gave me and Bruiser both a big hug. She was so fair-skinned, she looked like Snow White in general (but for the auburn hair). Today, you could tell she had been crying, and not sleeping, because there were dark circles, like a lavender thumbprint, in the delicate hollow under each eye. Her normally pale skin looked on the verge of gray. She asked about Pete; everyone was worried about him. She told me she was conflicted about Ferdy—she'd been angry with him, but she hadn't wanted him to die. We told her what he' said to us at the crypt, how Torstein was just supposed to get beat up and goaded into taking some action, going on television…It sounded so *stupid.* Could he really have been so blind?!

That made Maggie cry again, and I remembered Pete telling me that I was terrible at comforting women. I'd tried to learn something about it from Torstein, but I was still not very good at it. At least this time I put my arm around Maggie's shoulder .

When she stopped crying, she said someone had made a beautiful chalk drawing of the dragonfly coat in the center square of Patriots Park, and people had brought flowers and cards and left them there. Ariel Prince had been there, she said, recording new footage for her retrospective on Torstein. She'd done two news pieces on him, and this was sure to be a beautiful cap to them. The plan had worked out for her, either way.

Maggie said Len had taken Angel and Sully to the shore for the day, to try to get Angel's mind off her grief. Caroline had actually called her parents for the first time in 10 years, and asked them if she could come home and bring her son. They'd never even seen their grandson.

"Jack called me and said everyone is invited to go fishing tomorrow. Fishing!" She snorted.

"I'm going," I said. "Why not? Get out of the city. You should come. Bring Van and Sully. We need the break."

"Maybe," she said. "I'm not getting up at dark-thirty though."

"Aren't you?" Bruiser said. "I was up at dark-thirty this morning."

"Yeah," she said. "Maybe I will. But I want to visit the grave again. I keep thinking: this isn't real. He can't be dead. How could he be? He was more alive than any of us. Maybe if I go there, and see the crypt again, I'll believe it. Angel wants to go, too."

78

While we were sitting there at De Caf Bar, pretending to drink our java, Maggie trying not to start crying again, a man we didn't know approached our table. Had Torstein been with us, he would have jumped up and taken the man by the hand, offered him a seat at the table, asked him what troubled him. He *did* look troubled: his face was pale, his eyes red-rimmed, his hair was a bit wild. He looked as if he hadn't slept in a while. He was dressed nicely in a rather overdone tan sport-coat that verged on mustard color, and the hair that wasn't falling into his eyes was caught into a ponytail at the back of his head. Not the usual homeless guy who might ask to join us in hope of a hand-out if Torstein were there.

We all just looked up at him as he stood there, and he didn't speak. He wasn't—one of us, I guess you could say, we didn't know him—and yet he stared at us with this kind of intensity that made it seem as if perhaps he knew us, or really badly wanted to. Maggie recovered her manners first, and said, "Won't you join us?"

It was a thin greeting compared with the one he might have gotten from Torstein, but we were all so dazed, I think, we didn't mind about that.

The man sat down, set his cup of coffee on the table, looked at it for a few seconds, glanced around the table at us, and finally said:

"Who was he?"

"Who was *who?*" Bruiser asked.

"The green coat," he choked out. "Who was he?"

"Torstein," Maggie said. "His name was Torstein."

"But, who *was* he?" the man asked again.

"A friend of ours," I said. "Did you know him?"

"I was there," he said quietly.

"You were...where?" Bruiser asked.

"There. I was there when they killed him."

I think I flinched. Bruiser's face blanched. Maggie's face had already been milky, so no more blood could drain out of it. And yet, there was a reaction. The bright intensity of her blue-eyed gaze seemed to lock on the face of this man. Why would he come here and tell us this? Now that we were wholly caught up in staring at him, it was easy to imagine who he was, one of Nikolai's lieutenants, maybe—that explained the loud coat, the curly ponytail, his overall appearance of being ex-gun-runner euro trash. But it didn't explain why he would have stayed up all night in apparent anxiety and sought us out this morning.

"What do you mean?" Maggie said. "How could you have been there?"

"My job," he said. "It's my job. I was in charge."

"Do you mean to say you killed him?" Bruiser said, and I could see his knuckles as white as his face as he gripped the edge of the table. Maggie's small hand reached across and covered the back of his.

"No, I didn't do it, not personally," the man said. "But my guys did."

I thought he would begin to tell us that it was his job, that if he hadn't, someone else would have, that working for a mobster you had to follow orders or die. But he didn't. He just sat there, staring at his coffee cup.

"So what do you want?" Bruiser said. It amazed me that he and I were still sitting here with this guy and not knocking the top of his freaking head off. Maybe if Pete had been there...but then it occurred to me, what had happened to Ferdy, as much as we might think he deserved it, had hurt Bruiser the same way it had me. We felt like, no matter what Ferdy had done, he had still been one of us, and he'd deserved better *from us*. We hadn't been able to give him what he needed, and he'd killed himself. I think we both felt that was enough blood on our hands. So we waited for this man to tell us what his problem was.

"Nikolai wanted it to be bad, to be a message, like the thing with the Dunker. He doesn't want people making trouble for him. He wanted you all to know ..."

"You can skip that part," Maggie said. "Just tell us why you're here."

"He knew he was going to die, and he knew it was going to be brutal," the man said. "And he didn't say anything, and he didn't do anything. He didn't fight us. He reached into his jacket, at one point, and my guys drew down on him—we thought he was going for a gun, you know. But he pulled out a bag of sunflower seeds. He offered the guys some sunflower seeds."

I could see it all as he described it. I knew he was telling the truth.

"The guys, they thought this was hysterical, and they were laughing about it, like what kind of an idiot offers a snack to the people that are about to murder him? These guys that do this kind of work, they're not the most intelligent people in the world, and they don't live in a very emotionally healthy place."

This caused me to stare again at the man. What kind of talk was that for a mobster, a thug? He looked fit, and he wasn't a small man in stature, but he didn't look like hired muscle, not brawny like our Bruiser. Maybe that's how he got to be in the position he was in—not a trigger guy, but a captain, say. Because of his brains. I still had my doubts about *his* emotional health, though.

If there'd been a choice, I would have preferred not to hear his story. But I couldn't turn away from it.

"It didn't strike me as an idiot trying to buy off his antagonists with sunflower seeds," he went on, still staring at his hands around the cup. "It struck me, the way he did it, the look on his face, the confidence in his eyes...It struck me like someone with some trick up his sleeve, some vital bit of knowledge that we didn't have. His eyes locked onto mine, and he said, 'Mateo, have some sunflower seeds'."

He stopped again, and finally looked up from his coffee cup to look each one of us in the eyes. We waited...I don't think we thought there would ever be an end to waiting now. Torstein was gone. And we were all just waiting now. But this guy, Mateo was his name, he seemed to be waiting for us, too—waiting for us to fill in the blanks and understand what he was trying to tell us. But so far he had only revealed what we might have imagined: Torstein had offered some strangers sunflower seeds.

Mateo's eyebrows wrinkled, his whole forehead wrinkled, and his face seemed to question us, to beg us to make some response, to explain something. Finally Maggie said, "Did you take some?"

"Yes!" He huffed his reply out in a sort of quiet exclamation. "I did."

79

e stopped again. I didn't think we'd ever get the story out of him.

"So you took some sunflower seeds ..." Bruiser urged him on.

"That's all," he said. "But when I did, the way he looked at me, he smiled at me. He wasn't stupid. He knew what was about to happen. But he smiled at me, and he said, 'It's all right. No one can take my life from me unless I lay it down. But now, Mateo, what will *you* do from now on?' And I ..."

He paused again. I wanted to scream at him, *Oh for God's sake, just tell your story!*

But I didn't. I waited. Maggie waited. Bruiser waited.

Maybe for one minute, maybe two. That's a long time to wait in silence for someone to continue telling a story. He gulped, and then he said:

"I've killed people before. My line of work that's how you get noticed. I don't have any fairy tale notions that there's no blood on my hands, and I'm not squeamish about it."

OK, that part of the story, I could have done without, but I guess he wanted to impress on us what a tough guy he was, or had been, anyway.

"But when he said that, when he smiled, I felt like he *knew me,* and he *loved me,* despite what I was, even knowing what I was. And when he said that, when he asked me what I was going to do from now on...I couldn't take it. I ran away. I gave the order, and I left the room, and

Jaxn Hill

I heard the boys get started, and then it was like my life caved in on me. How could I go on doing what I do, after he looked at me like that? I couldn't go to sleep after that. I could always see his face when he handed me those sunflower seeds, it's burned on my eyeballs now. I couldn't stay at work. After the job was done, I just left, and I haven't been back. I don't know what to do now. I thought you could help me."

He looked around at us again, desperate.

"What do I do now? That's what he asked me. What would I do from now on?"

He hadn't killed Torstein, but he hadn't saved him, either. He'd given the order! Now he came to us to ask what to do? All I could think was: *why don't you do what Ferdy did?* But then, as soon as I thought it, I wanted to un-think it, because it had killed me what Ferdy did.

Bruiser reached over and put his hand on Mateo's shoulder.

"If you're asking, what would Torstein have told you to do, if you hadn't killed him, he would say that love is always the answer to every question."

Mateo looked at him, that desperation shining in his eyes, and said, "What does that mean? How does that work?"

"That's the part you have to figure out for yourself, I guess," Bruiser said. "I used to work in Nikolai's organization, too. I understand what violence and intimidation can do, but I'm only just learning now what love can do."

Maggie gave a tentative half-smile to Bruiser. She said to Mateo, "We had a friend, Ferdy. He was the one who lured Torstein into the garage so your guys could capture him. Yesterday, he felt so bad about what he'd done, he killed himself. What he didn't understand was, that was the last thing Torstein would have wanted. Torstein would have wanted Ferdy to forgive himself, and he would have wanted us to forgive Ferdy."

Tears were seeping out of her eyes. She reached for Mateo's hand and squeezed it, but she couldn't say more. When she opened her mouth to speak again, the words didn't come. More tears did. I realized it was up to me to finish what she'd begun, but I didn't know if I could.

Honestly I didn't know. Torstein made forgiveness, love and mercy look easy. But I'm only human. What had he been?

I cleared my throat and said, "I don't know what Torstein would have told you to do, if he were here. But I *do know* what he would have told Maggie and Bruiser and me. He would have said that he loved you, and he wants us to love you. We screwed up with Ferdy, but we won't let you get away. If you're looking for forgiveness, that's ours to give, because Torstein made it ours."

He pushed the coffee cup away, and laid his head down, pillowed on his arms on the table. He heaved a huge sigh of relief. And I think he said, "It's a start."

Bruiser said, "We're a man down with Ferdy gone anyway, brother. Why don't you stick with us? We'll square it with the other guys."

"Yes," Maggie said. "Why don't you come fishing with us tomorrow?"

80

That Sunday morning, it was Easter. That meant nothing to me. My dreams were dead. I'd told Jack and Jazz that Pete and I would come fishing, and that I thought the girls were coming, too, Maggie, Caroline and Marigold. I didn't tell them about Mateo. I figured I'd introduce him when we got there. Jazz told me Franz and Tawny were coming, and that Angel was bringing Sully, too. Len, he'd been called back to work—some crisis at the rehab—but he would be back, he'd promised Angel, by the time we got back from fishing in the evening.

Maggie and Angel and Caroline had gone to the cemetery early.

They wanted to see the grave again, for it to be real.

I didn't care if I never saw that place again.

Pete surprised me by getting up that morning and saying he would go fishing. He'd been in bed practically the entire time since the funeral. If you could call it a funeral. I didn't know how to reach him, but I understood how he felt. What he'd always relied on—his own strength and power—had failed him in the clutch. He didn't think there was anything left for him. He said he might as well go fishing. It was one thing he still knew how to do.

And that's what it felt like. Since the day we'd sold the fish market, we'd lived this extraordinary life on the high wire, learning to laugh and love and dance up there. Then, on Friday afternoon, we'd all tumbled off the tightrope and came crashing back into reality. Time to get back to real life. Time to go fishing.

Dragonfly

When I introduced Mateo to Pete, Jazz and Jack on the dock, they didn't ask any questions. They just shook hands and said he was welcome to come fishing. There would be 12 adults on the boat counting Mateo plus the two boys...I tried to think back to the summer, the last time we'd been out on the water together, and who all had been there. We'd been so happy just to be together. And we'd had such good luck that day.

A far cry from this gray morning.

We were waiting for the girls on the dock. They pulled up in Maggie's car, and the three ladies climbed out looking rather...happy... all things considered.

Maggie dashed up to Pete, grabbed the front of his shirt to pull his face down toward her, and nearly shouted at him, "Pete—he's all right! He's all right, and he's coming to find you. He said, 'Go tell Pete and the guys that I'm coming.' Everything is going to be okay." She grinned at him with idiot satisfaction, while the rest of us stared at her, bewildered.

"We went to the grave!" Marigold cried out, sounding every bit as happy and rejuvenated as Maggie. "But he's not there—he's not in the grave. Because he's *not dead!*"

Sully and Van had climbed out of the car, too, and they were doing a little two-step that Torstein had taught them sometime in the spring. They were laughing and dancing.

"You are all freaking nuts," Pete said.

"No we are not," Caroline said. "We saw him. We spoke to him! He told Maggie to tell you that he's all right, and he'll find you soon. Right, Angel?"

Angel just stood there, beaming at us, saying nothing. It was as if she had a secret so potent, so powerful, to speak it would diminish it.

"What are you talking about?" Phyllis said. "What on earth do you mean?" I could tell what she was thinking. She was thinking they'd gotten into someone's happy pills.

Maggie let go of Pete's shirt-front, threw her arms around Phyllis and said, "Torstein's alive! We saw him—we went to the grave, and the crypt was all demolished, and the casket was lying open on its side, and there was nobody in it."

"No *body* in it!" Marigold echoed, sounding slightly hysterical. She giggled at her own joke and then joined the boys in their little line dance.

"Oh, God," Jack said. You could tell he was daring to hope that somehow what Torstein had said was true, and he'd found a way to come back to us. I just feared that Nikolai's goons had come back to do something worse to the body than they'd already done.

"C'mon," Jack said. "Let's go, let's go see."

He sped off toward the street and his car, Pete running hard beside him and Jazz following along.

Bruiser and I grabbed Phyllis and pulled her into Bruiser's car with us and Mateo while Pete, Jazz and Jack piled into Jack's car. As we dashed away, we heard Maggie calling to Mateo, "You didn't kill him after all!" I was left to wonder what anyone else who heard it would think...I hadn't told them how Mateo came to be with us that morning.

It was still early morning, the sun had only just risen. Easter or no, the streets were empty, and we sped all the way to Green Lawn. The cars screeched into empty parking spaces and we ran full-out to the crypt.

Maggie was right. It was demolished. The heavy marble door had been splintered like an explosion. The east-facing wall looked like it had imploded, and the casket had been blown off it's pedestal, laid on its side, open, empty.

"What the hell?" Pete said. "What the hell?"

"What have they done with him?" Jazz said, touching the lining of the coffin where his head had laid.

"He said he'd come back," Jack said. "He said he'd find us!"

"It's not possible, Jack," I said. "It's not possible he could come back..."

81

We drove back to the docks. Tawny and Franz had arrived, and Maggie and the other ladies had told them what they'd seen, the demolished crypt, the empty casket, the vision of Torstein who told them he would find us later today.

"Not a vision," Angel said. "He was there. We touched him."

"Yeah," Sully said. "Van thought he was a ghost."

"I did not," Van said.

"But he wasn't. He was real."

Pete confirmed the scene at the cemetery, but said, "We didn't see him. We didn't see anything."

Our new friend, Mateo, was following along with us like someone in a dream. I could see that he *wanted* Torstein to be alive, of all the murders he'd done or ordered done, I knew this was the one he would most like to undo. But how could it be possible? How could they have seen Torstein today after the devastation in the red jacket we'd seen on Friday?

"He's alive," Maggie said. "You *will* see."

Franz shook his head. Clearly he didn't believe it.

"Let's go fishing," he said.

Jack powered up the engines. Jazz cast off the lines. We set out to sea.

The sun was rising over the city behind us as we chugged out into the open water. We were facing gray seas just beginning to color pale pink and orange where the first rays of morning lit them up. But that sunrise was behind us, and we were looking, and heading, west and slightly south—the girls, Van and Sully were standing at the rail on the bow, smiling and laughing, Mari and the boys still dancing, the chilly wind causing them not so much as a goose bump, so contented and happy they seemed. Jack had joined them, making them tell him again and again what they had seen.

Mateo, Pete and I were with Phyllis and Bruiser in the wheelhouse, Jazz was in the captain's chair.

Maggie worked her way back to the wheelhouse and said, "The funny thing was his jacket."

None of us were going to bite. We didn't believe it, couldn't bear to believe it, and then have our outlandish hopes dashed.

"His jacket wasn't green. It was sort of tan, golden you could say. Somehow, it was even more becoming ..."

"Did he tell you, did he really tell you to find me, Pete?" Pete asked. "Or did he just say, 'Go tell the guys'?"

I tried to keep my jaw from dropping. Could Pete really think there was some possibility it wasn't just Maggie's imagination? Did he really think she had talked to Torstein, alive?

"I told you!" Maggie said. "He said go tell Pete and the guys. He wanted you to know, specifically, Pete, that he was coming."

Pete had been looking gray ever since those thugs beat us up in the parking garage, but now he positively blanched. I couldn't figure it—on the wild, wacky chance that what Maggie said could possibly be true in this world, it would be *good news!* It would be the *best possible news.* And yet Pete looked like he was scared to death that it might, in fact, be so.

"Dear God," he murmured, and sat down on one of benches that ran around the inside of the wheelhouse. Mateo was already seated on one, slumped a little bit, staring straight ahead, clearly dazed by the notion that perhaps Torstein wasn't dead.

"Pete, it won't matter," Phyllis said. "Don't you see, if he's alive, then everything is all right! Nothing else matters as long as he's alive."

Pete leaned over and put his head in his hands. Phyllis sat beside him and put her arm around his shoulder. I still couldn't figure what was happening. I didn't think what Maggie was telling us could be true, but even if somehow Pete thought it was, his reaction was off.

Jazz said, "We were all there, Pete, Jack and me, and Andy. None of us stopped them. None of us saved him. If he told Maggie he's coming to find us, he's not going to blame us."

"None of you swore you'd protect him, either," Pete muttered into his hands. "None of you told that stinking Waverling that you didn't even know him!"

"Pete, it doesn't matter," said a strange, new voice in the wheelhouse. We'd been joined by a gorgeous guy in a shining golden coat. Where he came from, I can't say. How long he'd been there, I don't know. He was not very tall and built like Torstein, sort of muscular, but lithe—he even had Torstein's straight, black hair and hooked nose. Come to think of it, he had the shining blue eyes and dazzling smile, too.

82

He was smiling at us, the picture of health, of something beyond health, the picture of resurrection. Maggie had been right! His jacket was golden, his wounds were healed, and if anything he was *more alive* than we'd ever seen him before. He was ultra-alive, to the point where he was almost too much, too big, to be in the wheelhouse.

Maggie threw herself into his arms, then Phyllis did. I think my knees buckled, because suddenly I was sitting on the bench opposite Pete, and I think this time my jaw *had* dropped. I was just staring. I wasn't alone, though. Bruiser was staring, too, and Franz and Mateo.

It was as if the sun had come up behind us...and climbed right into the boat with us! The two boys and the ladies came running from the bow, with Jack leading them, and he threw himself at Torstein as shamelessly as Maggie and Phyllis had. Torstein was embracing them all, somehow, when Marigold and Caroline and Tawny piled in.

I'll tell you something. At a moment like this, you don't really have the time or ability to think: *This can't be happening.* And it's not *at all* like those dreams you sometimes have of dead people where it seems normal they're there, and you ask them about being dead, but they're real casual about it. You knew, in some remote and impoverished corner of your mind, that *this can't be,* and yet at the same time, you were overwhelmed by the warmth, the brightness, the life, the love—everything that used to emanate from Torstein before—now just poured out of him in waves. It swept us all up in him.

Dragonfly

Pete, he had just been sitting and staring, like me. But he was squinting, almost as if Torstein *were* too bright to look at.

Torstein was kissing everyone on the forehead, and then pushing them, gently, away from him. He turned to Bruiser and me, and kissed us, too. It felt like the touch of a cool breeze, it smelt like the salt of the sea air, and then, I think, I slumped back against the wall, amazed, and happy.

"Mateo, you came," Torstein said. I watched as he took Mateo's face in his hands, kissed his forehead, and smiled at him. "I knew you would."

Mateo's eyes began to shine. The pale and desperate man from the previous morning was completely banished, and the former mobster's man looked like Sully or Van, like a kid at Christmas.

Then Torstein was standing in front of Pete, who was still looking down at his knees where he sat.

"Pete, Pete," Torstein said softly. "Don't you love me?"

"Of course I love you," Pete said to his knees. "But I —"

"But nothing! *Do* you love me?"

"You know I love you."

"*Do* you—more than the rest of my friends?"

"Yes! Of course, yes," Pete said, looking up miserably now.

Torstein was smiling at him, that brilliant smile now kicked up a thousand watts. "I know you do," he said. "Do you know what your name means, Peter? It's from *petra,* Greek for rock. You're my rock now. I think before, you thought you were a rock because you were strong, and you were tough, and you were fearless. But that's not your foundation Pete. That's not what makes you a rock. It's love. Love is your greatest weapon, and love is your firmest foundation. Forget what you used to believe about yourself, and embrace this instead. Embrace love."

He reached out and gripped Pete's shoulders, pulling him up to standing, hugging him hard, slapping his back.

83

The sun had risen now, the day was bright. The blue water bobbed in white caps that sparkled like no shining ocean I'd ever seen before. The boat was drifting as Jazz stared in wonder at Torstein—and Pete, who drew away from him a new man, standing taller even than before. The awful pallor, that had colored him from the moment those thugs had driven away with Torstein, was now replaced by a flushed radiance of joy that reflected the glow of our amazing friend.

The ladies were crying, so touched were they by Torstein's words. I guess I was still staring, silent, mute.

"Look here," Torstein said. "I'm going away. To my Father—and your Father. You'll follow me there in his good timing, but until we meet again, you know what you have to do. Love is your common bond. Joy is your strength. Beauty, grace, forgiveness, mercy. That's all I can leave with you. And it's all you need."

"Do you have to go?" Sully said.

Kneeling down to face the boys, Torstein replied:

"I'm already gone. Look at me. I'm already too *alive* to be here. Did you ever see anyone glow like this?"

"You always glowed ..." Sully said.

"So do you," Torstein said, pulling both boys close, hugging them. "Now you've got to go on glowing, and glow even more, because I won't be here. You've got to be the sunflowers that spring up from my seeds. That's what I'm asking you to do. Will you do it?"

Dragonfly

Both boys agreed they would, though I doubt they understood what he was asking.

He stood up, buoyant, full of life, and it was easy to see that what he'd told the boys was true. He wasn't dead anymore, but he was too alive for this place. His vigor was overwhelming the clothes he wore, even somehow the body he inhabited—and we could tell that wherever this vitality came from, it was bursting to get back there. It was too much for this world. It was something huge and powerful, beautiful, but just too much.

"It's all right," he said. "you'll be like this, too, when you continue on the way of love. Your body may wither and die, maybe you'll perish violently like I did, but the spirit you've inherited from me today will grow and abound and expand until you'll be too big and too alive to stay here. Looking back from the other side, you'll see this world was a cold, dead place compared to the world to come, the world that is, waiting for you—where I am."

"I thought you said we created the world we'd always wanted when we acted in love," Tawny said.

"Exactly! You're changing this world, and you're *being changed* by it. You'll find that in the end you come to the same place, the place of life that's more *living* than any life you've ever lived." He grinned as if he were making sense, and all the light around us on this bright spring morning seemed to coalesce in his eyes. "That place is pulling me back. And right now, it's beginning to pull at you, too. From this moment on, you'll only be growing more and more homesick for this place of abundance where you've never been. But I'm there, and I'm with you."

I can't begin to tell you what happened after that. I don't think I rightly know. There was an enormous amount of light, but of a kind that didn't seem to hurt our eyes. And there was a wonderful sea breeze with a tangy taste and smell of salt that somehow cooled and refreshed. There was a hole in the sky where the clouds made way for a glimpse of deepest blue, like dark night beyond. And there was Torstein, over all, above all, in all...And then he was gone.

Jazz turned the boat around, to take us back to the mainland. In our eyes, and in our hearts, each of us carried a little bit of the

astonishing glow that had leapt from Torstein's smile. We had begun
to live in the corners of that smile. We'd begun to be called to another
land, another world, only reached by militant loving...radical caring...
outrageous giving...furious forgiving. And we wanted it so badly, we
were committed to pursue it, and to share it, with all our lives. Heaven
in a handful of sunflower seeds.

Afterword

You wouldn't think that a message of love would be so controversial. I don't want this to read like Foxe's *Book of Martyrs,* but of the 12 adults on the boat that day, only Jack is still living. (He's in virtual exile in China, rather like Napoleon on Elba. He's a political prisoner...an old man who wrote a tremendous book that swept up millions into the idea that love *is* the answer, and that we are, all of us, severely, exceptionally loved by God...and so, capable of loving each other. Maybe you've read it? It was a kind of Gospel. In the sense that it was tremendous Good News.)

But the rest of our crew...as Torstein predicted, they mostly died violently, in proclaiming the most dangerous message known to man— the message of love.

Andy, your narrator for this story, became a priest and got involved in the New Sanctuary movement that you probably heard about. Instead of helping illegals cross the border from Mexico to the USA, they started founding missions, schools and hospitals along the border so that those who were drawn north could find what they were looking for, still in their own country. His dad and step-mom were his bankroll at first, but when people saw that it worked, more money rolled in. Part of the mission was also to monitor the border and try to convince people *not* to go with the coyotes...and that's how Andrew got killed. One of the coyotes shot him.

His brother Pete got shot, too. He went to Washington, D.C. He said the best place to get our new message out was in the capital of the USA. He joined up with the Salvation Army there, and spent a lot of his free time in the parks, talking to the homeless and the drunks, just like

Torstein used to do. He really did many of the same things Torstein had done, and he had a great response with literally hundreds of followers throughout the capital. He directed them into other good works, and of course, directed his drunk and homeless friends to the Salvation Army. The other thing he did, in honor of Angel, was befriend a lot of crack addicts. He'd take food to their kids and talk to them about their future. And people listened to him! It was as if, after Torstein appeared to us, there were new light inside Pete that made him stronger and braver, but gentler and more authentic, too. He and Phyllis helped a lot of women and men get the help they needed to get off crack.

They were both found murdered in the tiny apartment they had in DC. Police suspected a robbery gone bad. I suspect the crack dealers were taking back what they thought was theirs. Pete and Phyllis' kids, the red-headed twins, who by then were both working as marine biologists in Hawaii, came back to DC, moved into the apartment, and started doing the work their parents had done. I'm pretty sure that would have made Phyllis and Pete pretty proud.

Franz and Tawny didn't have any kids of their own, but they moved to Sudan and started working in an orphanage, so for many years they had dozens of kids. The African people in southern Sudan had been devastated by genocidal attacks from their northern neighbors, and lots of children enslaved and/or orphaned, so there was plenty of business for Franz and Tawny. One night the *Janjaweed* militia—or some other terrorists—swept down on the village where the orphanage was and carried off a lot of the kids, and killed Tawny and Franz.

Marigold and Maggie joined an organization working to set women and children free from the sex trade. They were fearless. They'd go anywhere, face anyone down, and bring those poor souls into freedom. Through the years, they helped hundreds of women and children get a new start at life. But they were a big thorn in the side of the traffickers, and one day the Jeep they had rented just blew up when they turned the ignition key.

That one hit me hard. All those people had been like parents to me, and to Van, but Maggie especially had given me a new start in life, when I was so small.

My mom, Angel, and Len, my step-dad, took me back to the

mountains where the rehab center was. We lived there a long time, and Len eventually became the director. Angel, she had a program all her own, visiting shelters to talk to other moms addicted to crack and help them find a way out. That stuff is bad. It makes nice people into animals. It makes ladies who could be good moms into neglectful, abusive parents. One day Angel was running into traffic after some feral kid—that probably reminded her of me, truth be told—and she got hit by a car.

Van and I were in college then. We were so stunned...We wanted to be a sunflower like Torstein had asked us to...but it turned out to be a perilous profession. I'd lost my mom.

Jazz became a missionary. Once I asked him why he'd followed this path, and he told me:

"Jesus said the two most important things in the world are to love God, and love your neighbor as yourself. He said everything else hangs on those two mandates. What better gift to give the next generation?"

He was right.

But it proved to be a difficult path for him He was serving in some backwoods of Russia—in the Baryatia Autonomous Region—where the primitive people still believed in death-wish curses and consulted the shaman about what day to start building a house...someone didn't dig this message of love that set people free from the fear of witchcraft. Jazz went missing for about a year. Someone found his body decomposing in the tree tops.

Bruiser hooked up with a compassionate relief organization. He was on an advance team that went to evaluate the needs after that last big earthquake... and perished in an aftershock. He was in some tilting building trying to pull trapped kids out.

Mateo, who'd been there when they killed Torstein, he joined up with a prison ministry and spent a lot of his years behind bars, showing convicts and criminals the way to a better life. And of course, he got killed behind bars, too. It happens all the time.

Van's mom, Caroline, she got married a few years down the road, to a great guy back in her old hometown. Her parents, Van's grandparents, became like grandparents to me, too. Caroline lost her husband to

Jaxn Hill

cancer when she was about 60. She sold the house and took the little money she'd been left with, went to India. At 60 years old. She said she'd learned to tend sick people while her husband was dying, so she supposed they could use her in Calcutta to help the poorest of the poor. And they did. Fifteen years later, she wouldn't even come back to the USA when she needed treatment for cancer, herself.

As wretched and tragic as it all sounds...as wretched and tragic as it all *was*...I think Van and I both agree: every one of those dear souls would have wanted to go out the way they did: my mom breathed her last breath helping some other mother's son to safety. Caroline laid down her life bringing healing to other desperate people. Bruiser's final act was one of rescue. Jazz's life ended after a day of telling children how love sets you free. Mari and Maggie, Franz and Tawny, Mateo, Andy, Pete and Phyllis: all of them spent their lives, after Torstein, living Torstein's message, and it brought them to Torstein's end. It's the end I think they would have chosen!

In giving their lives away, they found more life, and more abundant, than ever before. They were becoming like him, becoming *too alive* for this world.

Between Caroline and her husband, Angel and Len, and Van's grandparents, he and I had a good few years growing up. You'd have thought that we'd forget Torstein, and the extraordinary events of that year—because we'd been so small. But I think with each passing year, the memories somehow became brighter, and more vivid. Perhaps because of the way the adults lived out his life again and again, before our eyes.

Today when Van and I look back on that time, it's with a sense of awe...that we ran and danced and sang and went fishing with Someone not of this world. That he loved us, and held us, and gave us a mission. Neither of us remembers that Terrible Day in anything but the vaguest terms—but we can both describe in great detail how Torstein appeared on the boat on the Last Day, and the way he breathed life, and love into us.

Van and I were too young, like the apostle said, "born out of time," but Torstein's impact on us was extreme. We've followed our extraordinary group of parents in their extraordinary lives. I figure we're due to follow them in death, in God's good timing.

Van never heard from his father, Nikolai, again. But he never forgot him, either. He lights candles for all three of his parents at St. Xavier church, where he's the leader of our Order. Torstein laughed when Andy first suggested we all start wearing Green Coats in his honor... but that's exactly what we've done. It's a vocation now, and wearing the Green Coat lets people know you believe that love is the answer, you're committed to loving God and people.

About 150,000 of us have accepted the call full-out and donned the Coat...and millions more are living the lifestyle. We're all poor as dirt—and as far as I can tell—happy as clams. Our *original* members may have disappeared, but the legacy they left continues to impact the world. You're welcome to join us, anytime. Here. Have some sunflower seeds.

About the Author ...

Jaxn Hill has worked as a writer for 20 years and more, mostly specializing in direct-mail marketing, video and audio scripts, brochures, advertising and fund-raising. She has learned that nothing engages a reader more, or communicates the truth better than a good story...and that all good stories reflect the truth of the One Good Story of our universe. It's her hope that this *Dragonfly* story, and her whole life and work, always retell that Story.

Jaxn lives outside Houston, Texas, with her husband Mike and good dog Barney. You can drop her a line at jaxy@jaxysdragonfly.com and read her blog at www.jesusandjaxyworld.com.